Dashiell

THE MALTESE FALCON

UNIFORM EDITION

CASSELL · LONDON

CASSELL & COMPANY LTD
35 Red Lion Square, London WC1R 4SG
*Sydney, Auckland, Toronto,
Johannesburg*

First published in this edition 1974

ISBN 0 304 29313 X

Printed in Great Britain by
Northumberland Press Limited,
Gateshead
1073

Chapter One

Spade and Archer

Samuel Spade's jaw was long and bony, his chin a jutting v under the more flexible v of his mouth. His nostrils curved back to make another, smaller, v. His yellow-grey eyes were horizontal. The v *motif* was picked up again by thickish brows rising outward from twin creases above a hooked nose, and his pale brown hair grew down—from high flat temples—in a point on his forehead. He looked rather pleasantly like a blond Satan.

He said to Effie Perine: 'Yes, sweetheart?'

She was a lanky sunburned girl whose tan dress of thin woollen stuff clung to her with an effect of dampness. Her eyes were brown and playful in a shiny boyish face. She finished shutting the door behind her, leaned against it, and said: 'There's a girl wants to see you. Her name's Wonderly.'

'A customer?'

'I guess so. You'll want to see her anyway: she's a knockout.'

'Shoo her in, darling,' said Spade. 'Shoo her in.'

Effie Perine opened the door again, following it back into the outer office, standing with a hand on the knob while saying: 'Will you come in, Miss Wonderly?'

A voice said, 'Thank you,' so softly that only the purest articulation made the words intelligible, and a young woman came through the doorway. She advanced slowly, with tentative steps, looking at Spade with cobalt-blue eyes that were both shy and probing.

She was tall and pliantly slender, without angularity anywhere. Her body was erect and high-breasted, her legs long, her hands and feet narrow. She wore two shades of blue that had been selected because of her eyes. The hair curling from under her blue hat was darkly red, her full lips more brightly red. White teeth glistened in the crescent her timid smile made.

Spade rose bowing and indicating with a thick-fingered hand the oaken armchair beside his desk. He was quite six feet tall. The steep rounded slope of his shoulders made his body seem almost conical—no broader than it was thick—and kept his freshly pressed grey coat from fitting very well.

Miss Wonderly murmured, 'Thank you,' softly as before and sat down on the edge of the chair's wooden seat.

Spade sank into his swivel-chair, made a quarter-turn to face her, smiled politely. He smiled without separating his lips. All the v's in his face grew longer.

The tappity-tap-tap and the thin bell and muffled whirr of Effie Perine's typewriting came through the closed door. Somewhere in a neighbouring office a power-driven machine vibrated dully. On Spade's desk a limp cigarette smouldered in a brass tray filled with the remains of limp cigarettes. Ragged grey flakes of cigarette-ash dotted the yellow top of the desk and the green blotter and the papers that were there. A buff-curtained window, eight or ten inches open, let in from the court a current of air faintly scented with ammonia. The ashes on the desk twitched and crawled in the current.

Miss Wonderly watched the grey flakes twitch and crawl. Her eyes were uneasy. She sat on the very edge of the chair. Her feet were flat on the floor, as if she were about to rise. Her hands in dark gloves clasped a flat dark handbag in her lap.

Spade rocked back in his chair and asked: 'Now what can I do for you, Miss Wonderly?'

She caught her breath and looked at him. She swallowed and said hurriedly: 'Could you——? I thought—— I—that is——' Then she tortured her lower lip with glistening teeth and said nothing. Only her dark eyes spoke now, pleading.

Spade smiled and nodded as if he understood her, but pleasantly, as if nothing serious were involved. He said: 'Suppose you tell me about it, from the beginning, and then we'll know what needs doing. Better begin as far back as you can.'

'That was in New York.'

'Yes.'

'I don't know where she met him. I mean I don't know where in New York. She's five years younger than I—only seventeen—and we didn't have the same friends. I don't suppose we've ever been as close as sisters should be. Mama and Papa are in Europe. It would kill them. I've got to get her back before they come home.'

'Yes,' he said.

'They're coming home the first of the month.'

Spade's eyes brightened. 'Then we've got two weeks,' he said.

'I didn't know what she had done until her letter came. I was frantic.' Her lips trembled. Her hands mashed the dark handbag in her lap. 'I was too afraid she had done something like this to go to the police, and the fear that something had happened to her kept urging me to go. There wasn't anyone I could go to for advice. I didn't know what to do. What could I do?'

'Nothing, of course,' Spade said, 'but then her letter came?'

'Yes, and I sent her a telegram asking her to come home. I sent it to General Delivery here. That was the only address she gave me. I waited a whole week, but no answer came, not another word from her. And Mama and Papa's return was drawing nearer and nearer. So I came to San Francisco to get her. I wrote her I was coming. I shouldn't have done that, should I?'

'Maybe not. It's not always easy to know what to do. You haven't found her?'

'No, I haven't. I wrote her that I would go to the St. Mark, and I begged her to come and let me talk to her even if she didn't intend to go home with me. But she didn't come. I waited three days, and she didn't come, didn't even send me a message of any sort.'

Spade nodded his blond Satan's head, frowned sympathetically, and tightened his lips together.

'It was horrible,' Miss Wonderly said, trying to smile. 'I couldn't sit there like that—waiting—not knowing what had happened to her, what might be happening to her.' She stopped trying to smile. She shuddered. 'The only address I had was General Delivery. I wrote her another letter, and yesterday afternoon I went to the Post Office. I stayed there until after dark, but I didn't see her. I went there again this morning, and still didn't see Corinne, but I saw Floyd Thursby.'

Spade nodded again. His frown went away. In its place came a look of sharp attentiveness.

'He wouldn't tell me where Corinne was,' she went on, hopelessly. 'He wouldn't tell me anything except that she was well and happy. But how can I believe that? That is what he would tell me anyhow, isn't it?'

'Sure,' Spade agreed. 'But it might be true.'

'I hope it is. I do hope it is,' she exclaimed. 'But I can't go back home like this, without having seen her, without even having talked to her on the phone. He wouldn't take me to her. He said she didn't want to see me. I can't believe that. He promised to tell her he had seen me, and to bring her to see me—if she would come—this evening at the hotel. He said he knew she wouldn't. He promised to come himself if she wouldn't. He——'

She broke off with a startled hand to her mouth as the door opened.

The man who had opened the door came in a step, said, 'Oh excuse me!' hastily took his brown hat from his head, and backed out.

'It's all right, Miles,' Spade told him. 'Come in. Miss Wonderly, this is Mr. Archer, my partner.'

Miles Archer came into the office again, shutting the door behind him, ducking his head and smiling at Miss Wonderly, making a vaguely polite gesture with the hat in his hand. He was of medium height, solidly built, wide in the shoulders, thick in the neck, with a jovial heavy-jawed red face and some grey in his close-trimmed hair. He was apparently as many years past forty as Spade was past thirty.

Spade said: 'Miss Wonderly's sister ran away from New York with a fellow named Floyd Thursby. They're here. Miss Wonderly has seen Thursby and has a date with him to-night. Maybe he'll bring the sister with him. The chances are he won't. Miss Wonderly wants us to find the sister and get her away from him and back home.' He looked at Miss Wonderly. 'Right?'

'Yes,' she said indistinctly. The embarrassment that had gradually been driven away by Spade's ingratiating smiles and nods and assurances was pinkening her face again. She looked at

the bag in her lap and picked nervously at it with a gloved finger.

Spade winked at his partner.

Miles Archer came forward to stand at a corner of the desk. While the girl looked at the bag he looked at her. His little brown eyes ran their bold appraising gaze from her lowered face to her feet and up to her face again. Then he looked at Spade and made a silent whistling mouth of appreciation.

Spade lifted two fingers from the arm of his chair in a brief warning gesture and said:

'We shouldn't have any trouble with it. It's simply a matter of having a man at the hotel this evening to shadow him away when he leaves, and shadow him until he leads us to your sister. If she comes with him, and you persuade her to return with you, so much the better. Otherwise—if she doesn't want to leave him after we've found her—well, we'll find a way of managing that.'

Archer said: 'Yeh.' His voice was heavy, coarse.

Miss Wonderly looked up at Spade, quickly, puckering her forehead between her eyebrows.

'Oh, but you must be careful!' Her voice shook a little, and her lips shaped the words with nervous jerkiness. 'I'm deathly afraid of him, of what he might do. She's so young and his bringing her here from New York is such a serious—— Mightn't he —mightn't he do—something to her?'

Spade smiled and patted the arms of his chair.

'Just leave that to us,' he said. 'We'll know how to handle him.'

'But mightn't he?' she insisted.

'There's always a chance,' Spade nodded judicially. 'But you can trust us to take care of that.'

'I do trust you,' she said earnestly, 'but I want you to know that he's a dangerous man. I honestly don't think he'd stop at anything. I don't believe he'd hesitate to—to kill Corinne if he thought it would save him. Mightn't he do that?'

'You didn't threaten him, did you?'

'I told him that all I wanted was to get her home before Mama and Papa came so they'd never know what she had done. I promised him I'd never say a word to them about it if he helped me, but if he didn't Papa would certainly see that he was punished. I—I don't suppose he believed me, altogether.'

'Can he cover up by marrying her?' Archer asked.

The girl blushed and replied in a confused voice: 'He has a wife and three children in England. Corinne wrote me that, to explain why she had gone off with him.'

'They usually do,' Spade said, 'though not always in England.' He leaned forward to reach for a pencil and a pad of paper. 'What does he look like?'

'Oh, he's thirty-five years old, perhaps, and as tall as you, and either naturally dark or quite sunburned. His hair is dark too, and he has thick eyebrows. He talks in a rather loud, blustery way and has a nervous, irritable manner. He gives the impression of being—of violence.'

Spade, scribbling on the pad, asked without looking up: 'What colour eyes?'

'They're blue-grey and watery, though not in a weak way. And—oh yes—he has a marked cleft in his chin.'

'Thin, medium, or heavy build?'

'Quite athletic. He's broad-shouldered and carries himself erect, has what could be called a decidedly military carriage. He was wearing a light-grey suit and a grey hat when I saw him this morning.'

'What does he do for a living?' Spade asked as he laid down his pencil.

'I don't know,' she said. 'I haven't the slightest idea.'

'What time is he coming to see you?'

'After eight o'clock.'

'All right, Miss Wonderly, we'll have a man there. It'll help if——'

'Mr. Spade, could either you or Mr. Archer?' She made an appealing gesture with both hands. 'Could either of you look after it personally? I don't mean that the man you'd send wouldn't be capable, but—oh!—I'm so afraid of what might happen to Corinne. I'm afraid of him. Could you? I'd be—I'd expect to be charged more, of course.' She opened her handbag with nervous fingers and put two hundred-dollar bills on Spade's desk. 'Would that be enough?'

'Yeh,' Archer said, 'and I'll look after it myself.'

Miss Wonderly stood up, impulsively holding a hand out to him.

'Thank you! Thank you!' she exclaimed, and then gave

Spade her hand, repeating : 'Thank you !'

'Not at all,' Spade said over it. 'Glad to. It'll help some if you either meet Thursby downstairs or let yourself be seen in the lobby with him at some time.'

'I will,' she promised, and thanked the partners again.

'And don't look for me,' Archer cautioned her. 'I'll see you all right.'

Spade went to the corridor-door with Miss Wonderly. When he returned to his desk Archer nodded at the hundred-dollar bills there, growled complacently, 'They're right enough,' picked one up, folded it, and tucked it into a vest pocket. 'And they had brothers in her bag.'

Spade pocketed the other bill before he sat down. Then he said : 'Well, don't dynamite her too much. What do you think of her?'

'Sweet! And you telling me not to dynamite her.' Archer guffawed suddenly without merriment. 'Maybe you saw her first, Sam, but I spoke first.' He put his hands in his trousers pockets and teetered on his heels.

'You'll play hell with her, you will.' Spade grinned wolfishly, showing the edges of teeth far back in his jaw. 'You've got brains, yes you have.' He began to make a cigarette.

Chapter Two

Death in the Fog

A telephone bell rang in darkness. When it had rung three times bed-springs creaked, fingers fumbled on wood, something small and hard thudded on a carpeted floor, the springs creaked again, and a man's voice said :

'Hello.... Yes, speaking.... Dead?... Yes.... Fifteen minutes. Thanks.'

A switch clicked and a white bowl hung on three gilded chains from the ceiling's centre filled the room with light. Spade, bare-footed in green and white checked pyjamas, sat on the side of his bed. He scowled at the telephone on the table while his hands took from beside it a packet of brown papers and a sack of Bull Durham tobacco.

Cold, steamy air blew in through two open windows, bringing with it half a dozen times a minute the Alcatraz foghorn's dull moaning. A tinny alarm clock, insecurely mounted on a corner of Duke's *Celebrated Criminal Cases of America*—face down on the table—held its hands at five minutes past two.

Spade's thick fingers made a cigarette with deliberate care, sifting a measured quantity of tan flakes down into curved paper, spreading the flakes so that they lay equal at the ends with a slight depression in the middle, thumbs rolling the paper's inner edge down and up under the outer edge as forefingers pressed it over, thumbs and fingers sliding to the paper cylinder's ends to hold it even while the tongue licked the flap, left forefinger and thumb pinching their end while right forefinger and thumb smoothed the damp seam, right forefinger and thumb twisting their end and lifting the other to Spade's mouth.

He picked up the pigskin-and-nickel lighter that had fallen to the floor, manipulated it, and with the cigarette burning in a corner of his mouth stood up. He took off his pyjamas. The smooth thickness of his arms, legs, and body, the sag of his big rounded shoulders, made his body like a bear's. It was like a shaved bear's: his chest was hairless. His skin was childishly soft and pink.

He scratched the back of his neck and began to dress. He put on a thin white union suit, grey socks, black garters, and dark brown shoes. When he had fastened his shoes he picked up the telephone, called Graystone 4500, and ordered a taxicab. He put on a green-striped white shirt, a soft white collar, a green necktie, the grey suit he had worn that day, a loose tweed overcoat, and a dark grey hat. The street-door bell rang as he stuffed tobacco, keys and money into his pockets.

Where Bush Street roofed Stockton before slipping downhill to Chinatown, Spade paid his fare and left the taxicab. San Francisco's night-fog, thin, clammy, and penetrant blurred the

street. A few yards from where Spade dismissed the taxicab
a small group of men stood looking up an alley. Two women
stood with a man on the other side of Bush Street, looking at the
alley. There were faces at windows.

Spade crossed the sidewalk between iron-railed hatchways that
opened above bare ugly stairs, went to the parapet, and, resting
his hands on the damp coping, looked down into Stockton Street.

An automobile popped out of the tunnel beneath him with
a roaring swish, as if it had been blown out, and ran away. Not
far from the tunnel's mouth a man was hunkered on his heels
before a billboard that held advertisements of a moving picture
and a gasoline across the front of a gap between two store build-
ings. The hunkered man's head was bent almost to the sidewalk so
he could look under the billboard. A hand flat on the paving, a
hand clenched on the billboard's green frame, held him in this
grotesque position. Two other men stood awkwardly together at
one end of the billboard, peeping through the few inches of
space between it and the building at that end. The building at
the other end had a blank grey sidewall that looked down on
the lot behind the billboard. Lights flickered on the sidewall, and
the shadows of men moving among lights.

Spade turned from the parapet and walked up Bush Street to
the alley where men were grouped. A uniformed policeman
chewing gum under an enamelled sign that said *Burritt St.* in
white against dark blue put out an arm and asked:

'What do you want here?'

'I'm Sam Spade. Tom Polhaus phoned me.'

'Sure you are.' The policeman's arm went down. 'I didn't
know you at first. Well, they're back there.' He jerked a thumb
over his shoulder. 'Bad business.'

'Bad enough,' Spade agreed, and went up the alley.

Half-way up it, not far from the entrance, a dark ambulance
stood. Behind the ambulance, to the left, the alley was bounded
by a waist-high fence, horizontal strips of rough boarding. From
the fence dark ground fell away steeply to the billboard on
Stockton Street below.

A ten-foot length of the fence's top rail had been torn from
a post at one end and hung dangling from the other. Fifteen feet
down the slope a flat boulder stuck out. In the notch between

boulder and slope Miles Archer lay on his back. Two men stood over him. One of them held the beam of an electric torch on the dead man. Other men with lights moved up and down the slope.

One of them hailed Spade, 'Hello, Sam,' and clambered up to the alley, his shadow running up the slope before him. He was a barrel-bellied tall man with shrewd small eyes, a thick mouth, and carelessly shaven dark jowls. His shoes, knees, hands, and chin were daubed with brown loam.

'I figured you'd want to see it before we took him away,' he said as he stepped over the broken fence.

'Thanks, Tom,' Spade said. 'What happened?' He put an elbow on the fence-post and looked down at the men below, nodding to those who nodded to him.

Tom Polhaus poked his own left breast with a dirty finger. 'Got him right through the pump—with this.' He took a fat revolver from his coat pocket and held it out to Spade. Mud inlaid the depressions in the revolver's surface. 'A Webley. English, ain't it?'

Spade took his elbow from the fence-post and leaned down to look at the weapon, but he did not touch it.

'Yes,' he said, 'Webley-Fosbery automatic revolver. That's it. Thirty-eight, eight shot. They don't make them any more. How many gone out of it?'

'One pill.' Tom poked his breast again. 'He must've been dead when he cracked the fence.' He raised the muddy revolver. 'Ever seen this before?'

Spade nodded. 'I've seen Webley-Fosberys,' he said without interest, and then spoke rapidly: 'He was shot up here, huh? Standing where you are, with his back to the fence. The man that shot him stands here.' He went around in front of Tom and raised a hand breast-high with levelled forefinger. 'Let's him have it and Miles goes back, taking the top off the fence and going on through and down till the rock catches him. That it?'

'That's it,' Tom replied slowly, working his brows together. 'The blast burnt his coat.'

'Who found him?'

'The man on the beat, Shilling. He was coming down Bush, and just as he got here a machine turning threw headlights up here, and he saw the top off the fence. So he came up to look at it, and found him.'

'What about the machine that was turning around?'

'Not a damned thing about it, Sam. Shilling didn't pay any attention to it, not knowing anything was wrong then. He says nobody didn't come out of here while he was coming down from Powell or he'd've seen them. The only other way out would be under the billboard on Stockton. Nobody went that way. The fog's got the ground soggy, and the only marks are where Miles slid down and where this here gun rolled.'

'Didn't anybody hear the shot?'

'For the love of God, Sam, we only just got here. Somebody must've heard it, when we find them.' He turned and put a leg over the fence. 'Coming down for a look at him before he's moved?'

Spade said: 'No.'

Tom halted astride the fence and looked back at Spade with surprised small eyes.

Spade said: 'You've seen him. You'd see everything I could.'

Tom, still looking at Spade, nodded doubtfully and withdrew his leg over the fence.

'His gun was tucked away on his hip,' he said. 'It hadn't been fired. His overcoat was buttoned. There's a hundred and sixty-some bucks in his clothes. Was he working, Sam?'

Spade, after a moment's hesitation, nodded.

Tom asked: 'Well?'

'He was supposed to be tailing a fellow named Floyd Thursby,' Spade said, and described Thursby as Miss Wonderly had described him.

'What for?'

Spade put his hands into his overcoat pockets and blinked sleepy eyes at Tom.

Tom repeated impatiently: 'What for?'

'He was an Englishman, maybe. I don't know what his game was exactly. We were trying to find out where he lived.' Spade grinned faintly and took a hand from his pocket to pat Tom's shoulder. 'Don't crowd me.' He put the hand in his pocket again. 'I'm going out to break the news to Miles's wife.' He turned away.

Tom, scowling, opened his mouth, closed it without having said anything, cleared his throat, put the scowl off his face, and spoke with a husky sort of gentleness:

'It's tough him getting it like that. Miles had his faults same as the rest of us, but I guess he must've had some good points too.'

'I guess so,' Spade agreed in a tone that was utterly meaningless, and went out of the alley.

In an all-night drugstore on the corner of Bush and Taylor Streets, Spade used a telephone.

'Precious,' he said into it a little while after he had given a number, 'Miles has been shot.... Yes, he's dead.... Now don't get excited.... Yes.... You'll have to break it to Iva.... No, I'm damned if I will. You've got to do it.... That's a good girl.... And keep her away from the office.... Tell her I'll see her—uh—some time.... Yes, but don't tie me up to anything.... That's the stuff. You're an angel. 'Bye.'

Spade's tinny alarm clock said three-forty when he turned on the light in the suspended bowl again. He dropped his hat and overcoat on the bed and went into his kitchen, returning to the bedroom with a wine-glass and a tall bottle of Bacardi. He poured a drink and drank it standing. He put bottle and glass on the table, sat on the side of the bed facing them, and rolled a cigarette. He had drunk his third glass of Bacardi and was lighting his fifth cigarette when the street-door bell rang. The hands of the alarm clock registered four-thirty.

Spade sighed, rose from the bed, and went to the telephone-box beside the bathroom door. He pressed the button that released the street-door lock. He muttered, 'Damn her,' and stood scowling at the black telephone-box, breathing irregularly while a dull flush grew in his cheeks.

The grating and rattling of the elevator-door opening and closing came from the corridor. Spade sighed again and moved towards the corridor door. Soft heavy footsteps sounded on the carpeted floor outside, the footsteps of two men. Spade's face brightened. His eyes were no longer harassed. He opened the door quickly.

'Hello, Tom,' he said to the barrel-bellied, tall detective with whom he had talked in Burritt Street, and, 'Hello, Lieutenant,' to the man beside Tom. 'Come in.'

They nodded together, neither saying anything, and came in. Spade shut the door and ushered them into his bedroom. Tom sat on the end of the sofa by the windows. The Lieutenant sat on a chair beside the table.

The Lieutenant was a compactly built man with a round head under short-cut grizzled hair and a square face behind a short-cut grizzled moustache. A five-dollar gold-piece was pinned to his necktie and there was a small elaborate diamond-set secret society emblem on his lapel.

Spade brought two wine-glasses in from the kitchen, filled them and his own with Bacardi, gave one to each of his visitors, and sat down with his on the side of the bed. His face was placid and uncurious. He raised his glass, and said, 'Success to crime,' and drank it down.

Tom emptied his glass, set it on the floor beside his feet, and wiped his mouth with a muddy forefinger. He stared at the foot of the bed as if trying to remember something of which it vaguely reminded him.

The Lieutenant looked at his glass for a dozen seconds, took a very small sip of its contents, and put the glass on the table at his elbow. He examined the room with hard deliberate eyes, and then looked at Tom.

Tom moved uncomfortably on the sofa and, not looking up, asked: 'Did you break the news to Miles's wife, Sam?'

Spade said: 'Uh-huh.'

'How'd she take it?'

Spade shook his head. 'I don't know anything about women.'

Tom said softly: 'The hell you don't.'

The Lieutenant put his hands on his knees and leaned forward. His greenish eyes were fixed on Spade in a peculiarly rigid stare, as if their focus were a matter of mechanics, to be changed only by pulling a lever or pressing a button.

'What kind of gun do you carry?' he asked.

'None. I don't like them much. Of course there are some in the office.'

'I'd like to see one of them,' the Lieutenant said. 'You don't happen to have one here?'

'No.'

'You sure of that?'

'Look around,' Spade smiled and waved his empty glass a little. 'Turn the dump upside-down if you want. I won't squawk —if you've got a search warrant.'

Tom protested: 'Oh, hell, Sam!'

Spade set his glass on the table and stood up facing the Lieutenant.

'What do you want, Dundy?' he asked in a voice hard and cold as his eyes.

Lieutenant Dundy's eyes had moved to maintain their focus on Spade's. Only his eyes had moved.

Tom shifted his weight on the sofa again, blew a deep breath out through his nose, and growled plaintively: 'We're not wanting to make any trouble, Sam.'

Spade, ignoring Tom, said to Dundy: 'Well, what do you want? Talk turkey. Who in hell do you think you are, coming in here trying to rope me?'

'All right,' Dundy said in his chest, 'sit down and listen.'

'I'll sit or stand as I damned please,' said Spade, not moving.

'For Christ's sake be reasonable,' Tom begged. 'What's the use of us having a row? If you want to know why we didn't talk turkey it's because when I asked you who this Thursby was you as good as told me it was none of my business. You can't treat us that way, Sam. It ain't right and it won't get you any-wheres. We got our work to do.'

Lieutenant Dundy jumped up, stood close to Spade, and thrust his square face up at the taller man's.

'I've warned you your foot was going to slip one of these days,' he said.

Spade made a depreciative mouth, raising his eyebrows. 'Everybody's foot slips sometime,' he replied with derisive mildness.

'And this is yours.'

Spade smiled and shook his head. 'No, I'll do nicely, thank you.' He stopped smiling. His upper lip, on the left side, twitched over his eyetooth. His eyes became narrow and sultry. His voice came out deep as the Lieutenant's. 'I don't like this. What are you sucking around for? Tell me, or get out and let me go to bed.'

'Who's Thursby?' Dundy demanded.

'I told Tom what I knew about him.'

'You told Tom damned little.'

'I knew damned little.'

'Why were you tailing him?'

'I wasn't. Miles was—for the swell reason that we had a client who was paying good United States money to have him tailed.'

'Who's the client?'

Placidity came back to Spade's face and voice. He said reprovingly: 'You know I can't tell you that until I've talked it over with the client.'

'You'll tell it to me or you'll tell it in court,' Dundy said hotly. 'This is murder and don't you forget it.'

'Maybe. And here's something for you to not forget, sweetheart. I'll tell it or not as I damned please. It's a long while since I burst out crying because policemen didn't like me.'

Tom left the sofa and sat on the foot of the bed. His carelessly shaven mud-smeared face was tired and lined.

'Be reasonable, Sam,' he pleaded. 'Give us a chance. How can we turn up anything on Miles's killing if you won't give us what you've got?'

'You needn't get a headache over that,' Spade told him. 'I'll bury my dead.'

Lieutenant Dundy sat down and put his hands on his knees again. His eyes were warm green discs.

'I thought you would,' he said. He smiled with grim content. 'That's just exactly why we came to see you. Isn't it, Tom?'

Tom groaned, but said nothing articulate.

Spade watched Dundy warily.

'That's just exactly what I said to Tom,' the Lieutenant went on. 'I said: "Tom, I've got a hunch that Sam Spade's a man to keep family troubles in the family." That's just what I said to him.'

The wariness went out of Spade's eyes. He made his eyes dull with boredom. He turned his face around to Tom and asked with great carelessness: 'What's itching your boy-friend now?'

Dundy jumped up and tapped Spade's chest with the ends of two bent fingers.

'Just this,' he said, taking pains to make each word distinct, emphasising them with his tapping finger-ends: 'Thursby was shot down in front of his hotel just thirty-five minutes after you left Burritt Street.'

Spade spoke, taking equal pains with his words: 'Keep your God-damned paws off me.'

Dundy withdrew the tapping fingers, but there was no change in his voice: 'Tom says you were in too much of a hurry to even stop for a look at your partner.'

Tom growled apologetically: 'Well, damn it, Sam, you did run off like that.'

'And you didn't go to Archer's house to tell his wife,' the Lieutenant said. 'We called up and that girl in your office was there, and she said you sent her.'

Spade nodded. His face was stupid in its calmness.

Lieutenant Dundy raised his two bent fingers towards Spade's chest, quickly lowered them, and said: 'I give you ten minutes to get to a phone and do your talking to the girl. I give you ten minutes to get to Thursby's joint—Geary near Leavenworth—you could do it easy in that time, or fifteen at the most. And that gives you ten or fifteen minutes of waiting before he showed up.'

'I knew where he lived?' Spade asked. 'And I knew he hadn't gone straight home from killing Miles?'

'You knew what you knew,' Dundy replied stubbornly. 'What time did you get home?'

'Twenty minutes to four. I walked around thinking things over.'

The Lieutenant wagged his round head up and down. 'We knew you weren't home at three-thirty. We tried to get you on the phone. Where'd you do your walking?'

'Out Bush Street a way and back.'

'Did you see anybody that——?'

'No, no witnesses,' Spade said and laughed pleasantly. 'Sit down, Dundy. You haven't finished your drink. Get your glass, Tom.'

Tom said: 'No, thanks, Sam.'

Dundy sat down, but paid no attention to his glass of rum.

Spade filled his own glass, drank, set the empty glass on the table and returned to his bedside seat.

'I know where I stand now,' he said, looking with friendly eyes from one of the police detectives to the other. 'I'm sorry I got up on my hind legs, but you birds coming in and trying to put the works on me made me nervous. Having Miles knocked off bothered me, and then you birds cracking foxy. That's all right now, though, now that I know what you're up to.'

Tom said: 'Forget it.'

The Lieutenant said nothing.

Spade asked: 'Thursby die?'

While the Lieutenant hesitated Tom said: 'Yes.'

Then the Lieutenant said angrily: 'And you might just as well know it—if you don't—that he died before he could tell anybody anything.'

Spade was rolling a cigarette. He asked, not looking up: 'What do you mean by that? You think I did know it?'

'I meant what I said,' Dundy replied bluntly.

Spade looked up at him and smiled, holding the finished cigarette in one hand, his lighter in the other.

'You're not ready to pinch me yet, are you, Dundy?' he asked.

Dundy looked with hard green eyes at Spade and did not answer him.

'Then,' said Spade, 'there's no particular reason why I should give a damn what you think, is there, Dundy?'

Tom said: 'Aw, be reasonable, Sam.'

Spade put the cigarette in his mouth, set fire to it, and laughed smoke out.

'I'll be reasonable, Tom,' he promised. 'How did I kill this Thursby? I've forgotten.'

Tom grunted in disgust. Lieutenant Dundy said: 'He was shot four times in the back, with a forty-four or forty-five, from across the street, when he started to go in the hotel. Nobody saw it, but that's the way it figures.'

'And he was wearing a Luger in a shoulder-holster,' Tom added. 'It hadn't been fired.'

'What do the hotel people know about him?' Spade asked.

'Nothing except that he'd been there a week.'

'Alone?'

'Alone.'

'What did you find on him, or in his room?'

Dundy drew his lips in and asked: 'What'd you think we'd find?'

Spade made a careless circle with his limp cigarette. 'Something to tell you who he was, what his store was. Did you?'

'We thought you could tell us that.'

Spade looked at the Lieutenant with yellow-grey eyes that held an almost exaggerated amount of candour. 'I've never seen Thursby, dead or alive.'

Lieutenant Dundy stood up looking dissatisfied. Tom rose yawning and stretching.

'We've asked what we came to ask,' Dundy said, frowning over eyes hard as green pebbles. He held his moustached upper lip tight to his teeth, letting his lower lip push the words out. 'We've told you more than you've told us. That's fair enough. You know me, Spade. If you did or you didn't you'll get a square deal out of me, and most of the breaks. I don't know that I'd blame you a hell of a lot—but that wouldn't keep me from nailing you.'

'Fair enough,' Spade replied evenly. 'But I'd feel better about it if you'd drink your drink.'   ,

Lieutenant Dundy turned to the table, picked up his glass, and slowly emptied it. Then he said, 'Good night,' and held out his hand. They shook hands ceremoniously. Tom and Spade shook hands ceremoniously. Spade let them out. Then he undressed, turned off the lights, and went to bed.

Chapter Three

Three Women

When Spade reached his office at ten o'clock the following morning Effie Perine was at her desk opening the morning's mail.

Her boyish face was pale under its sunburn. She put down the handful of envelopes and the brass paper-knife she held and said: 'She's in there.' Her voice was low and warning.

'I asked you to keep her away,' Spade complained. He too kept his voice low.

Effie Perine's brown eyes opened wide and her voice was irritable as his: 'Yes, but you didn't tell me how.' Her eyelids went together a little and her shoulders drooped. 'Don't be cranky, Sam,' she said wearily. 'I had her all night.'

Spade stood beside the girl, put a hand on her head, and smoothed her hair away from its parting. 'Sorry, angel, I haven't——' He broke off as the inner door opened. 'Hello, Iva,' he said to the woman who had opened it.

'Oh, Sam!' she said.

She was a blonde woman of a few more years than thirty. Her facial prettiness was perhaps five years past its best moment. Her body for all its sturdiness was finely modelled and exquisite. She wore black clothes from hat to shoes. They had as mourning an impromptu air. Having spoken, she stepped back from the door and stood waiting for Spade.

He took his hand from Effie Perine's head and entered the inner office shutting the door. Iva came quickly to him, raising her sad face for his kiss. Her arms were around him before his held her. When they had kissed he made a little movement as if to release her, but she pressed her face to his chest and began sobbing.

He stroked her round back, saying: 'Poor darling.' His voice was tender. His eyes, squinting at the desk that had been his partner's across the room from his own, were angry. He drew his lips back over his teeth in an impatient grimace and turned his chin aside to avoid contact with the crown of her hat. 'Did you send for Miles's brother?' he asked.

'Yes, he came over this morning.' The words were blurred by her sobbing and his coat against her mouth.

He grimaced again and bent his head for a surreptitious look at the watch on his wrist. His left arm was around her, the hand on her left shoulder. His cuff was pulled back far enough to leave the watch uncovered. It showed ten-ten.

The woman stirred in his arms and raised her face again. Her blue eyes were wet, round, and white-ringed. Her mouth was moist.

'Oh, Sam,' she moaned, 'did you kill him?'

Spade stared at her with bulging eyes. His bony jaw fell down. He took his arms from her and stepped back out of her arms. He scowled at her and cleared his throat.

She held her arms up as he had left them. Anguish clouded her eyes, partly closed them under eyebrows pulled up at the inner ends. Her soft, damp, red lips trembled.

Spade laughed a harsh syllable, 'Ha!' and went to the buff-curtained window. He stood there with his back to her looking through the curtain into the court until she started towards him. Then he turned quickly and went to his desk. He sat down, put his elbows on the desk, his chin between his fists, and looked at her. His yellowish eyes glittered between narrowed lids.

'Who,' he asked coldly, 'put that bright idea in your head?'

'I thought——' She lifted a hand to her mouth and fresh tears came to her eyes. She came to stand beside the desk, moving with easy sure-footed grace in black slippers whose smallness and heel-height were extreme. 'Be kind to me, Sam,' she said humbly.

He laughed at her, his eyes still glittering. 'You killed my husband, Sam, be kind to me.' He clapped his palms together and said: 'Jesus Christ.'

She began to cry audibly, holding a white handkerchief to her face.

He got up and stood close behind her. He put his arms around her. He kissed her neck between ear and coat collar. He said: 'Now, Iva, don't.' His face was expressionless. When she had stopped crying he put his mouth to her ear and murmured: 'You shouldn't have come here to-day, precious. It wasn't wise. You can't stay. You ought to be home.'

She turned around in his arms to face him and asked: 'You'll come to-night?'

He shook his head gently. 'Not to-night.'

'Soon?'

'Yes.'

'How soon?'

'As soon as I can.'

He kissed her mouth, led her to the door, opened it, said, 'Good-bye, Iva,' bowed her out, shut the door, and returned to his desk.

He took tobacco and cigarette papers from his vest pockets, but did not roll a cigarette. He sat holding the papers in one hand, the tobacco in the other, and looked with brooding eyes at his dead partner's desk.

Effie Perine opened the door and came in. Her brown eyes were uneasy. Her voice was careless. She asked: 'Well?'

Spade said nothing. His brooding gaze did not move from his partner's desk.

The girl frowned and came around to his side. 'Well,' she asked in a louder voice, 'how did you and the widow make out?'

'She thinks I shot Miles,' he said. Only his lips moved.

'So you could marry her?'

Spade made no reply to that.

The girl took his hat from his head and put it on the desk. Then she leaned over and took the tobacco sack and the papers from his inert fingers.

'The police think I shot Thursby,' he said.

'Who is he?' she asked, separating a cigarette paper from the packet, sifting tobacco into it.

'Who do you think I shot?' he asked.

When she ignored that question he said: 'Thursby's the guy Miles was supposed to be tailing for the Wonderly girl.'

Her thin fingers finished shaping the cigarette. She licked it, smoothed it, twisted its ends, and placed it between Spade's lips. He said, 'Thanks, honey,' put an arm around her slim waist, and rested his cheek wearily against her hip, shutting his eyes.

'Are you going to marry Iva?' she asked, looking down at his pale brown hair.

'Don't be silly,' he muttered. The unlighted cigarette bobbed up and down with the movement of his lips.

'She doesn't think it's silly. Why should she—the way you've played around with her?'

He sighed and said: 'I wish to God I'd never seen her.'

'Maybe you do now.' A trace of spitefulness came into the girl's voice. 'But there was a time.'

'I never know what to do or say to a woman except that way,' he grumbled, 'and then I didn't like Miles.'

'That's a lie, Sam,' the girl said. 'You know I think she's a louse, but I'd be a louse too if it would give me a body like hers.'

Spade rubbed his face impatiently against her hip, but said nothing.

Effie Perine bit her lip, wrinkled her forehead, and, bending over for a better view of his face, asked: 'Do you suppose she could have killed him?'

Spade sat up straight and took his arm from her waist. He smiled at her. His smile held nothing but amusement. He took out his lighter, snapped on the flame, and applied it to the end of his cigarette. 'You're an angel,' he said tenderly through smoke, 'a nice rattle-brained angel.'

She smiled a bit wryly. 'Oh, am I? Suppose I told you that your Iva hadn't been home many minutes when I arrived to break the news at three o'clock this morning?'

'Are you telling me?' he asked. His eyes had become alert though his mouth continued to smile.

'She kept me waiting at the door while she undressed or finished undressing. I saw her clothes where she had dumped them on a chair. Her hat and coat were underneath. Her singlette, on top, was still warm. She said she had been asleep, but she hadn't. She had wrinkled up the bed, but the wrinkles weren't mashed down.'

Spade took the girl's hand and patted it. 'You're a detective, darling, but'—he shook his head— 'she didn't kill him.'

Effie Perine snatched her hand away. 'That louse wants to marry you, Sam,' she said bitterly.

He made an impatient gesture with his head and one hand.

She frowned at him and demanded: 'Did you see her last night?'

'No.'

'Honestly?'

'Honestly. Don't act like Dundy, sweetheart. It ill becomes you.'

'Has Dundy been after you?'

'Uh-huh. He and Tom Polhaus dropped in for a drink at four o'clock.'

'Do they really think you shot this what's-his-name?'

'Thursby.' He dropped what was left of his cigarette into the brass tray and began to roll another.

'Do they?' she insisted.

'God knows.' His eyes were on the cigarette he was making. 'They did have some such notion. I don't know how far I talked them out of it.'

'Look at me, Sam.'

He looked at her and laughed so that for the moment merriment mingled with the anxiety in her face.

'You worry me,' she said, seriousness returning to her face as she talked. 'You always think you know what you're doing, but you're too slick for your own good, and some day you're going to find it out.'

He sighed mockingly and rubbed his cheek against her arm. 'That's what Dundy says, but you keep Iva away from me, sweet, and I'll manage to survive the rest of my troubles.' He stood up and put on his hat. 'Have the *Spade & Archer* taken off the door and *Samuel Spade* put on. I'll be back in an hour, or phone you.'

Spade went through the St. Mark's long purplish lobby to the desk and asked a red-haired dandy whether Miss Wonderly was in. The red-haired dandy turned away, and then back, shaking his head. 'She checked out this morning, Mr. Spade.'

'Thanks.'

Spade walked past the desk to an alcove off the lobby where a plump young-middle-aged man in dark clothes sat at a flat-topped mahogany desk. On the edge of the desk facing the lobby was a triangular prism of mahogany and brass inscribed *Mr. Freed*.

The plump man got up and came around the desk holding out his hand.

'I was awfully sorry to hear about Archer, Spade,' he said in the tone of one trained to sympathise readily without intrusiveness. 'I've just seen it in the *Call*. He was here last night, you know.'

'Thanks, Freed. Were you talking to him?'

'No. He was sitting in the lobby when I came in early in the evening. I didn't stop. I thought he was probably working and I know you fellows like to be left alone when you're busy. Did that have anything to do with his——?'

'I don't think so, but we don't know yet. Anyway, we won't mix the house up in it if it can be helped.'

'Thanks.'

'That's all right. Can you give me some dope on an ex-guest, and then forget that I asked for it?'

'Surely.'

'A Miss Wonderly checked out this morning. I'd like to know the details.'

'Come along,' Freed said, 'and we'll see what we can learn.'

Spade stood still, shaking his head. 'I don't want to show in it.'

Freed nodded and went out of the alcove. In the lobby he halted suddenly and came back to Spade.

'Harriman was the house-detective on duty last night,' he said. 'He's sure to have seen Archer. Shall I caution him not to mention it?'

Spade looked at Freed from the corners of his eyes. 'Better not. That won't make any difference as long as there's no connection shown with this Wonderly. Harriman's all right, but he likes to talk, and I'd as lief not have him think there's anything to be kept quiet.'

Freed nodded again and went away. Fifteen minutes later he returned.

'She arrived last Tuesday, registering from New York. She hadn't a trunk, only some bags. There were no phone calls charged to her room, and she doesn't seem to have received much, if any, mail. The only one anybody remembers having seen her with was a tall dark man of thirty-six or so. She went out at half-past nine this morning, came back an hour later, paid her bill, and had her bags carried out to a car. The boy who carried them says it was a Nash touring car, probably a hired one. She left a forwarding address—the Ambassador, Los Angeles.'

Spade said, 'Thanks a lot, Freed,' and left the St. Mark.

*   *   *

When Spade returned to his office Effie Perine stopped typing a letter to tell him: 'Your friend Dundy was in. He wanted to look at your guns.'

'And?'

'I told him to come back when you were here.'

'Good girl. If he comes back again let him look at them.'

'And Miss Wonderly called up.'

'It's about time. What did she say?'

'She wants to see you.' The girl picked up a slip of paper from her desk and read the memorandum pencilled on it: 'She's at the Coronet, on California Street, apartment one thousand and one. You're to ask for Miss Leblanc.'

Spade said, 'Give me,' and held out his hand. When she had given him the memorandum he took out his lighter, snapped on the flame, set it to the slip of paper, held the paper until all but one corner was curling black ash, dropped it on the linoleum floor, and mashed it under his shoe sole.

The girl watched him with disapproving eyes.

He grinned at her, said, 'That's just the way it is, dear,' and went out again.

Chapter Four

The Black Bird

Miss Wonderly, in a belted green crêpe silk dress, opened the door of apartment 1001 at the Coronet. Her face was flushed. Her dark red hair, parted on the left side, swept back in loose waves over her right temple, was somewhat tousled.

Spade took off his hat and said: 'Good morning.'

His smile brought a fainter smile to her face. Her eyes, of blue that was almost violet, did not lose their troubled look. She lowered her head and said in a hushed, timid, voice: 'Come in, Mr. Spade.'

She led him past open kitchen, bathroom, and bedroom doors

into a cream-and-red living-room, apologising for its confusion: 'Everything is upside down. I haven't even finished unpacking.'

She laid his hat on a table and sat down on a walnut settee. He sat on a brocaded oval-backed chair facing her.

She looked at her fingers, working them together, and said: 'Mr. Spade, I've a terrible, terrible confession to make.'

Spade smiled a polite smile, which she did not lift her eyes to see, and said nothing.

'That—that story I told you yesterday was all—a story,' she stammered, and looked up at him now with miserable frightened eyes.

'Oh, that,' Spade said lightly. 'We didn't exactly believe your story.'

'Then——?' Perplexity was added to the misery and fright in her eyes.

'We believed your two hundred dollars.'

'You mean——?' She seemed not to know what he meant.

'I mean that you paid us more than if you'd been telling the truth,' he explained blandly, 'and enough more to make it all right.'

Her eyes suddenly lighted up. She lifted herself a few inches from the settee, settled down again, smoothed her skirt, leaned forward and spoke eagerly: 'And even now you'd be willing to—— ?'

Spade stopped her with a palm-up motion of one hand. The upper part of his face frowned. The lower part smiled. 'That depends,' he said. 'The hell of it is, Miss—— Is your name Wonderly or Leblanc?'

She blushed and murmured: 'It's really O'Shaughnessy— Brigid O'Shaughnessy.'

'The hell of it is, Miss O'Shaughnessy, that a couple of murders' —she winced—'coming together like this get everybody stirred up, make the police think they can go the limit, make everybody hard to handle and expensive. It's not——'

He stopped talking because she had stopped listening and was waiting for him to finish.

'Mr. Spade, tell me the truth.' Her voice quivered on the verge of hysteria. Her face had become haggard around desperate eyes. 'Am I to blame for—for last night?'

Spade shook his head. 'Not unless there are things I don't know about,' he said. 'You warned us that Thursby was dangerous. Of course you lied to us about your sister and all, but that doesn't count: we didn't believe you.' He shrugged his sloping shoulders. 'I wouldn't say it was your fault.'

She said, 'Thank you,' very softly, and then moved her head from side to side. 'But I'll always blame myself.' She put a hand to her throat. 'Mr. Archer was so—so alive yesterday afternoon, so solid and hearty and——'

'Stop it,' Spade commanded. 'He knew what he was doing. They're the chances we take.'

'Was—was he married?'

'Yes, with ten thousand insurance, no children, and a wife who didn't like him.'

'Oh, please don't!' she whispered.

Spade shrugged again. 'That's the way it was.' He glanced at his watch and moved from his chair to the settee beside her. 'There's no time for worrying about that now.' His voice was pleasant but firm. 'Out there a flock of policemen and assistant district attorneys and reporters are running around with their noses to the ground. What do you want to do?'

'I want you to save me from—from it all,' she replied in a thin tremulous voice. She put a timid hand on his sleeve. 'Mr. Spade, do they know about me?'

'Not yet. I wanted to see you first.'

'What—what would they think if they knew about the way I came to you with those lies?'

'It would make them suspicious. That's why I've been stalling them till I could see you. I thought maybe we wouldn't have to let them know all of it. We ought to be able to fake a story that will rock them to sleep, if necessary.'

'You don't think I had anything to do with the—the murders —do you?'

Spade grinned at her and said: 'I forgot to ask you that. Did you?'

'No.'

'That's good. Now what are we going to tell the police?'

She squirmed on her end of the settee and her eyes wavered between heavy lashes, as if trying and failing to free their gaze from his. She seemed smaller, and very young and oppressed.

'Must they know about me at all?' she asked. 'I think I'd rather die than that, Mr. Spade. I can't explain now, but can't you somehow manage so that you can shield me from them, so I won't have to answer their questions? I don't think I could stand being questioned now. I think I would rather die. Can't you, Mr. Spade?'

'Maybe,' he said, 'but I'll have to know what it's all about.'

She went down on her knees at his knees. She held her face up to him. Her face was wan, taut, and fearful over tight-clasped hands.

'I haven't lived a good life,' she cried. 'I've been bad—worse than you could know—but I'm not all bad. Look at me, Mr. Spade. You know I'm not all bad, don't you? You can see that, can't you? Then can't you trust me a little? Oh, I'm so alone and afraid, and I've got nobody to help me if you won't help me. I know I've no right to ask you to trust me if I won't trust you. I do trust you, but I can't tell you. I can't tell you now. Later I will, when I can. I'm afraid, Mr. Spade. I'm afraid of trusting you. I don't mean that. I do trust you, but—I trusted Floyd and—I've nobody else, nobody else, Mr. Spade. You can help me. You've said you can help me. If I hadn't believed you could save me I would have run away to-day instead of sending for you. If I thought anybody else could save me would I be down on my knees like this? I know this isn't fair of me. But be generous Mr. Spade, don't ask me to be fair. You're strong, you're resourceful, you're brave. You can spare me some of that strength and resourcefulness and courage, surely. Help me, Mr. Spade. Help me because I need help so badly, and because if you don't where will I find anyone who can, no matter how willing? Help me. I've no right to ask you to help me blindly, but I do ask you. Be generous, Mr. Spade. You can help me. Help me.'

Spade, who had held his breath through much of this speech, now emptied his lungs with a long sighing exhalation between pursed lips and said: 'You won't need much of anybody's help. You're good. You're very good. It's chiefly in your eyes, I think, and that throb you get into your voice when you say things like "Be generous, Mr. Spade."'

She jumped up on her feet. Her face crimsoned painfully,

but she held her head erect and she looked Spade straight in the eyes.

'I deserve that,' she said. 'I deserve it, but—oh!—I did want your help so much. I do want it, and need it, so much. And the lie was in the way I said it, and not at all in what I said.' She turned away, no longer holding herself erect. 'It is my own fault that you can't believe me now.'

Spade's face reddened and he looked down at the floor, muttering: 'Now you are dangerous.'

Brigid O'Shaughnessy went to the table and picked up his hat. She came back and stood in front of him holding the hat, not offering it to him, but holding it for him to take if he wished. Her face was white and thin.

Spade looked at his hat and asked: 'What happened last night?'

'Floyd came to the hotel at nine o'clock, and we went out for a walk. I suggested that so Mr. Archer could see him. We stopped at a restaurant in Geary Street, I think it was, for supper and to dance, and came back to the hotel at about half-past twelve. Floyd left me at the door and I stood inside and watched Mr. Archer follow him down the street on the other side.'

'Down? You mean towards Market Street?'

'Yes.'

'Do you know what they'd be doing in the neighbourhood of Bush and Stockton, where Archer was shot?'

'Isn't that near where Floyd lived?'

'No. It would be nearly a dozen blocks out of his way if he was going from your hotel to his. Well, what did you do after they had gone?'

'I went to bed. And this morning when I went out for breakfast I saw the headlines in the papers and read about—you know. Then I went up to Union Square, where I had seen automobiles for hire, and got one and went to the hotel for my luggage. After I found my room had been searched yesterday I knew I would have to move, and I found this place yesterday afternoon. So I came up here and then telephoned your office.'

'Your room at the St. Mark was searched?' he asked.

'Yes, while I was at your office.' She bit her lip. 'I didn't mean to tell you that.'

'That means I'm not supposed to question you about it?'
She nodded shyly.

He frowned.

She moved his hat a little in her hands.

He laughed impatiently and said: 'Stop waving the hat in my face. Haven't I offered to do what I can?'

She smiled contritely, returned the hat to the table, and sat beside him on the settee again.

He said: 'I've got nothing against trusting you blindly except that I won't be able to do you much good if I haven't some idea of what it's all about. For instance, I've got to have some sort of a line on your Floyd Thursby.'

'I met him in the Orient.' She spoke slowly, looking down at a pointed finger tracing eights on the settee between them. 'We came here from Hongkong last week. He was—he had promised to help me. He took advantage of my helplessness and dependence on him to betray me.'

'Betray you how?'

She shook her head and said nothing.

Spade, frowning with impatience, asked: 'Why did you want him shadowed?'

'I wanted to learn how far he had gone. He wouldn't even let me know where he was staying. I wanted to find out what he was doing, whom he was meeting, things like that.'

'Did he kill Archer?'

She looked up at him, surprised. 'Yes, certainly,' she said.

'He had a Luger in a shoulder-holster. Archer wasn't shot with a Luger.'

'He had a revolver in his overcoat pocket,' she said.

'You saw it?'

'Oh, I've seen it often. I know he always carries one there. I didn't see it last night, but I know he never wears an overcoat without it.'

'Why all the guns?'

'He lived by them. There was a story in Hongkong that he had come out there, to the Orient, as bodyguard to a gambler who had had to leave the States, and that the gambler had since disappeared. They said Floyd knew about his disappearing. I don't know. I do know that he always went heavily armed and that he never went to sleep without covering the floor around his bed with crumpled newspapers so nobody could come silently into his room.'

'You picked a nice sort of playmate.'

'Only that sort could have helped me,' she said simply, 'if he had been loyal.'

'Yes, if.' Spade pinched his lower lip between finger and thumb and looked gloomily at her. The vertical creases over his nose deepened, drawing his brows together. 'How bad a hole are you actually in?'

'As bad,' she said, 'as could be.'

'Physical danger?'

'I'm not heroic. I don't think there's anything worse than death.'

'Then it's that?'

'It's that as surely as we're sitting here'—she shivered—'unless you help me.'

He took his fingers away from his mouth and ran them through his hair. 'I'm not God,' he said irritably. 'I can't work miracles out of thin air.' He looked at his watch. 'The day's going and you're giving me nothing to work with. Who killed Thursby?'

She put a crumpled handkerchief to her mouth and said, 'I don't know,' through it.

'Your enemies or his?'

'I don't know. His, I hope, but I'm afraid—I don't know.'

'How was he supposed to be helping you? Why did you bring him here from Hongkong?'

She looked at him with frightened eyes and shook her head in silence. Her face was haggard and pitifully stubborn.

Spade stood up, thrust his hands into the pockets of his jacket, and scowled down at her. 'This is hopeless,' he said savagely. 'I can't do anything for you. I don't know what you want done. I don't even know if you know what you want.'

She hung her head and wept.

He made a growling animal noise in his throat and went to the table for his hat.

'You won't,' she begged in a small choked voice, not looking up, 'go to the police?'

'Go to them!' he exclaimed, his voice loud with rage. 'They've been running me ragged since four o'clock this morning. I've made myself God knows how much trouble standing them off. For what? For some crazy notion that I could help you. I can't. I won't try.' He put his hat on his head and pulled it down tight. 'Go to them? All I've got to do is stand still and they'll be swarming all over me. Well, I'll tell them what I know and you'll have to take your chances.'

She rose from the settee and held herself straight in front of him though her knees were trembling, and she held her white panic-stricken face up high though she couldn't hold the twitching muscles of mouth and chin still. She said: 'You've been patient. You've tried to help me. It is hopeless, and useless, I suppose.' She stretched out her right hand. 'I thank you for what you have done. I—I'll have to take my chances.'

Spade made the growling animal noise in his throat again and sat down on the settee. 'How much money have you got?' he asked.

The question startled her. Then she pinched her lower lip between her teeth and answered reluctantly: 'I've about five hundred dollars left.'

'Give it to me.'

She hesitated, looking timidly at him. He made angry gestures with mouth, eyebrows, hands and shoulders. She went into her bedroom, returning almost immediately with a sheaf of paper money in one hand.

He took the money from her, counted it, and said: 'There's only four hundred here.'

'I had to keep some to live on,' she explained meekly, putting a hand to her breast.

'Can't you get any more?'

'No.'

'You must have something you can raise money on,' he insisted.

'I've some rings, a little jewellery.'

'You'll have to hock them,' he said, and held out his hand. 'The Remedial's the best place—Mission and Fifth.'

She looked pleadingly at him. His yellowish-grey eyes were hard and implacable. Slowly she put her hand inside the neck of her dress, brought out a slender roll of bills, and put them in his waiting hand.

He smoothed the bills out and counted them—four twenties, four tens, and a five. He returned two of the tens and the five to her. The others he put in his pocket. Then he stood up and said: 'I'm going out and see what I can do for you. I'll be back as soon as I can with the best news I can manage. I'll ring four times—long, short, long, short—so you'll know it's me. You needn't go to the door with me. I can let myself out.'

He left her standing in the centre of the floor looking after him with dazed blue eyes.

Spade went into a reception room whose door bore the legend *Wise, Merican & Wise*. The red-haired girl at the switchboard said: 'Oh, hello, Mr. Spade.'

'Hello, darling,' he replied. 'Is Sid in?'

He stood beside her with a hand on her plump shoulder while she manipulated a plug and spoke into the mouthpiece: 'Mr. Spade to see you, Mr. Wise.' She looked up at Spade. 'Go right in.'

He squeezed her shoulder by way of acknowledgment, crossed the reception room to a dully lighted inner corridor, and passed down the corridor to a frosted glass door at its far end. He opened the frosted glass door and went into an office where a small olive-skinned man with a tired oval face under thin dark hair dotted with dandruff sat behind an immense desk on which bales of paper were heaped.

The small man flourished a cold cigar-stub at Spade and said: 'Pull a chair around. So Miles got the big one last night?' Neither his tired face nor his rather shrill voice held any emotion.

'Uh-huh, that's what I came in about.' Spade frowned and cleared his throat. 'I think I'm going to have to tell a coroner to go to hell, Sid. Can I hide behind the sanctity of my clients' secrets and identities and what-not, all the same priest or lawyer?'

Sid Wise lifted his shoulders and lowered the ends of his mouth. 'Why not? An inquest is not a court-trial. You can try, anyway. You've gotten away with more than that before this.'

'I know, but Dundy's getting snotty, and maybe it is a little bit thick this time. Get your hat, Sid, and we'll go see the right people. I want to be safe.'

Sid Wise looked at the papers massed on his desk and groaned, but he got up from his chair and went to the closet by the window.

'You're a son of a gun, Sammy,' he said as he took his hat from its hook.

Spade returned to his office at ten minutes past five that evening. Effie Perine was sitting at his desk reading *Time*. Spade sat on the desk and asked: 'Anything stirring?'

'Not here. You look like you'd swallowed the canary.'

He grinned contentedly. 'I think we've got a future. I always had an idea that if Miles would go off and die somewhere we'd stand a better chance of thriving. Will you take care of sending flowers for me?'

'I did.'

'You're an invaluable angel. How's your woman's intuition to-day?'

'Why?'

'What do you think of Wonderly?'

'I'm for her,' the girl replied without hesitation.

'She's got too many names,' Spade mused, 'Wonderly, Leblanc, and she says the right one's O'Shaughnessy.'

'I don't care if she's got all the names in the phone book. That girl is all right, and you know it.'

'I wonder.' Spade blinked sleepily at Effie Perine. He chuckled. 'Anyway she's given up seven hundred smacks in two days, and that's all right.'

Effie Perine sat up straight and said: 'Sam, if that girl's in trouble and you let her down, or take advantage of it to bleed her, I'll never forgive you, never have any respect for you, as long as I live.'

Spade smiled unnaturally. Then he frowned. The frown was unnatural. He opened his mouth to speak, but the sound of someone's entrance through the corridor-door stopped him.

Effie Perine rose and went into the outer office. Spade took off his hat and sat in his chair. The girl returned with an engraved card—*Mr. Joel Cairo*.

'This guy is queer,' she said.

'In with him, then, darling,' said Spade.

Mr. Joel Cairo was a small-boned, dark man of medium height. His hair was black and smooth and very glossy. His features were Levantine. A square-cut ruby, its sides paralleled by four baguette diamonds, gleamed against the deep green of his cravat. His black coat, cut tight to narrow shoulders, flared a little over slightly plump hips. His trousers fitted his round legs more snugly than was the current fashion. The uppers of his patent-leather shoes were hidden by fawn spats. He held a black derby hat in a chamois-gloved hand and came towards Spade with short mincing, bobbing steps. The fragrance of *chypre* came with him.

Spade inclined his head at his visitor and then at a chair, saying: 'Sit down, Mr. Cairo.'

Cairo bowed elaborately over his hat, said, 'I thank you,' in a high-pitched thin voice and sat down. He sat down primly, crossing his ankles, placing his hat on his knees, and began to draw off his yellow gloves.

Spade rocked back in his chair and asked: 'Now what can I do for you, Mr. Cairo?' The amiable negligence of his tone, his motion in the chair, were precisely as they had been when he had addressed the same question to Brigid O'Shaughnessy on the previous day.

Cairo turned his hat over, dropping his gloves into it, and placed it bottom-up on the corner of the desk nearest him. Diamonds twinkled on the second and fourth fingers of his left hand, a ruby that matched the one in his tie even to the surrounding diamonds on the third finger of his right hand. His hands were soft and well cared for. Though they were not large their flaccid bluntness made them seem clumsy. He rubbed his palms together and said over the whispering sound they made: 'May a stranger offer condolences for your partner's unfortunate death?'

'Thanks.'

'May I ask, Mr. Spade, if there was, as the newspapers inferred, a certain—ah—relationship between that unfortunate happening and the death a little later of the man Thursby?'

Spade said nothing in a blank-faced definite way.

Cairo rose and bowed. 'I beg your pardon.' He sat down and placed his hands side by side, palms down, on the corner of the desk. 'More than idle curiosity made me ask that, Mr. Spade. I am trying to recover an—ah—ornament that has been—shall we say?—mislaid. I thought, and hoped, you could assist me.'

Spade nodded with eyebrows lifted to indicate attentiveness.

'The ornament is a statuette,' Cairo went on, selecting and mouthing his words carefully, 'the black figure of a bird.'

Spade nodded again, with courteous interest.

'I am prepared to pay, on behalf of the figure's rightful owner, the sum of five thousand dollars for its recovery.' Cairo raised one hand from the desk corner and touched a spot in the air with the broad-nailed tip of an ugly forefinger. 'I am prepared to promise that—what is the phrase?—no questions will be asked.' He put his hand on the desk again beside the other and smiled blandly over them at the private detective.

'Five thousand is a lot of money,' Spade commented, looking thoughtfully at Cairo. 'It——'

Fingers drummed lightly on the door.

When Spade had called, 'Come in,' the door opened far enough to admit Effie Perine's head and shoulders. She had put on a small dark felt hat and a dark coat with a grey fur collar.

'Is there anything else?' she asked.

'No. Good night. Lock the door when you go, will you?'

'Good night,' she said and disappeared behind the closing door.

Spade turned in his chair to face Cairo again, saying: 'It's an interesting figure.'

The sound of the corridor door's closing behind Effie Perine came to them.

Cairo smiled and took a short compact flat black pistol out of an inner pocket. 'You will please,' he said, 'clasp your hands together at the back of your neck.'

Chapter Five

The Levantine

Spade did not look at the pistol. He raised his arms and, leaning back in his chair, intertwined the fingers of his two hands behind his head. His eyes, holding no particular expression remained focused on Cairo's dark face.

Cairo coughed a little apologetic cough and smiled nervously with lips that had lost some of their redness. His dark eyes were humid and bashful and very earnest. 'I intend to search your offices, Mr. Spade. I warn you that if you attempt to prevent me I shall certainly shoot you.'

'Go ahead,' Spade's voice was as empty of expression as his face.

'You will please stand,' the man with the pistol instructed him at whose thick chest the pistol was aimed. 'I shall have to make sure that you are not armed.'

Spade stood up pushing the chair back with his calves as he straightened his legs.

Cairo went around behind him. He transferred the pistol from his right hand to his left. He lifted Spade's coat-tail and looked under it. Holding the pistol close to Spade's back, he put his right hand around Spade's side and patted his chest. The Levantine's face was then no more than six inches below and behind Spade's right elbow.

Spade's elbow dropped as Spade spun to the right. Cairo's face jerked back not far enough : Spade's right heel on the patent-leathered toes anchored the smaller man in the elbow's path. The elbow struck him beneath the cheek-bone, staggering him so that he must have fallen had he not been held by Spade's foot on his foot. Spade's elbow went on past the astonished dark face and straightened when Spade's hand struck down at the pistol. Cairo let the pistol go the instant that Spade's fingers touched it. The pistol was small in Spade's hand.

Spade took his foot off Cairo's to complete his about-face. With his left hand Spade gathered together the smaller man's coat lapels—the ruby-set green tie bunching out over his knuckles —while his right hand stowed the captured weapon away in a coat pocket. Spade's yellow-grey eyes were sombre. His face was wooden, with a trace of sullenness around the mouth.

Cairo's face was twisted by pain and chagrin. There were tears in his dark eyes. His skin was the complexion of polished lead except where the elbow had reddened his cheeks.

Spade by means of his grip on the Levantine's lapels turned him slowly and pushed him back until he was standing close in front of the chair he had lately occupied. A puzzled look replaced the look of pain in the lead-coloured face. Then Spade smiled. His smile was gentle, even dreamy. His right shoulder raised a few inches. His bent right arm was driven up by the shoulder's lift. Fist, wrist, forearm, crooked elbow and upper arm seemed all one rigid piece, with only the limber shoulder giving them motion. The fist struck Cairo's face, covering for a moment one side of his chin, a corner of his mouth, and most of his cheek between cheek-bone and jaw-bone.

Cairo shut his eyes and was unconscious.

Spade lowered the limp body into the chair, where it lay with sprawled arms and legs, the head lolling back against the chair back, the mouth open.

Spade emptied the unconscious man's pockets one by one, working methodically, moving the lax body when necessary, making a pile of the pocket's contents on the desk. When the last pocket had been turned out he turned to his own chair, rolled and lighted a cigarette, and began to examine his spoils. He examined them with grave unhurried thoroughness.

There was a large wallet of dark soft leather. The wallet contained three hundred and sixty-five dollars in United States bills of several sizes; three five-pound notes; a much-viséd Greek passport bearing Cairo's name and portrait; five folded sheets of pinkish onion-skin paper covered with what seemed to be Arabic writing; a raggedly clipped newspaper account of the finding of Archer's and Thursby's bodies; a postcard photograph of a dusky woman with bold cruel eyes and a tender drooping mouth; a large silk handkerchief, yellow with age and somewhat cracked along its folds; a thin sheaf of Mr. Joel Cairo's engraved cards; and a ticket for an orchestra seat at the Geary Theatre that evening.

Besides the wallet and its contents there were three gaily coloured silk handkerchiefs fragrant of *chypre*; a platinum Longines watch on a platinum-and-red gold chain, attached at the other end to a small pear-shaped pendant of some white metal; a handful of United States, British, French, and Chinese coins; a ring holding half a dozen keys; a silver-and-onyx fountain pen; a metal comb in a leatherette case; a nail-file in a leatherette case; a small street-guide to San Francisco; a Southern Pacific baggage-check; a half-filled package of violet pastilles; a Shanghai insurance-broker's business card; and four sheets of Hotel Belvedere writing paper, on one of which was written in small precise letters Samuel Spade's name and the address of his office and his apartment.

Having examined these articles carefully—he even opened the back of the watch-case to see that nothing was hidden inside—Spade leaned over and took the unconscious man's wrist between finger and thumb, feeling his pulse. Then he dropped the wrist, settled back in his chair, and rolled and lighted another cigarette. His face while he smoked was, except for occasional slight and aimless movements of his lower lip, so still and reflective that it seemed stupid; but when Cairo presently moaned and fluttered his eyelids Spade's face became bland, and he put the beginning of a friendly smile into his eyes and mouth.

Joel Cairo awakened slowly. His eyes opened first, but a full minute passed before they fixed their gaze on any definite part of the ceiling. Then he shut his mouth and swallowed, exhaling heavily through his nose afterwards. He drew in one foot and turned a hand over on his thigh. Then he raised his head from the chair back, looked around the office in confusion, saw Spade, and sat up. He opened his mouth to speak, started, clapped a hand to his face where Spade's fist had struck and where there was now a florid bruise.

Cairo said through his teeth, painfully: 'I could have shot you, Mr. Spade.'

'You could have tried,' Spade conceded.

'I did not try.'

'I know.'

'Then why did you strike me after I was disarmed?'

'Sorry,' Spade said, and grinned wolfishly, showing his jaw-teeth, 'but imagine my embarrassment when I found that five-thousand-dollar offer was just hooey.'

'You are mistaken, Mr. Spade. That was, and is, a genuine offer.'

'What the hell?' Spade's surprise was genuine.

'I am prepared to pay five thousand dollars for the figure's return.' Cairo took his hand away from his bruised face and sat up prim and business-like again. 'You have it?'

'No.'

'If it is not here'—Cairo was very politely sceptical—'why should you have risked serious injury to prevent my searching for it?'

'I should sit around and let people come in and stick me up?' Spade flicked a finger at Cairo's possessions on the desk. 'You've got my apartment address. Been up there yet?'

'Yes, Mr. Spade. I am ready to pay five thousand dollars for the figure's return, but surely it is natural enough that I should try first to spare the owner that expense if possible.'

'Who is he?'

Cairo shook his head and smiled. 'You will have to forgive my not answering that question.'

'Will I?' Spade leaned forward smiling with tight lips. 'I've got you by the neck, Cairo. You've walked in and tied yourself up, plenty strong enough to suit the police, with last night's killings. Well, now you'll have to play with me or else.'

Cairo's smile was demure and not in any way alarmed. 'I made somewhat extensive inquiries about you before taking any action,' he said, 'and was assured that you were far too reasonable to allow other considerations to interfere with profitable business relations.'

Spade shrugged. 'Where are they?' he asked.

'I have offered you five thousand dollars for——'

Spade thumped Cairo's wallet with the backs of his fingers and said: 'There's nothing like five thousand dollars here. You're betting your eyes. You could come in and say you'd pay me a million for a purple elephant, but what in hell would that mean?'

'I see, I see,' Cairo said thoughtfully, screwing up his eyes.

'You wish some assurance of my sincerity.' He brushed his red lower lip with a finger-tip. 'A retainer, would that serve?'

'It might.'

Cairo put his hand out towards his wallet, hesitated, withdrew the hand, and said: 'You will take, say, a hundred dollars?'

Spade picked up the wallet and took out a hundred dollars. Then he frowned, said, 'Better make it two hundred,' and did.

Cairo said nothing.

'Your first guess was that I had the bird,' Spade said in a crisp voice when he had put the two hundred dollars into his pocket and had dropped the wallet on the desk again. 'There's nothing in that. What's your second?'

'That you know where it is, or, if not exactly that, that you know it is where you can get it.'

Spade neither denied nor affirmed that: he seemed hardly to have heard it. He asked: 'What sort of proof can you give me that your man is the owner?'

'Very little, unfortunately. There is this, though: nobody else can give you any authentic evidence of ownership at all. And if you know as much about the affair as I suppose—or I should not be here—you know that the means by which it was taken from him shows that his right to it was more valid than anyone else's—certainly more valid than Thursby's.'

'What about his daughter?' Spade asked.

Excitement opened Cairo's eyes and mouth, turned his face red, made his voice shrill. '*He* is not the owner!'

Spade said, 'Oh,' mildly and ambiguously.

'Is he here, in San Francisco, now?' Cairo asked in a less shrill, but still excited, voice.

Spade blinked his eyes sleepily and suggested: 'It might be better all around if we put our cards on the table.'

Cairo recovered composure with a little jerk. 'I do not think it would be better.' His voice was suave now. 'If you know more than I, I shall profit by your knowledge, and so will you to the extent of five thousand dollars. If you do not then I have made a mistake in coming to you, and to do as you suggest would be simply to make that mistake worse.'

Spade nodded indifferently and waved his hand at the articles on the desk, saying: 'There's your stuff'; and then, when Cairo was returning them to his pockets: 'It's understood that you're to pay my expenses while I'm getting this black bird for you, and five thousand dollars when it's done?'

'Yes, Mr. Spade; that is, five thousand dollars less whatever moneys have been advanced to you—five thousand in all.'

'Right. And it's a legitimate proposition.' Spade's face was solemn except for wrinkles at the corners of his eyes. 'You're not hiring me to do any murders or burglaries for you, but simply to get it back if possible in an honest and lawful way.'

'If possible,' Cairo agreed. His face also was solemn except for the eyes. 'And in any event with discretion.' He rose and picked up his hat. 'I am at the Hotel Belvedere when you wish to communicate with me—room six-thirty-five. I confidently expect the greatest mutual benefit from our association, Mr. Spade.' He hesitated. 'May I have my pistol?'

'Sure, I'd forgotten it.'

Spade took the pistol out of his coat pocket and handed it to Cairo.

Cairo pointed the pistol at Spade's chest.

'You will please keep your hands on the top of the desk,' Cairo said earnestly. 'I intend to search your offices.'

Spade said: 'I'll be damned.' Then he laughed in his throat and said: 'All right. Go ahead. I won't stop you.'

Chapter Six

The Undersized Shadow

For half an hour after Joel Cairo had gone Spade sat alone, still frowning, at his desk. Then he said aloud in the tone of one dismissing a problem, 'Well, they're paying for it,' and took a bottle of Manhattan cocktail and a paper drinking-cup from a desk drawer. He filled the cup two-thirds full, drank, returned the bottle to the drawer, tossed the cup into the waste-basket, put on his hat and overcoat, turned off the lights, and went down to the night-lit street.

An undersized youth of twenty or twenty-one in neat grey cap and overcoat was standing idly on the corner below Spade's building.

Spade walked up Sutter Street to Kearny, where he entered a cigar store to buy two sacks of Bull Durham. When he came out the youth was one of four people waiting for a street-car on the opposite corner.

Spade ate dinner at Herbert's Grill in Powell Street. When he left the Grill, at a quarter to eight, the youth was looking into a near-by haberdasher's window.

Spade went to the Hotel Belvedere, asking at the desk for Mr. Cairo. He was told that Cairo was not in. The youth sat in a chair in a far corner of the lobby.

Spade went to the Geary Theatre, failed to see Cairo in the lobby, and posted himself on the kerb in front, facing the theatre. The youth loitered with other loiterers before Marquard's restaurant below.

At ten minutes past eight Joel Cairo appeared, walking up Geary Street with his little mincing bobbling steps. Apparently he did not see Spade until the private detective touched his shoulder. He seemed moderately surprised for a moment, and then said: 'Oh, yes, of course you saw the ticket.'

'Uh-huh. I've got something I want to show you.' Spade drew Cairo back towards the kerb a little away from the other waiting theatre-goers. 'The kid in the cap down by Marquard's.'

Cairo murmured, 'I'll see,' and looked at his watch. He looked up Geary Street. He looked at a theatre sign in front of him on which George Arliss was shown costumed as Shylock, and then his dark eyes crawled sidewise in their sockets until they were looking at the kid in the cap, at his cool pale face with curling lashes hiding lowered eyes.

'Who is he?' Spade asked.

Cairo smiled up at Spade. 'I do not know him.'

'He's been tailing me around town.'

Cairo wet his lower lip with his tongue and asked: 'Do you think it was wise, then, to let him see us together?'

'How do I know?' Spade replied. 'Anyway, it's done.'

Cairo removed his hat and smoothed his hair with a gloved hand. He replaced his hat carefully on his head and said with every appearance of candour: 'I give you my word I do not know him, Mr. Spade. I give you my word I have nothing to do with him. I have asked nobody's assistance except yours, on my word of honour.'

'Then he's one of the others?'

'That may be.'

'I just wanted to know, because if he gets to be a nuisance I may have to hurt him.'

'Do as you think best. He is not a friend of mine.'

'That's good. There goes the curtain. Good night,' Spade said, and crossed the street to board a westbound street-car.

The youth in the cap boarded the same car.

Spade left the car at Hyde Street and went up to his apartment. His rooms were not greatly upset, but showed unmistakable signs of having been searched. When Spade had washed and had put on a fresh shirt and collar he went out again, walked up to Sutter Street and boarded a westbound car. The youth boarded it also.

Within half a dozen blocks of the Coronet, Spade left the car and went into the vestibule of a tall brown apartment building. He pressed three bell-buttons together. The street-door lock buzzed. He entered, passed the elevator and stairs, went down a long yellow-walled corridor to the rear of the building, found a back door fastened by a Yale lock, and let himself out into a narrow court. The court led to a dark back street, up which Spade walked for two blocks. Then he crossed over to California Street and went to the Coronet. It was not quite half-past nine o'clock.

The eagerness with which Brigid O'Shaughnessy welcomed Spade suggested that she had been not entirely certain of his coming. She had put on a satin gown of the blue shade called Artoise that season, with chalcedony shoulder-straps, and her stockings and slippers were Artoise.

The red and cream sitting-room had been brought to order and livened with flowers in squat pottery vases of black and silver. Three small rough-barked logs burned in the fireplace. Spade watched them burn while she put away his hat and coat.

'Do you bring me good news?' she asked when she came

into the room again. Anxiety looked through her smile, and she held her breath.

'We don't have to make anything public that hasn't already been made public.'

'The police won't have to know about me?'

'No.'

She sighed happily and sat on the walnut settee. Her face relaxed and her body relaxed. She smiled up at him with admiring eyes. 'However did you manage it?' she asked more in wonder than in curiosity.

'Most things in San Francisco can be bought or taken.'

'And you won't get into trouble? Do sit down.' She made room for him on the settee.

'I don't mind a reasonable amount of trouble,' he said with not too much complacence.

He stood beside the fireplace and looked at her with eyes that studied, weighed, judged her without pretence that they were not studying, weighing, judging her. She flushed slightly under the frankness of his scrutiny, but she seemed more sure of herself than before, though a becoming shyness had not left her eyes. He stood there until it seemed plain that he meant to ignore her invitation to sit beside her, and then crossed to the settee.

'You aren't,' he asked as he sat down, 'exactly the sort of person you pretend to be, are you?'

'I'm not sure I know what you mean,' she said in her hushed voice, looking at him with puzzled eyes.

'Schoolgirl manner,' he explained, 'stammering and blushing and all that.'

She blushed and replied hurriedly, not looking at him: 'I told you this afternoon that I've been bad—worse than you could know.'

'That's what I mean,' he said. 'You told me that this afternoon in the same words, same tone. It's a speech you've practised.'

After a moment in which she seemed confused almost to the point of tears she laughed and said: 'Very well, then, Mr. Spade, I'm not at all the sort of person I pretend to be. I'm eighty years old, incredibly wicked, and an iron-moulder by trade. But if it's a pose it's one I've grown into, so you won't expect me to drop it entirely, will you?'

'Oh, it's all right,' he assured her. 'Only it wouldn't be all right if you were actually that innocent. We'd never get anywhere.'

'I won't be innocent,' she promised with a hand on her heart.

'I saw Joel Cairo to-night,' he said in the manner of one making polite conversation.

Gaiety went out of her face. Her eyes, focused on his profile, became frightened, then cautious. He had stretched his legs out and was looking at his crossed feet. His face did not indicate that he was thinking about anything.

There was a long pause before she asked uneasily:

'You—you know him?'

'I saw him to-night.' Spade did not look up and he maintained his light conversational tone. 'He was going to see George Arliss.'

'You mean you talked to him?'

'Only for a minute or two, till the curtain-bell rang.'

She got up from the settee and went to the fireplace to poke the fire. She changed slightly the position of an ornament on the mantelpiece, crossed the room to get a box of cigarettes from a table in a corner, straightened a curtain, and returned to her seat. Her face now was smooth and unworried.

Spade grinned sidewise at her and said: 'You're good. You're very good.'

Her face did not change. She asked quietly: 'What did he say?'

'About what?'

She hesitated. 'About me.'

'Nothing,' Spade turned to hold his lighter under the end of her cigarette. His eyes were shiny in a wooden Satan's face.

'Well, what did he say?' she asked with half-playful petulance.

'He offered me five thousand dollars for the black bird.'

She started, her teeth tore the end of her cigarette, and her eyes, after a swift alarmed glance at Spade, turned away from him.

'You're not going to go around poking at the fire and straightening up the room again, are you?' he asked lazily.

She laughed a clear merry laugh, dropped the mangled cigarette into a tray, and looked at him with clear merry eyes. 'I won't,' she promised. 'And what did you say?'

'Five thousand dollars is a lot of money.'

She smiled, but when, instead of smiling, he looked gravely at her, her smile became faint, confused, and presently vanished. In it's place came a hurt, bewildered look. 'Surely you're not really considering it,' she said.

'Why not? Five thousand dollars is a lot of money.'

'But Mr. Spade, you promised to help me.' Her hands were on his arm. 'I trusted you. You can't——' She broke off, took her hands from his sleeve and worked them together.

Spade smiled gently into her troubled eyes. 'Don't let's try to figure out how much you've trusted me. I promised to help you—sure—but you didn't say anything about any black birds.'

'But you must've known or—or you wouldn't have mentioned it to me. You do know now. You won't—you can't—treat me like that.' Her eyes were cobalt-blue prayers.

'Five thousand dollars is,' he said it for the third time, 'a lot of money.

She lifted her shoulders and hands and let them fall in a gesture that accepted defeat. 'It is,' she agreed in a small dull voice. 'It is far more than I could ever offer you, if I must bid for your loyalty.'

Spade laughed. His laughter was brief and somewhat bitter. 'That is good,' he said, 'coming from you. What have you given me beside money? Have you given me any of your confidence, any of the truth, any help in helping you? Haven't you tried to buy my loyalty with money and nothing else? Well, if I'm peddling it, why shouldn't I let it go to the highest bidder?'

'I've given you all the money I have.' Tears glistened in her white-ringed eyes. Her voice was hoarse, vibrant. 'I've thrown myself on your mercy, told you that without your help I'm utterly lost. What else is there?' She suddenly moved close to him on the settee and cried angrily: 'Can I buy you with my body?'

Their faces were a few inches apart. Spade took her face between his hands and he kissed her mouth roughly and contemptuously. Then he sat back and said: 'I'll think it over.' His face was hard and furious.

She sat still holding her numb face where his hands had left it.

He stood up and said: 'Christ! there's no sense to this.' He took two steps towards the fireplace and stopped, glowering at the burning logs, grinding his teeth together.

She did not move.

He turned to face her. The two vertical lines above his nose were deep clefts between red weals. 'I don't give a damn about your honesty,' he told her, trying to make himself speak calmly. 'I don't care what kind of tricks you're up to, what your secrets are, but I've got to have something to show that you know what you're doing.'

'I do know. Please believe that I do, and that it's all for the best, and——'

'Show me,' he ordered. 'I'm willing to help you. I've done what I could so far. If necessary I'll go ahead blindfolded, but I can't do it without more confidence in you than I've got now. You've got to convince me that you know what it's all about, that you're not simply fiddling around by guess and by God, hoping it'll come out all right somehow in the end.'

'Can't you trust me just a little longer?'

'How much is a little? And what are you waiting for?'

She bit her lip and looked down. 'I must talk to Joel Cairo,' she said almost inaudibly.

'You can see him to-night,' Spade said, looking at his watch. 'His show will be out soon. We can get him on the phone at his hotel.'

She raised her eyes, alarmed. 'But he can't come here. I can't let him know where I am. I'm afraid.'

'My place,' Spade suggested.

She hesitated, working her lips together, then asked: 'Do you think he'd go there?'

Spade nodded.

'All right,' she exclaimed, jumping up, her eyes large and bright. 'Shall we go now?'

She went into the next room. Spade went to the table in the corner and silently pulled the drawer out. The drawer held two packs of playing cards, a pad of score-cards for bridge, a brass screw, a piece of red string, and a gold pencil. He had shut the drawer and was lighting a cigarette when she returned wearing a small dark hat and a grey kidskin coat, carrying his hat and coat.

Their taxicab drew up behind a dark sedan that stood directly in front of Spade's street-door. Iva Archer was alone in the sedan, sitting at the wheel. Spade lifted his hat to her and went indoors with Brigid O'Shaughnessy. In the lobby he halted beside one of the benches and asked: 'Do you mind waiting here a moment? I won't be long.'

'That's perfectly all right,' Brigid O'Shaughnessy said, sitting down. 'You needn't hurry.'

Spade went out to the sedan. When he opened the sedan's door Iva spoke quickly: 'I've got to talk to you, Sam. Can't I come in?' Her face was pale and nervous.

'Not now.'

Iva clicked her teeth together and asked sharply: 'Who is she?'

'I've only got a minute, Iva,' Spade said patiently. 'What is it?'

'Who is she?' she repeated, nodding at the street-door.

He looked away from her, down the street. In front of a garage on the next corner an undersized youth of twenty or twenty-one in neat grey cap and overcoat loafed with his back against a wall. Spade frowned and returned his gaze to Iva's insistent face. 'What's the matter?' he asked. 'Has anything happened? You oughtn't to be here at this time of night.'

'I'm beginning to believe that,' she complained. 'You told me I oughtn't to come to the office, and now I oughtn't to come here. Do you mean I oughtn't to chase after you? If that's what you mean why don't you say it right out?'

'Now, Iva, you've got no right to take that attitude.'

'I know I haven't. I haven't any rights at all, it seems, where you're concerned. I thought I had. I thought your pretending to love me gave me——'

Spade said wearily: 'This is no time to be arguing about that, precious. What was it you wanted to see me about?'

'I can't talk to you here, Sam. Can't I come in?'

'Not now.'

'Why can't I?'

Spade said nothing.

She made a thin line of her mouth, squirmed around straight behind the wheel, and started the sedan's engine, staring angrily ahead.

When the sedan began to move Spade said, 'Good night, Iva,'

shut the door, and stood at the kerb with his hat in his hand until it had been driven away. Then he went indoors again.

Brigid O'Shaughnessy rose smiling cheerfully from the bench and they went up to his apartment.

Chapter Seven

G in the Air

In his bedroom that was a living-room now the wall-bed was up, Spade took Brigid O'Shaughnessy's hat and coat, made her comfortable in a padded rocking-chair, and telephoned the Hotel Belvedere. Cairo had not returned from the theatre. Spade left his telephone number with the request that Cairo call him as soon as he came in.

Spade sat down in the armchair beside the table and without any preliminary, without an introductory remark of any sort, began to tell the girl about a thing that had happened some years before in the North-west. He talked in a steady matter-of-fact voice that was devoid of emphasis or pauses, though now and then he repeated a sentence slightly rearranged, as if it were important that each detail be related exactly as it had happened.

At the beginning Brigid O'Shaughnessy listened with only partial attentiveness, obviously more surprised by his telling the story than interested in it, her curiosity more engaged with his purpose in telling the story than with the story he told; but presently, as the story went on, it caught her more and more fully and she became still and receptive.

A man named Flitcraft had left his real estate office, in Tacoma, to go to luncheon one day and never returned. He did not keep an engagement to play golf after four that afternoon, though he had taken the initiative in making the engagement less than half an hour before he went out to luncheon. His wife and children never saw him again. His wife and he were supposed to be on the best of terms. He had two children, boys, one five and the other three. He owned his house in a Tacoma suburb, a new Packard, and the rest of the appurtenances of successful American living.

Flitcraft had inherited seventy thousand dollars from his father, and, with his success in real estate, was worth something in the neighbourhood of two hundred thousand dollars at the time he vanished. His affairs were in order, though there were enough loose ends to indicate that he had not been setting them in order preparatory to vanishing. A deal that would have brought him an attractive profit, for instance, was to have been concluded the day after the one on which he disappeared. There was nothing to suggest that he had more than fifty or sixty dollars in his immediate possession at the time of his going. His habits for months past could be accounted for too thoroughly to justify any suspicion of secret vices, or even of another woman in his life, though either was barely possible.

'He went like that,' Spade said, 'like a fist when you open your hand.'

When he had reached this point in his story the telephone bell rang.

'Hello,' Spade said into the instrument. 'Mr. Cairo? ... This is Spade. Can you come up to my place—Post Street—now? ... Yes, I think it is.' He looked at the girl, pursed his lips, and then said rapidly: 'Miss O'Shaughnessy is here and wants to see you.'

Brigid O'Shaughnessy frowned and stirred in her chair, but did not say anything.

Spade put the telephone down and told her: 'He'll be up in a few minutes. Well, that was in 1922. In 1927 I was with one of the big detective agencies in Seattle. Mrs. Flitcraft came in and told us somebody had seen a man in Spokane who looked a lot like her husband. I went over there. It was Flitcraft all right. He had been living in Spokane for a couple of years as Charles—that was his first name—Pierce. He had an automobile business that was netting him twenty or twenty-five thousand a year, a wife, a baby son, owned his home in a Spokane suburb, and usually got away to play golf after four in the afternoon during the season.'

Spade had not been told very definitely what to do when he

found Flitcraft. They talked in Spade's room at the Davenport. Flitcraft had no feeling of guilt. He had left his first family well provided for, and what he had done seemed to him perfectly reasonable. The only thing that bothered him was a doubt that he could make that reasonableness clear to Spade. He had never told anybody his story before, and thus had not had to attempt to make its reasonableness explicit. He tried now.

'I got it all right,' Spade told Brigid O'Shaughnessy, 'but Mrs. Flitcraft never did. She thought it was silly. Maybe it was. Anyway, it came out all right. She didn't want any scandal, and, after the trick he had played on her—the way she looked at it—she didn't want him. So they were divorced on the quiet and everything was swell all around.

'Here's what happened to him. Going to lunch he passed an office building that was being put up—just the skeleton. A beam or something fell eight or ten stories down and smacked the sidewalk alongside him. It brushed pretty close to him, but didn't touch him, though a piece of the sidewalk was chipped off and flew up and hit his cheek. It only took a piece of skin off, but he still had the scar when I saw him. He rubbed it with his finger—well, affectionately—when he told me about it. He was scared stiff of course, he said, but he was more shocked than really frightened. He felt like somebody had taken the lid off life and let him look at the works.'

Flitcraft had been a good citizen and a good husband and father, not by any outer compulsion, but simply because he was a man who was most comfortable in step with his surroundings. He had been raised that way. The people he knew were like that. The life he knew was a clean, orderly, sane, responsible affair. Now a falling beam had shown him that life was fundamentally none of these things. He, the good citizen-husband-father, could be wiped out between office and restaurant by the accident of a falling beam. He knew then that men died at haphazard like that, and lived only while blind chance spared them.

It was not, primarily, the injustice of it that disturbed him: he accepted that after the first shock. What disturbed him was the discovery that in sensibly ordering his affairs he had got out of step, and not into step, with life. He said he knew before he he had gone twenty feet from the fallen beam that he would never know peace again until he had adjusted himself to this new glimpse of life. By the time he had eaten his luncheon he had found his means of adjustment. Life could be ended for him at random by a falling beam: he would change his life at random by simply going away. He loved his family, he said, as much as he supposed was usual, but he knew he was leaving them adequately provided for, and his love for them was not of the sort that would make absence painful.

'He went to Seattle that afternoon,' Spade said, 'and from there by boat to San Francisco. For a couple of years he wandered around and then drifted back to the North-west, and settled in Spokane and got married. His second wife didn't look like the first but they were more alike than they were different. You know, the kind of women that play fair games of golf and bridge and like new salad recipes. He wasn't sorry for what he had done. It seemed reasonable enough to him. I don't think he even knew he had settled back naturally into the same groove he had jumped out of in Tacoma. But that's the part of it I always liked. He adjusted himself to beams falling, and then no more of them fell, and he adjusted himself to them not falling.'

'How perfectly fascinating,' Brigid O'Shaughnessy said. She left her chair and stood in front of him, close. Here eyes were wide and deep. 'I don't have to tell you how utterly at a disadvantage you'll have me, with him here, if you choose.'

Spade smiled slightly without separating his lips. 'No, you don't have to tell me,' he agreed.

'And you know I'd never have placed myself in this position if I hadn't trusted you completely.' Her thumb and forefinger twisted a black button on his blue coat.

Spade said, 'That again!' with mock resignation.

'But you know it's so,' she insisted.

'No, I don't know it.' He patted the hand that was twisting the button. 'My asking for reasons why I should trust you brought us here. Don't let's confuse things. You don't have to trust me, anyhow, as long as you can persuade me to trust you.'

She studied his face. Her nostrils quivered.

Spade laughed. He patted her hand again and said: 'Don't worry about that now. He'll be here in a moment. Get your business with him over, and then we'll see how we'll stand.'

'And you'll let me go about it—with him—in my own way?'

'Sure.'

She turned her hand under his so that her fingers pressed his. She said softly: 'You're a God-send.'

Spade said: 'Don't overdo it.'

She looked reproachfully at him, though smiling, and returned to the padded rocker.

Joel Cairo was excited. His dark eyes seemed all irises and his high-pitched thin-voiced words were tumbling out before Spade had the door half-open.

'That boy is out there watching the house, Mr. Spade, that boy you showed me, or to whom you showed me, in front of the theatre. What am I to understand from that, Mr. Spade? I came here in good faith, with no thought of tricks or traps.'

'You were asked in good faith.' Spade frowned thoughtfully. 'But I ought to've guessed he might show up. He saw you come in?'

'Naturally. I could have gone on, but that seemed useless, since you had already let him see us together.'

Brigid O'Shaughnessy came into the passage-way behind Spade and asked anxiously: 'What boy? What is it?'

Cairo removed his black hat from his head, bowed stiffly, and said in a prim voice: 'If you do not know, ask Mr. Spade. I know nothing about it except through him.'

'A kid who's been trying to tail me around town all evening,' Spade said carelessly over his shoulder, not turning to face the girl. 'Come on in, Cairo. There's no use standing here talking for all the neighbours.'

Brigid O'Shaughnessy grasped Spade's arm above the elbow and demanded: 'Did he follow you up to my apartment?'

'No. I shook him before that. Then I suppose he came back here to try to pick me up again.'

Cairo, holding his black hat to his belly with both hands, had come into the passage-way. Spade shut the corridor door behind him and they went into the living-room. There Cairo bowed stiffly over his hat once more and said: 'I am delighted to see you again, Miss O'Shaughnessy.'

'I was sure you would be, Joe,' she replied, giving him her hand.

He made a formal bow over her hand and released it quickly.

She sat in the padded rocker she had occupied before. Cairo sat in the armchair by the table. Spade, when he had hung Cairo's hat and coat in the closet, sat on an end of the sofa in front of the windows and began to roll a cigarette.

Brigid O'Shaughnessy said to Cairo: 'Sam told me about your offer for the falcon. How soon can you have the money ready?'

Cairo's eyebrows twitched. He smiled. 'It is ready.' He continued to smile at the girl for a while after he had spoken, and then looked at Spade.

Spade was lighting his cigarette. His face was tranquil.

'In cash?' the girl asked.

'Oh, yes,' Cairo replied.

She frowned, put her tongue between her lips, withdrew it, and asked: 'You are ready to give us five thousand dollars, now, if we give you the falcon?'

Cairo held up a wriggling hand. 'Excuse me,' he said. 'I expressed myself badly. I did not mean to say that I have the money in my pockets, but that I am prepared to get it on a very few minutes' notice at any time during banking hours.'

'Oh!' She looked at Spade.

Spade blew cigarette smoke down the front of his vest and said: 'That's probably right. He only had a few hundred in his pockets when I frisked him this afternoon.'

When her eyes opened round and wide he grinned.

The Levantine bent forward in his chair. He failed to keep eagerness from showing in his eyes and voice. 'I can be quite prepared to give you the money at, say, half-past ten in the morning. Eh?'

Brigid O'Shaughnessy smiled at him and said: 'But I haven't got the falcon.'

Cairo's face was darkened by a flush of annoyance. He put an ugly hand on either arm of his chair, holding his small-boned body erect and stiff between them. His dark eyes were angry. He did not say anything.

The girl made a mock-placatory face at him. 'I'll have it in a week at the most, though,' she said.

'Where is it?' Cairo used politeness of mien to express scepticism.

'Where Floyd hid it.'

'Floyd? Thursby?'

She nodded.

'And you know where that is?' he asked.

'I think I do.'

'Then why must we wait a week?'

'Perhaps not a whole week. Whom are you buying it for, Joe?'

Cairo raised his eyebrows. 'I told Mr. Spade. For its owner.'

Surprise illuminated the girl's face. 'So you went back to him?'

'Naturally I did.'

She laughed softly in her throat and said: 'I should have liked to have seen that.'

Cairo shrugged. 'That was the logical development.' He rubbed the back of one hand with the palm of the other. His upper lids came down to shade his eyes. 'Why, if I in turn may ask a question, are you willing to sell to me?'

'I'm afraid,' she said simply, 'after what happened to Floyd. That's why I haven't it now. I'm afraid to touch it except to turn it over to somebody else right away.'

Spade, propped on an elbow on the sofa, looked at and listened to them impartially. In the comfortable slackness of his body, in the easy stillness of his features, there was no indication of either curiosity or impatience.

'Exactly what,' Cairo asked in a low voice, 'happened to Floyd?'

The tip of Brigid O'Shaughnessy's right forefinger traced a swift G in the air.

Cairo said, 'I see,' but there was something doubting in his smile. 'Is he here?'

'I don't know.' She spoke impatiently. 'What difference does it make?'

The doubt in Cairo's smile deepened. 'It might make a world of difference,' he said, and rearranged his hands in his lap so that, intentionally or not, a blunt forefinger pointed at Spade.

The girl glanced at the pointing finger and made an impatient motion with her head. 'Or me,' she said, 'or you.'

'Exactly, and shall we add more certainly the boy outside?'

'Yes,' she agreed and laughed. 'Yes, unless he's the one you had in Constantinople.'

Sudden blood mottled Cairo's face. In a shrill enraged voice he cried: 'The one you couldn't make?'

Brigid O'Shaughnessy jumped up from the chair. Her lower lip was between her teeth. Her eyes were dark and wide in a tense white face. She took two quick steps towards Cairo. He started to rise. Her right hand went out and cracked sharply against his cheek, leaving the imprint of fingers there.

Cairo grunted and slapped her cheek, staggering her sidewise, bringing from her mouth a brief muffled scream.

Spade, wooden of face, was up from the sofa and close to them by then. He caught Cairo by the throat and shook him. Cairo gurgled and put a hand inside his coat. Spade grasped the Levantine's wrist, wrenched it away from the coat, forced it straight out to the side, and twisted until the clumsy flaccid fingers opened to let the black pistol fall down on the rug.

Brigid O'Shaughnessy quickly picked up the pistol.

Cairo, speaking with difficulty because of the fingers on his throat said: 'This is the second time you've put your hands on me.' His eyes, though the throttling pressure on his throat made them bulge, were cold and menacing.

'Yes,' Spade growled. 'And when you're slapped you'll take it and like it.' He released Cairo's wrist and with a thick open hand struck the side of his face three times, savagely.

Cairo tried to spit in Spade's face, but the dryness of his mouth made it only an angry gesture. Spade slapped the mouth, cutting the lower lip.

The door bell rang.

Cairo's eyes jerked into focus on the passage-way that led to the corridor door. His eyes had become unangry and wary. The girl had gasped and turned to face the passage-way. Her face was frightened. Spade stared gloomily for a moment at the blood trickling from Cairo's lip, and then stepped back, taking his hand from the Levantine's throat.

'Who is it?' the girl whispered, coming close to Spade; and Cairo's eyes jerked back to ask the same question.

Spade gave his answer irritably: 'I don't know.'

The bell rang again, more insistently.

'Well, keep quiet,' Spade said, and went out of the room, shutting the door behind him.

Spade turned on the light in the passage-way and opened the door to the corridor. Lieutenant Dundy and Tom Polhaus were there.

'Hello, Sam,' Tom said. 'We thought maybe you wouldn't've gone to bed yet.'

Dundy nodded, but said nothing.

Spade said good-naturedly: 'Hello. You guys pick swell hours to do your visiting in. What is it this time?'

Dundy spoke then, quietly: 'We want to talk to you, Spade.'

'Well?' Spade stood in the doorway, blocking it. 'Go ahead and talk.'

Tom Polhaus advanced saying: 'We don't have to do it standing here, do we?'

Spade stood in the doorway and said: 'You can't come in.' His tone was very slightly apologetic.

Tom's thick-featured face, even in height with Spade's, took on an expression of friendly scorn, though there was a bright gleam in his small shrew eyes. 'What the hell, Sam?' he protested and put a big hand playfully on Spade's chest.

Spade leaned against the pushing hand, grinned wolfishly, and asked: 'Going to strong-arm me, Tom?'

Tom grumbled, 'Aw, for God's sake,' and took his hand away.

Dundy clicked his teeth together and said through them: 'Let us in.'

Spade's lip twitched over his eyetooth. He said: 'You're not coming in. What do you want to do about it? Try to get in? Or do your talking here? Or go to hell?'

Tom groaned.

Dundy, still speaking through his teeth, said: 'It'd pay you to play along with us a little, Spade. You've got away with this and you've got away with that, but you can't keep it up forever.'

'Stop me when you can,' Spade replied arrogantly.

'That's what I'll do.' Dundy put his hands behind him and thrust his hard face up towards the private detective's. 'There's talk going around that you and Archer's wife were cheating on him.'

Spade laughed. 'That sounds like something you thought up yourself.'

'Then there's not anything to it?'

'Not anything.'

'The talk is,' Dundy said, 'that she tried to get a divorce out of him so's she could put in with you, but he wouldn't give it to her. Anything to that?'

'No.'

'There's even talk,' Dundy went on stolidly, 'that that's why he was put on the spot.'

Spade looked mildly amused. 'Don't be a hog,' he said. 'You oughtn't to try to pin more than one murder at a time on me. Your first idea that I knocked Thursby off because he'd killed Miles falls apart if you blame me for killing Miles too.'

'You haven't heard me say you killed anybody,' Dundy replied. 'You're the one that keeps bringing that up. But suppose I did. You could have blipped them both. There's a way of figuring it.'

'Uh-huh. I could've butchered Miles to get his wife, and then Thursby so I could hang Miles's killing on him. That's a hell of a swell system, or will be when I can give somebody else the bump and hang Thursby's on them. How long am I supposed to keep that up? Are you going to put your hand on my shoulder for all the killings in San Francisco from now on?'

Tom said: 'Aw, cut the comedy, Sam. You know damned well we don't like this any more than you do, but we got our work to do.'

'I hope you've got something to do besides pop in here early every morning with a lot of damned fool questions.'

'And get damned lying answers,' Dundy added deliberately.

'Take it easy,' Spade cautioned him.

Dundy looked him up and down and then looked him straight in the eyes. 'If you say there was nothing between you and Archer's wife,' he said, 'you're a liar, and I'm telling you so.'

A startled look came into Tom's small eyes.

Spade moistened his lips with the tip of his tongue and asked: 'Is that the hot tip that brought you here at this ungodly time of night?

'That's one of them.'

'And the others?'

Dundy pulled down the corners of his mouth. 'Let us in.' He nodded significantly at the doorway in which Spade stood.

Spade frowned and shook his head.

Dundy's mouth corners lifted in a smile of grim satisfaction. 'There must've been something to it,' he told Tom.

Tom shifted his feet and, not looking at either man, mumbled: 'God knows.'

'What's this?' Spade asked. 'Charades?'

'All right, Spade, we're going.' Dundy buttoned his over-coat. 'We'll be in to see you now and then. Maybe you're right in bucking us. Think it over.'

'Uh-huh,' Spade said, grinning. 'Glad to see you any time, Lieutenant, and whenever I'm not busy I'll let you in.'

A voice in Spade's living-room screamed: 'Help! Help! Police! Help!' The voice, high and thin and shrill, was Joel Cairo's.

Lieutenant Dundy stopped turning away from the door, con-fronted Spade again, and said decisively: 'I guess we're going in.'

The sounds of a brief struggle, of a blow, of a subdued cry, came to them.

Spade's face twisted into a smile that held little joy. He said, 'I guess you are,' and stood out of the way.

When the police detectives had entered he shut the corridor door and followed them back into the living-room.

Chapter Eight

Horse Feathers

Brigid O'Shaughnessy was huddled in the armchair by the table. Her forearms were up over her cheeks, her knees drawn up until they hid the lower part of her face. Her eyes were white-circled and terrified.

Joel Cairo stood in front of her, bending over her, holding in one hand the pistol Spade had twisted out of his hand. His other hand was clapped to his forehead. Blood ran through the fingers of that hand and down under them to his eyes. A smaller trickle from his cut lip made three wavy lines across his chin.

Cairo did not heed the detectives. He was glaring at the girl huddled in front of him. His lips were working spasmodically, but no coherent sound came from between them.

Dundy, the first of the three into the living-room, moved swiftly to Cairo's side, put a hand on his own hip under his overcoat, a hand on the Levantine's wrist, and growled: 'What are you up to here?'

Cairo took the red-smeared hand from his head and flourished it close to the Lieutenant's face. Uncovered by the hand, his forehead showed a three-inch ragged tear. 'This is what she has done,' he cried. 'Look at it.'

The girl put her feet down on the floor and looked warily from Dundy, holding Cairo's wrist, to Tom Polhaus, standing a little behind them, to Spade, leaning against the door-frame. Spade's face was placid. When his gaze met hers his yellow-grey eyes glinted for an instant with malicious humour and then became expressionless again.

'Did you do that?' Dundy asked the girl, nodding at Cairo's cut head.

She looked at Spade again. He did not in any way respond to the appeal in her eyes. He leaned against the door-frame and observed the occupants of the room with the polite detached air of a disinterested spectator.

The girl turned her eyes up to Dundy's. Her eyes were wide and dark and earnest. 'I had to,' she said in a low throbbing voice. 'I was all alone in here with him when he attacked me. I couldn't—I tried to keep him off. I—I couldn't make myself shoot him.'

'Oh, you liar!' Cairo cried, trying unsuccessfully to pull the arm that held his pistol out of Dundy's grip. 'Oh, you dirty filthy liar!' He twisted himself around to face Dundy. 'She's lying awfully. I came here in good faith and was attacked by both of them, and when you came he went out to talk to you, leaving her here with this pistol, and then she said they were going to kill me after you left, and I called for help, so you wouldn't leave me here to be murdered, and then she struck me with the pistol.'

'Here, give me this thing,' Dundy said, and took the pistol from Cairo's hand. 'Now let's get this straight. What'd you come here for?'

'He sent for me.' Cairo twisted his head around to stare defiantly at Spade. 'He called me up on the phone and asked me to come here.'

Spade blinked sleepily at the Levantine and said nothing.

Dundy asked: 'What'd he want you for?'

Cairo withheld his reply until he had mopped his bloody forehead and chin with a lavender-barred silk handkerchief. By then some of the indignation in his manner had been replaced by caution. 'He said he wanted—they wanted—to see me. I didn't know what about.'

Tom Polhaus lowered his head, sniffed the odour of *chypre* that the mopping handkerchief had released in the air, and turned his head to scowl interrogatively at Spade. Spade winked at him and went on rolling a cigarette.

Dundy asked: 'Well, what happened then?'

'Then they attacked me. She struck me first, and then he choked me and took the pistol out of my pocket. I don't know what they would have done next if you hadn't arrived at that moment. I dare say they would have murdered me then and there. When he went to answer the bell he left her here with the pistol to watch over me.'

Brigid O'Shaughnessy jumped out of the armchair crying, 'Why don't you make him tell the truth?' and slapped Cairo on the cheek.

Cairo yelled inarticulately.

Dundy pushed the girl back into the chair with the hand that was not holding the Levantine's arm and growled: 'None of that now.'

Spade, lighting his cigarette, grinned softly through smoke and told Tom: 'She's impulsive.'

'Yeah,' Tom agreed.

Dundy scowled down at the girl and asked: 'What do you want us to think the truth is?'

'Not what he said,' she replied. 'Not anything he said.' She turned to Spade. 'Is it?'

'How do I know?' Spade responded. 'I was out in the kitchen

mixing an omelette when it all happened, wasn't I?'

She wrinkled her forehead, studying him with eyes that perplexity clouded.

Tom grunted in disgust.

Dundy, still scowling at the girl, ignored Spade's speech and asked her: 'If he's not telling the truth, how come he did the squawking for help, and not you?'

'Oh, he was frightened to death when I struck him,' she replied, looking contemptuously at the Levantine.

Cairo's face flushed where it was not blood-stained. He exclaimed: 'Pfoo! Another lie!'

She kicked his leg, the high heel of her blue slipper striking him just below the knee. Dundy pulled him away from her while big Tom came to stand close to her, rumbling: 'Behave, sister. That's no way to act.'

'Then make him tell the truth,' she said defiantly.

'We'll do that all right,' he promised. 'Just don't get rough.'

Dundy, looking at Spade with green eyes hard and bright and satisfied, addressed his subordinate: 'Well, Tom, I don't guess we'll go wrong pulling the lot of them in.'

Tom nodded gloomily.

Spade left the door and advanced to the centre of the room, dropping his cigarette into a tray on the table as he passed it. His smile and manner were amiably composed. 'Don't be in a hurry,' he said. 'Everything can be explained.'

'I bet you,' Dundy agreed, sneering.

Spade bowed to the girl. 'Miss O'Shaughnessy,' he said, 'may I present Lieutenant Dundy and Detective-Sergeant Polhaus.' He bowed to Dundy. 'Miss O'Shaughnessy is an operative in my employ.'

Joel Cairo said indignantly: 'That isn't so. She——'

Spade interrupted him in a quite loud, but still genial voice: 'I hired her just recently, yesterday. This is Mr. Joel Cairo, a friend—an acquaintance, at any rate—of Thursby's. He came to me this afternoon and tried to hire me to find something Thursby was supposed to have on him when he was bumped off. It looked funny, the way he put it to me, so I wouldn't touch it. Then he pulled a gun—well, never mind that unless it comes to a point of laying charges against each other. Anyway, after talking it over with Miss O'Shaughnessy, I thought maybe I could get something out of him about Miles's and Thursby's killings, so I asked him to come up here. Maybe we put the questions to him a little rough, but he wasn't hurt any, not enough to have to cry for help. I'd already had to take his gun away from him again.'

As Spade talked anxiety came into Cairo's reddened face. His eyes moved jerkily up and down, shifting their focus uneasily between the floor and Spade's bland face.

Dundy confronted Cairo and brusquely demanded: 'Well, what've you got to say to that?'

Cairo had nothing to say for nearly a minute while he stared at the Lieutenant's chest. When he lifted his eyes they were shy and wary. 'I don't know what I should say,' he murmured. His embarrassment seemed genuine.

'Try telling the facts,' Dundy suggested.

'The facts?' Cairo's eyes fidgeted, though their gaze did not actually leave the Lieutenant's. 'What assurance have I that the facts will be believed?'

'Quit stalling. All you've got to do is swear to a complaint that they took a poke at you and the warrant-clerk will believe you enough to issue a warrant that'll let us throw them in the can.'

Spade spoke in an amused tone: 'Go ahead, Cairo. Make him happy. Tell him you'll do it, and then we'll swear to one against you, and he'll have the lot of us.'

Cairo cleared his throat and looked nervously around the room, not into the eyes of anyone there.

Dundy blew breath through his nose in a puff that was not quite a snort and said: 'Get your hats.'

Cairo's eyes, holding worry and a question, met Spade's mocking gaze. Spade winked at him and sat on the arm of the padded rocker. 'Well, boys and girls,' he said, grinning at the Levantine and at the girl with nothing but delight in his voice and grin, 'we put it over nicely.'

Dundy's hard square face darkened the least of shades. He repeated peremptorily: 'Get your hats.'

Spade turned his grin on the Lieutenant, squirmed into a more comfortable position on the chair-arm, and asked lazily: 'Don't you know when you're being kidded?'

Tom Polhaus's face became red and shiny.

Dundy's face, still darkening, was immobile except for lips moving stiffly to say: 'No, but we'll let that wait till we get down to the Hall.'

Spade rose and put his hands in his trousers pockets. He stood erect so he might look that much farther down at the Lieutenant. His grin was a taunt and self-certainty spoke in every line of his posture.

'I dare you to take us in, Dundy,' he said. 'We'll laugh at you in every newspaper in San Francisco. You don't think any of us is going to swear to any complaints against the others, do you? Wake up. You've been kidded. When the bell rang I said to Miss O'Shaughnessy and Cairo: "It's those damned bulls again. They're getting to be nuisances. Let's play a joke on them. When you hear them going one of you scream, and then we'll see how far we can string them along before they tumble." And——'

Brigid O'Shaughnessy bent forward in her chair and began to laugh hysterically.

Cairo started and smiled. There was no vitality in his smile, but he held it fixed on his face.

Tom, glowering, grumbled: 'Cut it out, Sam.'

Spade chuckled and said: 'But that's the way it was. We——'

'And the cut on his head and mouth?' Dundy asked scornfully. 'Where'd they come from?'

'Ask him,' Spade suggested. 'Maybe he cut himself shaving.'

Cairo spoke quickly, before he could be questioned, and the muscles of his face quivered under the strain of holding his smile in place while he spoke. 'I fell. We intended to be struggling for the pistol when you came in, but I fell. I tripped on the end of the rug and fell while we were pretending to struggle.'

Dundy said: 'Horse feathers.'

Spade said: 'That's all right, Dundy, believe it or not. The point is that that's our story and we'll stick to it. The newspapers will print it whether they believe it or not, and it'll be just as funny one way as the other, or more so. What are you going to do about it? It's no crime to kid a copper, is it? You haven't got anything on anybody here. Everything we told you was part of the joke. What are you going to do about it?'

Dundy put his back to Spade and gripped Cairo by the shoulders.

'You can't get away with that,' he snarled, shaking the Levantine. 'You belched for help and you've got to take it.'

'No, sir,' Cairo sputtered. 'It was a joke. He said you were friends of his and would understand.'

Spade laughed.

Dundy pulled Cairo roughly around, holding him now by one wrist and the nape of his neck. 'I'll take you along for packing the gun, anyway,' he said. 'And I'll take the rest of you along to see who laughs at the joke.'

Cairo's alarmed eyes jerked sidewise to focus on Spade's face.

Spade said: 'Don't be a sap, Dundy. The gun was part of the plant. It's one of mine.' He laughed. 'Too bad it's only a thirty-two, or maybe you could find it was the one Thursby and Miles were shot with.'

Dundy released Cairo, spun on his heel, and his right fist clicked on Spade's chin.

Brigid O'Shaughnessy uttered a short cry.

Spade's smile flickered out at the instant of the impact, but returned immediately with a dreamy quality added. He steadied himself with a short backward step and his thick sloping shoulders writhed under his coat. Before his fist could come up Tom Polhaus had pushed himself between the two men, facing Spade, encumbering Spade's arms with the closeness of his barrel-like belly and his own arms.

'No, no for God's sake!' Tom begged.

After a long moment of motionlessness Spade's muscles relaxed. 'Then get him out of here quick,' he said. His smile had gone away again, leaving his face sullen and somewhat pale.

Tom, staying close to Spade, keeping his arms on Spade's arms, turned his head to look over his shoulder at Lieutenant Dundy. Tom's small eyes were reproachful.

Dundy's fists were clenched in front of his body and his feet were planted firm and a little apart on the floor, but the truculence in his face was modified by thin white rims of white showing between green irises and upper eyelids.

'Get their names and addresses,' he ordered.

Tom looked at Cairo, who said quickly: 'Joel Cairo, Hotel Belvedere.'

Spade spoke before Tom could question the girl. 'You can

always get in touch with Miss O'Shaughnessy through me.'

Tom looked at Dundy. Dundy growled: 'Get her address.'

Spade said: 'Her address is in care of my office.'

Dundy took a step forward, halting in front of the girl. 'Where do you live?' he asked.

Spade addressed Tom: 'Get him out of here. I've had enough of this.'

Tom looked at Spade's eyes—hard and glittering—and mumbled: 'Take it easy, Sam.' He buttoned his coat and turned to Dundy, asking, in a voice that aped casualness, 'Well, is that all?' and taking a step towards the door.

Dundy's scowl failed to conceal indecision.

Cairo moved suddenly towards the door, saying: 'I'm going too, if Mr. Spade will be kind enough to give me my hat and coat.'

Spade asked: 'What's the hurry?'

Dundy said angrily: 'It was all in fun, but just the same you're afraid to be left here with them.'

'Not at all,' the Levantine replied, fidgeting, looking at neither of them, 'but it's quite late—and I'm going. I'll go out with you if you don't mind.'

Dundy put his lips together firmly and said nothing. A light was glinting in his green eyes.

Spade went to the closet in the passage-way and fetched Cairo's hat and coat. Spade's face was blank. His voice held the same blankness when he stepped back from helping the Levantine into his coat and said to Tom: 'Tell him to leave the gun.'

Dundy took Cairo's pistol from his overcoat pocket and put it on the table. He went out first, with Cairo at his heels. Tom halted in front of Spade, muttering, 'I hope to God you know what you're doing,' got no response, sighed, and followed the others out. Spade went after them as far as the bend in the passage-way, where he stood until Tom had closed the corridor-door.

Chapter Nine

Brigid

Spade returned to the living-room and sat on an end of the sofa, elbows on knees, cheeks in hand, looking at the floor and not at Brigid O'Shaughnessy smiling weakly at him from the armchair. His eyes were sultry. The creases between brows over his nose were deep. His nostrils moved in and out with his breathing.

Brigid O'Shaughnessy, when it became apparent that he was not going to look up at her, stopped smiling and regarded him with growing uneasiness.

Red rage came suddenly into his face and he began to talk in a harsh guttural voice. Holding his maddened face in his hands, glaring at the floor, he cursed Dundy for five minutes without break, cursed him obscenely, blasphemously, repetitiously, in a harsh guttural voice.

Then he took his face out of his hands, looked at the girl, grinned sheepishly, and said: 'Childish, huh? I know, but, by God, I do hate being hit without hitting back.' He touched his chin with careful fingers. 'Not that it was so much of a sock at that.' He laughed and lounged back on the sofa crossing his legs. 'A cheap enough price to pay for winning.' His brows came together in a fleeting scowl. 'Though I'll remember it.'

The girl, smiling again, left her chair and sat on the sofa beside him. 'You're absolutely the wildest person I've ever known,' she said. 'Do you always carry on so high-handed?'

'I let him hit me, didn't I?'

'Oh, yes, but a police official.'

'It wasn't that,' Spade explained, 'It was that in losing his head and slugging me he overplayed his hand. If I'd mixed it with him then he couldn't't've backed down. He'd've had to go through with it, and we'd've had to tell that goofy story at headquarters.' He stared thoughtfully at the girl, and asked:

'What did you do to Cairo?'

'Nothing.' Her face became flushed. 'I tried to frighten him into keeping still until they had gone and he either got too frightened or stubborn and yelled.'

'And then you smacked him with the gun?'

'I had to. He attacked me.'

'You don't know what you're doing.' Spade's smile did not hide his annoyance. 'It's just what I told you: you're fumbling along by guess and by God.'

'I'm sorry,' she said, face and voice soft with contrition, 'Sam.'

'Sure you are.' He took tobacco and papers from his pockets and began to make a cigarette. 'Now you've had your talk with Cairo. Now you can talk to me.'

She put a finger-tip to her mouth, staring across the room at nothing with widened eyes, and then, with narrower eyes, glanced quickly at Spade. He was engrossed in the making of his cigarette. 'Oh, yes,' she began, 'of course——' She took the finger away from her mouth and smoothed her blue dress over her knees. She frowned at her knees.

Spade licked his cigarette, sealed it, and asked, 'Well?' while he felt for his lighter.

'But I didn't,' she said, pausing between words as if she were selecting them with great care, 'have time to finish talking to him.' She stopped frowning at her knees and looked at Spade with clear candid eyes. 'We were interrupted almost before we had begun.'

Spade lighted his cigarette and laughed his mouth empty of smoke. 'Want me to phone him and ask him to come back?'

She shook her head, not smiling. Her eyes moved back and forth between her lids as she shook her head, maintaining their focus on Spade's eyes. Her eyes were inquisitive.

Spade put an arm across her back, cupping his hand over the smooth bare white shoulder farthest from him. She leaned back into the bend of his arm. He said: 'Well, I'm listening.'

She twisted her head around to smile up at him with playful insolence, asking: 'Do you need your arm there for that?'

'No.' He removed his hand from her shoulder and let his arm drop down behind her.

'You're altogether unpredictable,' she murmured.

He nodded and said amiably: 'I'm still listening.'

'Look at the time!' she exclaimed, wriggling a finger at the alarm clock perched atop the book saying two-fifty with its clumsily shaped hands.

'Uh-huh, it's been a busy evening.'

'I must go.' She rose from the sofa. 'This is terrible.'

Spade did not rise. He shook his head and said: 'Not until you've told me about it.'

'But look at the time,' she protested, 'and it would take hours to tell you.'

'It'll have to take them then.'

'Am I a prisoner?' she asked gaily.

'Besides, there's the kid outside. Maybe he hasn't gone home to sleep yet.'

Her gaiety vanished. 'Do you think he's still there?'

'It's likely.'

She shivered. 'Could you find out?'

'I could go down and see.'

'Oh, that's—will you?'

Spade studied her anxious face for a moment and then got up from the sofa saying: 'Sure.' He got a hat and overcoat from the closet. 'I'll be gone about ten minutes.'

'Do be careful,' she begged as she followed him to the corridor-door.

He said, 'I will,' and went out.

Post Street was empty when Spade issued into it. He walked east a block, crossed the street, walked west two blocks on the other side, re-crossed it, and returned to his building without having seen anyone except two mechanics working on a car in a garage.

When he opened his apartment door Brigid O'Shaughnessy was standing at the bend in the passage-way, holding Cairo's pistol straight down at her side.

'He's still there,' Spade said.

She bit the inside of her lip and turned slowly, going back into the living-room. Spade followed her in, put his hat and overcoat on a chair, said, 'So we'll have time to talk,' and went into the kitchen.

He had put the coffee-pot on the stove when she came to the door, and was slicing a slender loaf of French bread. She stood in the doorway and watched him with preoccupied eyes. The fingers of her left hand idly caressed the body and barrel of the pistol her right hand still held.

'The tablecloth's in there,' he said, pointing the bread-knife at a cupboard that was one breakfast-nook partition.

She set the table while he spread liverwurst on, or put cold corned beef between, the small ovals of bread he had sliced. Then he poured the coffee, added brandy to it from a squat bottle, and they sat at the table. They sat side by side on one of the benches. She put the pistol down on the end of the bench nearer her.

'You can start now, between bites,' he said.

She made a face at him, complained, 'You're the most insistent person,' and bit a sandwich.

'Yes, and wild and unpredictable. What's this bird, this falcon, that everybody's all steamed up about?'

She chewed the beef and bread in her mouth, swallowed it, looked attentively at the small crescent its removal had made in the sandwich's rim, and asked: 'Suppose I wouldn't tell you? Suppose I wouldn't tell you anything at all about it? What would you do?'

'You mean about the bird?'

'I mean about the whole thing.'

'I wouldn't be too surprised,' he told her, grinning so that the edges of his jaw-teeth were visible, 'to know what to do next.'

'And that would be?' She transferred her attention from the sandwich to his face. 'That's what I wanted to know: what would you do next?'

He shook his head.

Mockery rippled in a smile on her face. 'Something wild and unpredictable?'

'Maybe. But I don't see what you've got to gain by covering up now. It's coming out bit by bit anyhow. There's a lot of it I don't know, but there's some of it I do, and some more that I can guess at, and, give me another day like this, I'll soon be knowing things about it that you don't know.'

'I suppose you do now,' she said, looking at her sandwich again, her face serious. 'But—oh!—I'm so tired of it, and I do so hate having to talk about it. Wouldn't it—wouldn't it be just as well to wait and let you learn about it as you say you will?'

Spade laughed. 'I don't know. You'll have to figure that out for yourself. My way of learning is to heave a wild and unpredictable monkey-wrench into the machinery. It's all right with me, if you're sure none of the flying pieces will hurt you.'

She moved her bare shoulders uneasily, but said nothing. For several minutes they ate in silence, he phlegmatically, she thoughtfully. Then she said in a hushed voice: 'I'm afraid of you, and that's the truth.'

He said: 'That's not the truth.'

'It is,' she insisted in the same low voice. 'I know two men I'm afraid of and I've seen both of them to-night.'

'I can understand your being afraid of Cairo,' Spade said. 'He's out of your reach.'

'And you aren't?'

'Not that way,' he said and grinned.

She blushed. She picked up a slice of bread encrusted with grey liverwurst. She put it down on her plate. She wrinkled her white forehead and she said: 'It's a black figure, as you know, smooth and shiny, of a bird, a hawk or falcon, about that high.' She held her hands a foot apart.

'What makes it important?'

She sipped coffee and brandy before she shook her head. 'I don't know,' she said. 'They'd never tell me. They promised me five hundred pounds if I helped them get it. Then Floyd said afterwards, after we'd left Joe, that he'd give me seven hundred and fifty.'

'So it must be worth more than seventy-five hundred dollars?'

'Oh, much more than that,' she said. 'They didn't pretend that they were sharing equally with me. They were simply hiring me to help them.'

'To help them how?'

She lifted her cup to her lips again. Spade, not moving the domineering stare of his yellow-grey eyes from her face, began to make a cigarette. Behind them the percolator bubbled on the stove.

'To help them get it from the man who had it,' she said slowly when she had lowered her cup, 'a Russian named Kemidov.'

'How?'

'Oh, but that's not important,' she objected, 'and wouldn't help you'—she smiled impudently—'and is certainly none of your business.'

'This was in Constantinople?'

She hesitated, nodded, and said: 'Marmora.'

He waved a cigarette at her, saying: 'Go ahead, what happened then?'

'But that's all. I've told you. They promised me five hundred pounds to help them and I did and then we found that Joe Cairo meant to desert us, taking the falcon with him and leaving us nothing. So we did exactly that to him, first. But then I wasn't any better off than I had been before, because Floyd hadn't any intention at all of paying me the seven hundred and fifty pounds he had promised me. I had learned that by the time we got here. He said we would go to New York, where he would sell it and give me my share, but I could see he wasn't telling me the truth.' Indignation had darkened her eyes to violet. 'And that's why I came to you to get you to help me learn where the falcon was.'

'And suppose you'd got it? What then?'

'Then I'd have been in a position to talk terms with Mr. Floyd Thursby.'

Spade squinted at her and suggested: 'But you wouldn't have known where to take it to get more money than he'd give you, the larger sum that you knew he expected to sell it for?'

'I did not know,' she said.

Spade scowled at the ashes he had dumped on his plate. 'What makes it worth all that money?' he demanded. 'You must have some idea, at least be able to guess.'

'I haven't the slightest idea.'

He directed the scowl at her. 'What's it made of?'

'Porcelain or black stone. I don't know. I've never touched it. I've only seen it once, for a few minutes. Floyd showed it to me when we'd first got hold of it.'

Spade mashed the end of his cigarette in his plate and made one draught of the coffee and brandy in his cup. His scowl had gone away. He wiped his lips with his napkin, dropped it crumpled on the table, and spoke casually: 'You *are* a liar.'

She got up and stood at the end of the table, looking down

at him with dark abashed eyes in a pinkening face. 'I am a liar,' she said. 'I've always been a liar.'

'Don't brag about it. It's childish.' His voice was good-humoured. He came out from between table and bench. 'Was there any truth at all in that yarn?'

She hung her head. Dampness glistened on her dark lashes. 'Some,' she whispered.

'How much?'

'Not—not very much.'

Spade put a hand under her chin and lifted her head. He laughed into her wet eyes and said: 'We've got all night before us. I'll put some more brandy in some more coffee and we'll try again.'

Her eyelids drooped. 'Oh, I'm so tired,' she said tremulously, 'so tired of it all, of myself, of lying and thinking up lies, and of not knowing what is a lie and what is the truth. I wish I——'

She put her hands up to Spade's cheeks, put her open mouth hard against his mouth, her body flat against his body.

Spade's arms went around her, holding her to him, muscles bulging his blue sleeves, a hand cradling her head, its fingers half lost among red hair, a hand moving groping fingers over her slim back. His eyes burned yellowly.

Chapter Ten

The Belvedere Divan

Beginning day had reduced night to a thin smokiness when Spade sat up. At his side Brigid O'Shaughnessy's soft breathing had the regularity of utter sleep. Spade was quiet leaving bed and bedroom and shutting the bedroom door. He dressed in the bathroom. Then he examined the sleeping girl's clothes, took a flat brass key from the pocket of her coat, and went out.

He went to the Coronet, letting himself into the building and into her apartment with the key. To the eye there was nothing furtive about his going in: he entered boldly and directly. To the ear his going in was almost unnoticeable: he made as little sound as might be.

In the girl's apartment he switched on all the lights. He searched the place from wall to wall. His eyes and thick fingers moved without apparent haste, and without ever lingering or fumbling or going back, from one inch of their fields to the next, probing, scrutinising, testing with expert certainty. Every drawer, cupboard, cubbyhole, box, bag, trunk—locked or unlocked—was opened and its contents subjected to examination by eyes and fingers. Every piece of clothing was tested by hands that felt for tell-tale bulges, and ears that listened for the crinkle of paper between pressing fingers. He stripped the bed of bedclothes. He looked under rugs and at the underside of each piece of furniture. He pulled down blinds to see that nothing had been rolled up in them for concealment. He leaned through windows to see that nothing hung below them on the outside. He poked with a fork into powder and cream-jars on the dressing-table. He held atomisers and bottles up against the light. He examined dishes and pans and food and food-containers. He emptied the garbage-can on spread sheets of newspaper. He opened the top of the flush-box in the bathroom, drained the box, and peered down into it. He examined and tested the metal screens over the drains of bath-tub, wash-bowl, sink, and laundry-tub.

He did not find the black bird. He found nothing that seemed to have any connection with a black bird. The only piece of writing he found was a week-old receipt for the month's apart-ment-rent Brigid O'Shaughnessy had paid. The only thing he found that interested him enough to delay his search while he looked at it was a double-handful of rather fine jewellery in a polychrome box in a locked dressing-table drawer.

When he had finished he made and drank a cup of coffee. Then he unlocked the kitchen window, scarred the edge of its lock a little with his pocket-knife, opened the window—over a fire-escape—got his hat and overcoat from the settee in the living-room and left the apartment as he had come.

On his way home he stopped at a store that was being opened by a puffy-eyed, shivering, plump grocer and bought oranges, eggs, rolls, butter and cream.

Spade went quietly into his apartment, but before he had shut the corridor-door behind him Brigid O'Shaughnessy cried: 'Who is that?'

'Young Spade bearing breakfast.'

'Oh, you frightened me!'

The bedroom door he had shut was open. The girl sat on the side of the bed, trembling, with her right hand out of sight under a pillow.

Spade put his packages on the kitchen table and went into the bedroom. He sat on the bed beside the girl, kissed her smooth shoulder, and said: 'I wanted to see if that kid was still on the job and to get stuff for breakfast.'

'Is he?'

'No.'

She sighed and leaned against him. 'I awakened and you weren't here and then I heard someone coming in. I was terrified.'

Spade combed her red hair back from her face with his fingers and said: 'I'm sorry, angel. I thought you'd sleep through it. Did you have that gun under your pillow all night?'

'No. You know I didn't. I jumped up and got it when I was frightened.'

He cooked breakfast—and slipped the flat brass key into her coat pocket again—while she bathed and dressed.

She came out of the bathroom whistling *En Cuba*. 'Shall I make the bed?' she asked.

'That'd be swell. The eggs need a couple of minutes more.'

Their breakfast was on the table when she returned to the kitchen. They sat where they had sat the night before and ate heartily.

'Now about the bird?' Spade suggested presently as they ate.

She put her fork down and looked at him. She drew her eyebrows together and made her mouth small and tight. 'You can't ask me to talk about that this morning of all mornings,' she protested. 'I don't want to and I won't.'

'It's a stubborn damned hussy,' he said sadly and put a piece of roll into his mouth.

The youth who had shadowed Spade was not in sight when Spade and Brigid O'Shaughnessy crossed the sidewalk to the waiting taxicab. The taxicab was not followed. Neither the youth nor another loiterer was visible in the vicinity of the Coronet when the taxicab arrived there.

Brigid O'Shaughnessy would not let Spade go in with her. 'It's bad enough to be coming home in evening dress at this hour without bringing company. I hope I don't meet anybody.'

'Dinner to-night?'

'Yes.'

They kissed. She went into the Coronet. He told the chauffeur: 'Hotel Belvedere.'

When he reached the Belvedere he saw the youth who had shadowed him sitting in the lobby on a divan from which the elevators could be seen. Apparently the youth was reading a newspaper.

At the desk Spade learned that Cairo was not in. He frowned and pinched his lower lip. Points of yellow light began to dance in his eyes. 'Thanks,' he said softly to the clerk and turned away.

Sauntering, he crossed the lobby to the divan from which the elevators could be seen and sat down beside—not more than a foot from—the young man who was apparently reading a newspaper.

The young man did not look up from his newspaper. Seen at this scant distance, he seemed certainly less than twenty years old. His features were small, in keeping with his stature, and regular. His skin was very fair. The whiteness of his cheeks was as little blurred by any considerable growth of beard as by the glow of blood. His clothing was neither new nor of more than ordinary quality, but it, and his manner of wearing it, were marked by a hard masculine neatness.

Spade asked casually, 'Where is he?' while shaking tobacco down into a brown paper curved to catch it.

The boy lowered his paper and looked around, moving with a purposeful sort of slowness, as of a more natural swiftness restrained. He looked with small hazel eyes under somewhat long curling lashes at Spade's chest. He said, in a voice as colourless and composed and cold as his young face: 'What?'

'Where is he?' Spade was busy with his cigarette.

'Who?'

'The fairy.'

The hazel eyes' gaze went up Spade's chest to the knot of his maroon tie and rested there. 'What do you think you're doing, Jack?' the boy demanded. 'Kidding me?'

'I'll tell you when I am.' Spade licked his cigarette and smiled amiably at the boy. 'New York, aren't you?'

The boy stared at Spade's tie and did not speak. Spade nodded as if the boy had said yes and asked: 'Baumes rush?'

The boy stared at Spade's tie for a moment longer, then raised his newspaper and returned his attention to it. 'Shove off,' he said from the side of his mouth.

Spade lighted his cigarette, leaned back comfortably on the divan, and spoke with good-natured carelessness: 'You'll have to talk to me before you're through, sonny—some of you will— and you can tell G. I said so.'

The boy put his paper down quickly and faced Spade, staring at his necktie with bleak hazel eyes. The boy's small hands were spread flat over his belly. 'Keep asking for it and you're going to get it,' he said, 'plenty.' His voice was low and flat and menacing. 'I told you to shove off. Shove off.'

Spade waited until a bespectacled pudgy man and a thin-legged blonde girl had passed out of hearing. Then he chuckled and said: 'That would go over big back on Seventh Avenue. But you're not in Romeville now. You're in my burg.' He inhaled cigarette smoke and blew it out in a long pale cloud. 'Well, where is he?'

The boy spoke two words, the first a short guttural verb, the second 'you.'

'People lose teeth talking like that.' Spade's voice was still amiable though his face had become wooden. 'If you want to hang around you'll be polite.'

The boy repeated his two words.

Spade dropped his cigarette into a tall stone jar beside the divan and with a lifted hand caught the attention of a man who had been standing at the end of the cigar-stand for several minutes. The man nodded and came towards them. He was a middle-aged man of medium height, round and sallow of face, compactly built, tidily dressed in dark clothes.

'Hello, Sam,' he said as he came up.

'Hello, Luke.'

They shook hands and Luke said: 'Say, that's too bad about Miles.'

'Uh-huh, a bad break.' Spade jerked his head to indicate the boy on the divan beside him. 'What do you let these cheap gunmen hang about in your lobby for, with their tools bulging their clothes?'

'Yes?' Luke examined the boy with crafty brown eyes set in a suddenly hard face. 'What do you want here?' he asked.

The boy stood up. Spade stood up. The boy looked at the two men, at their neckties, from one to the other. Luke's necktie was black. The boy looked like a schoolboy standing in front of them.

Luke said: 'Well, if you don't want anything, beat it, and don't come back.'

The boy said, 'I won't forget you guys,' and went out.

They watched him go out. Spade took off his hat and wiped his damp forehead with a handkerchief.

The hotel detective asked: 'What is it?'

'Damned if I know,' Spade replied. 'I just happened to spot him. Know anything about Joel Cairo—six-thirty-five?'

'Oh, that one!' the hotel detective leered.

'How long's he been here?'

'Four days. This is the fifth.'

'What about him?'

'Search me, Sam. I got nothing against him but his looks.'

'Find out if he came in last night?'

'Try to,' the hotel detective promised and went away. Spade sat on the divan until he returned. 'No,' Luke reported, 'he didn't sleep in his room. What is it?'

'Nothing.'

'Come clean. You know I'll keep my clam shut, but if there's anything wrong we ought to know about it so's we can collect our bill.'

'Nothing like that,' Spade assured him. 'As a matter of fact, I'm doing a little work for him. I'd tell you if he was wrong.'

'You'd better. Want me to kind of keep an eye on him?'

'Thanks, Luke. It wouldn't hurt. You can't know too much about the men you're working for these days.'

*　　*　　*

It was twenty-one minutes past eleven by the clock over the elevator doors when Joel Cairo came in from the street. His forehead was bandaged. His clothes had the limp unfreshness of too many hours' consecutive wear. His face was pasty, with sagging mouth and eyelids.

Spade met him in front of the desk. 'Good morning,' Spade said easily.

Cairo drew his tired body up straight and the drooping lines of his face tightened. 'Good morning,' he responded without enthusiasm.

There was a pause.

Spade said: 'Let's go some place where we can talk.'

Cairo raised his chin. 'Please excuse me,' he said. 'Our conversations in private have not been such that I am anxious to continue them. Pardon my speaking bluntly, but it is the truth.'

'You mean last night?' Spade made an impatient gesture with head and hands. 'What in hell else could I do? I thought you'd see that. If you pick a fight with her, or let her pick one with you, I've got to throw in with her. I don't know where that damned bird is. You don't. She does. How in hell are we going to get it if I don't play along with her?'

Cairo hesitated, said dubiously: 'You have always, I must say, a smooth explanation ready.'

Spade scowled. 'What do you want me to do? Learn to stutter? Well, we can talk over here.' He led the way to the divan. When they were seated he asked: 'Dundy take you down to the Hall?'

'Yes.'

'How long did they work on you?'

'Until a very little while ago, and very much against my will.' Pain and indignation were mixed in Cairo's face and voice. 'I shall certainly take the matter up with the Consulate General of Greece and with an attorney.'

'Go ahead, and see what it gets you. What did you let the police shake out of you?'

There was prim satisfaction in Cairo's smile. 'Not a single thing. I adhered to the course you indicated earlier in your rooms.' His smile went away. 'Though I certainly wish you had devised a more reasonable story. I felt decidedly ridiculous repeating it.'

Spade grinned mockingly. 'Sure,' he said, 'but its goofiness is what makes it good. You sure you didn't give them anything?'

'You may rely upon it, Mr. Spade, I did not.'

Spade drummed with his fingers on the leather seat between them. 'You'll be hearing from Dundy again. Stay dummied-up on him and you'll be all right. Don't worry about the story's goofiness. A sensible one would've had us all in the cooler.' He rose to his feet. 'You'll want sleep if you've been standing up under a police storm all night. See you later.'

Effie Perine was saying, 'No, not yet,' into the telephone when Spade entered his outer office. She looked around at him and her lips shaped a silent word: 'Iva.' He shook his head. 'Yes, I'll have him call you as soon as he comes in,' she said aloud and replaced the receiver on its prong. 'That's the third time she's called up this morning,' she told Spade.

He made an impatient growling noise.

The girl moved her brown eyes to indicate the inner office. 'Your Miss O'Shaughnessy's in there. She's been waiting since a few minutes after nine.'

Spade nodded as if he had expected that and asked. 'What else?'

'Sergeant Polhaus called up. He didn't leave any message.'

'Get him for me.'

'And G. called up.'

Spade's eyes brightened. He asked: 'Who?'

'G. That's what he said.' Her air of personal indifference to the subject was flawless. 'When I told him you weren't in he said: "When he comes in, will you please tell him that G., who got his message, phoned and will phone again?"'

Spade worked his lips together as if tasting something he liked. 'Thanks, darling,' he said. 'See if you can get Tom Polhaus.' He opened the inner door and went into his private office, pulling the door to behind him.

Brigid O'Shaughnessy, dressed as on her first visit to the office, rose from a chair beside his desk and came quickly towards him. 'Somebody has been in my apartment,' she exclaimed. 'It is all upside-down, every which way.'

He seemed moderately surprised. 'Anything taken?'

'I don't think so. I don't know. I was afraid to stay. I changed as fast as I could and came down here. Oh, you must've let that boy follow you there!'

Spade shook his head. 'No, angel.' He took an early copy of an afternoon paper from his pocket, opened it, and showed her a quarter column headed SCREAM ROUTS BURGLAR.

A young woman named Carolin Beale, who lived alone in a Sutter Street apartment, had been awakened at four that morning by the sound of somebody moving in her bedroom. She had screamed. The mover had run away. Two other women who lived alone in the same building had discovered, later in the morning, signs of the burglar's having visited their apartments. Nothing had been taken from any of the three.

'That's where I shook him,' Spade explained. 'I went into that building and ducked out the back door. That's why all three were women who lived alone. He tried the apartments that had women's names in the vestibule register, hunting for you under an alias.'

'But he was watching your place when we were there,' she objected.

Spade shrugged. 'There's no reason to think he's working alone. Or maybe he went to Sutter Street after he had begun to think you were going to stay all night in my place. There are a lot of maybes, but I didn't lead him to the Coronet.'

She was not satisfied. 'But he found it, or somebody did.'

'Sure.' He frowned at her feet. 'I wonder if it could have been Cairo. He wasn't at his hotel all night, didn't get in till a few minutes ago. He told me he had been standing up under a police grilling all night. I wonder.' He turned, opened the door, and asked Effie Perine: 'Got Tom yet?'

'He's not in. I'll try again in a few minutes.'

'Thanks.' Spade shut the door and faced Brigid O'Shaughnessy.

She looked at him with cloudy eyes. 'You went to see Joe this morning?' she asked.

'Yes.'

She hesitated. 'Why?'

'Why?' He smiled down at her. 'Because, my own true love, I've got to keep in some sort of touch with all the loose ends of this dizzy affair if I'm ever going to make heads or tails of it.' He put an arm around her shoulders and led her over to his swivel-chair. He kissed the tip of her nose lightly and set her down in the chair. He sat on the desk in front of her. He said: 'Now we've got to find a new home for you, haven't we?'

She nodded with emphasis. 'I won't go back there.'

He patted the desk beside his thighs and made a thoughtful face. 'I think I've got it,' he said presently. 'Wait a minute.' He went into the outer office, shutting the door.

Effie Perine reached for the telephone, saying: 'I'll try again.'

'Afterwards. Does your woman's intuition still tell you that she's a madonna or something?'

She looked sharply up at him. 'I still believe that no matter what kind of trouble she's gotten into she's all right, if that's what you mean.'

'That's what I mean,' he said. 'Are you strong enough for her to give her a lift?'

'How?'

'Could you put her up for a few days?'

'You mean at home?'

'Yes. Her joint's been broken into. That's the second burglary she's had this week. It'd be better for her if she wasn't alone. It would help a lot if you could take her in.'

Effie Perine leaned forward, asking earnestly: 'Is she really in danger, Sam?'

'I think she is.'

She scratched her lip with a fingernail. 'That would scare Ma into a green haemorrhage. I'll have to tell her she's a surprise witness or something that you're keeping under cover till the last minute.'

'You're a darling,' Spade said. 'Better take her out there now. I'll get a key from her and bring whatever she needs over from her apartment. Let's see. You oughtn't to be seen leaving here together. You go home now. Take a taxi, but make sure you aren't followed. You probably won't be, but make sure. I'll send her out in another in a little while, making sure she isn't followed.'

Chapter Eleven

The Fat Man

The telephone bell was ringing when Spade returned to his office after sending Brigid O'Shaughnessy off to Effie Perine's house. He went to the telephone.

'Hello.... Yes, this is Spade.... Yes, I got it. I've been waiting to hear from you.... Who? ... Mr. Gutman? Oh, yes, sure! ... Now—the sooner the better.... Twelve C.... Right. Say fifteen minutes.... Right.'

Spade sat on the corner of his desk beside the telephone and rolled a cigarette. His mouth was a hard complacent v. His eyes, watching his fingers make the cigarette, smouldered over lower lids drawn up straight.

The door opened and Iva Archer came in.

Spade said, 'Hello, honey,' in a voice as lightly amiable as his face had suddenly become.

'Oh, Sam, forgive me! forgive me!' she cried in a choked voice. She stood just inside the door, wadding a black-bordered handkerchief in her small gloved hands, peering into his face with frightened red and swollen eyes.

He did not get up from his seat on the desk corner. He said: 'Sure. That's all right. Forget it.'

'But, Sam,' she wailed, 'I sent those policemen there. I was mad, crazy with jealousy, and I phoned them that if they'd go there they'd learn something about Miles's murder.'

'What made you think that?'

'Oh, I didn't! But I was mad, Sam, and I wanted to hurt you.'

'It made things damned awkward.' He put his arm around her and drew her nearer. 'But it's all right now, only don't get any more crazy notions like that.'

'I won't,' she promised, 'ever. But you weren't nice to me

last night. You were cold and distant and wanted to get rid of me, when I had come down there and waited so long to warn you, and you——'

'Warn me about what?'

'About Phil. He's found out about—about your being in love with me, and Miles had told him about my wanting a divorce, though of course *he* never knew what for, and now Phil thinks we—you killed his brother because he wouldn't give me the divorce so we could get married. He told me he believed that, and yesterday he went and told the police.'

'That's nice,' Spade said softly. 'And you came to warn me, and because I was busy you got up on your ear and helped this damned Phil Archer stir things up.'

'I'm sorry,' she whimpered, 'I know you won't forgive me. I—I'm sorry, sorry, sorry.'

'You ought to be,' he agreed, 'on your own account as well as mine. Has Dundy been to see you since Phil did his talking? Or anybody from the bureau?'

'No.' Alarm opened her eyes and mouth.

'They will,' he said, 'and it'd be just as well not to let them find you here. Did you tell them who you were when you phoned?'

'Oh, no! I simply told them that if they'd go to your apartment right away they'd learn something about the murder and hung up.'

'Where'd you phone from?'

'The drugstore up above your place. Oh, Sam, dearest, I——'

He patted her shoulder and said pleasantly: 'It was a dumb trick, all right, but it's done now. You'd better run along home and think up things to tell the police. You'll be hearing from them. Maybe it'd be best to say "no" right across the board.' He frowned at something distant. 'Or maybe you'd better see Sid Wise first.' He removed his arm from around her, took a card out of his pocket, scribbled three lines on its back, and gave it to her. 'You can tell Sid everything.' He frowned. 'Or almost everything. Where were you the night Miles was shot?'

'Home,' she replied without hesitating.

He shook his head, grinning at her.

'I was,' she insisted.

'No,' he said, 'but if that's your story it's all right with me. Go see Sid. It's up on the next corner, the pinkish building, room eight-twenty-seven.'

Her blue eyes tried to probe his yellow-grey ones. 'What makes you think I wasn't home?' she asked slowly.

'Nothing except that I know you weren't.'

'But I was, I was.' Her lips twisted and anger darkened her eyes. 'Effie Perine told you that,' she said indignantly. 'I saw her looking at my clothes and snooping around. You know she doesn't like me, Sam. Why do you believe things she tells you when you know she'd do anything to make trouble for me?'

'Jesus, you women,' Spade said mildly. He looked at the watch on his wrist. 'You'll have to trot along, precious. I'm late for an appointment now. You do what you want, but if I were you I'd tell Sid the truth or nothing. I mean leave out the parts you don't want to tell him, but don't make up anything to takes its place.'

'I'm not lying to you, Sam,' she protested.

'Like hell you're not,' he said and stood up.

She strained on tiptoe to hold her face nearer his. 'You don't believe me?' she whispered.

'I don't believe you.'

'And you won't forgive me for—for what I did?'

'Sure I do.' He bent his head and kissed her mouth. 'That's all right. Now run along.'

She put her arms around him. 'Won't you go with me to see Mr. Wise?'

'I can't, and I'd only be in the way.' He patted her arms, took them from around his body, and kissed her left wrist between glove and sleeve. He put his hands on her shoulders, turned her to face the door, and released her with a little push. 'Beat it,' he ordered.

The mahogany door of suite 12C at the Alexandria Hotel was opened by the boy Spade had talked to in the Belvedere lobby. Spade said, 'Hello,' good-naturedly. The boy did not say anything. He stood aside holding the door open.

Spade went in. A fat man came to meet him.

The fat man was flabbily fat with bulbous pink cheeks and lips and chins and neck, with a great soft egg of a belly that was all his torso, and pendant cones for arms and legs. As he advanced to meet Spade all his bulbs rose and shook and fell separately with each step, in the manner of clustered soap-bubbles not yet released from the pipe through which they had been blown. His eyes, made small by fat puffs around them, were dark and sleek. Dark ringlets thinly covered his broad scalp. He wore a black cutaway coat, black vest, black satin Ascot tie holding a pinkish pearl, striped grey worsted trousers, and patent-leather shoes.

His voice was a throaty purr. 'Ah, Mr. Spade,' he said with enthusiasm and held out a hand like a fat pink star.

Spade took the hand and smiled and said: 'How do you do, Mr. Gutman?'

Holding Spade's hand, the fat man turned beside him, put his other hand to Spade's elbow, and guided him across a green rug to a green plush chair beside a table that held a siphon, some glasses, and a bottle of Johnnie Walker whisky on a tray, a box of cigars—Coronas del Ritz—two newspapers, and a small and plain yellow soapstone box.

Spade sat in the green chair. The fat man began to fill two glasses from bottle and siphon. The boy had disappeared. Doors set in three of the room's walls were shut. The fourth wall, behind Spade, was pierced by two windows looking out over Geary Street.

'We begin well, sir,' the fat man purred, turning with a proffered glass in his hand. 'I distrust a man that says when. If he's got to be careful not to drink too much it's because he's not to be trusted when he does.'

Spade took the glass and, smiling, made the beginning of a bow over it.

The fat man raised his glass and held it against a window's light. He nodded approvingly at the bubbles running up in it. He said: 'Well, sir, here's to plain speaking and clear under-standing.'

They drank and lowered their glasses.

The fat man looked shrewdly at Spade and asked: 'You're a close-mouthed man?'

Spade shook his head. 'I like to talk.'

'Better and better!' the fat man exclaimed. 'I distrust a close-mouthed man. He generally picks the wrong time to talk and says the wrong things. Talking's something you can't do judiciously unless you keep in practice.' He beamed over his glass. 'We'll get along, sir, that we will.' He set his glass on the table and held the box of Coronas del Ritz out to Spade. 'A cigar, sir.'

Spade took a cigar, trimmed the end of it, and lighted it. Meanwhile the fat man pulled another green plush chair around to face Spade's within convenient distance and placed a smoking-stand within reach of both chairs. Then he took his glass from the table, took a cigar from the box and lowered himself into his chair. His bulbs stopped jouncing and settled into flabby rest. He sighed comfortably and said: 'Now, sir, we'll talk if you like. And I'll tell you right out that I'm a man who likes talking to a man that likes to talk.'

'Swell. Will we talk about the black bird?'

The fat man laughed and his bulbs rode up and down on his laughter. 'Will we?' he asked and, 'We will,' he replied. His pink face was shiny with delight. 'You're the man for me, sir, a man along my own lines. No beating about the bush, but right to the point. "Will we talk about the black bird?" We will. I like that, sir. I like that way of doing business. Let us talk about the black bird by all means, but first, sir, answer me a question, please, though maybe it's an unnecessary one, so we'll understand each other from the beginning. You're here as Miss O'Shaughnessy's representative?'

Spade blew smoke over the fat man's head in a long slanting plume. He frowned thoughtfully at the ash-tipped end of his cigar. He replied deliberately: 'I can't say yes or no. There's nothing certain about it either way, yet.' He looked up at the fat man and stopped frowning. 'It depends.'

'It depends on——?'

Spade shook his head. 'If I knew what it depends on I could say yes or no.'

The fat man took a mouthful from his glass, swallowed it, and suggested: 'Maybe it depends on Joel Cairo?'

Spade's prompt 'Maybe' was noncommittal. He drank.

The fat man leaned forward until his belly stopped him. His smile was ingratiating and so was his purring voice. 'You could say, then, that the question is which one of them you'll represent?'

'You could put it that way.'

'It will be one or the other?'

'I didn't say that.'

The fat man's eyes glistened. His voice sank to a throaty whisper asking: 'Who else is there?'

Spade pointed his cigar at his own chest. 'There's me,' he said.

The fat man sank back in his chair and let his body go flaccid. He blew his breath out in a long contented gust. 'That's wonderful, sir,' he purred. 'That's wonderful. I do like a man that tells you right out he's looking out for himself. Don't we all? I don't trust a man that says he's not. And the man that's telling the truth when he say's he's not I distrust most of all, because he's an ass and an ass that's going contrary to the laws of nature.'

Spade exhaled smoke. His face was politely attentive. He said: 'Uh-huh. Now let's talk about the black bird.'

The fat man smiled benevolently. 'Let's,' he said. He squinted so that fat puffs crowding together left nothing of his eyes but a dark gleam visible. 'Mr. Spade, have you any conception of how much money can be made out of that black bird?'

'No.'

The fat man leaned forward again and put a bloated pink hand on the arm of Spade's chair. 'Well, sir, if I told you—by Gad, if I told you half!—you'd call me a liar.'

Spade smiled. 'No,' he said, 'not even if I thought it. But if you won't take the risk just tell me what it is and I'll figure out the profits.'

The fat man laughed. 'You couldn't do it, sir. Nobody could do it that hadn't had a world of experience with things of that sort, and'—he paused impressively—'there aren't any other things of that sort.' His bulbs jostled one another as he laughed again. He stopped laughing, abruptly. His fleshy lips hung open as laughter had left them. He stared at Spade with an intentness that suggested myopia. He asked: 'You mean you don't know what it is?' Amazement took the throatiness out of his voice.

Spade made a careless gesture with his cigar. 'Oh, hell,' he said lightly, 'I know what it's supposed to look like. I know the value in life you people put on it. I don't know what it is.'

'She didn't tell you?'

'Miss O'Shaughnessy?'

'Yes. A lovely girl, sir.'

'Uh-huh. No.'

The fat man's eyes were dark gleams in ambush behind pink puffs of flesh. He said indistinctly, 'She must know,' and then, 'And Cairo didn't either?'

'Cairo is cagey. He's willing to buy it, but he won't risk telling me anything I don't know already.'

The fat man moistened his lips with his tongue. 'How much is he willing to buy it for?' he asked.

'Ten thousand dollars.'

The fat man laughed scornfully. 'Ten thousand, and dollars, mind you, not even pounds. That's the Greek for you. Humph! And what did you say to that?'

'I said if I turned it over to him I'd expect the ten thousand.'

'Ah, yes, *if*! Nicely put, sir.' The fat man's forehead squirmed in a flesh-blurred frown. 'They must know,' he said only partly aloud, then: 'Do they? Do they know what the bird is, sir? What was your impression?'

'I can't help you there,' Spade confessed. 'There's not much to go by. Cairo didn't say he did and he didn't say he didn't. She said she didn't, but I took it for granted that she was lying.'

'That was not an injudicious thing to do,' the fat man said, but his mind was obviously not on his words. He scratched his head. He frowned until his forehead was marked by raw red creases. He fidgeted in his chair as much as his size and the size of the chair permitted fidgeting. He shut his eyes, opened them suddenly—wide—and said to Spade: 'Maybe they don't.' His bulbous pink face slowly lost its worried frown and then, more quickly, took on an expression of ineffable happiness. 'If they don't,' he cried, and again: 'If they don't I'm the only one in the whole wide sweet world who does!'

Spade drew his lips back in a tight smile. 'I'm glad I came to the right place,' he said.

The fat man smiled too, but somewhat vaguely. Happiness had gone out of his face, though he continued to smile, and caution had come into his eyes. His face was a watchful-eyed smiling mask held up between his thoughts and Spade. His eyes, avoiding Spade's, shifted to the glass at Spade's elbow. His face brightened. 'By Gad, sir,' he said, 'your glass is empty.' He got up and went to the table and clattered glasses and siphon and bottle mixing two drinks.

Spade was immobile in his chair until the fat man, with a flourish and a bow and a jocular 'Ah, sir, this kind of medicine will never hurt you!' had handed him his refilled glass. Then Spade rose and stood close to the fat man, looking down at him, and Spade's eyes were hard and bright. He raised his glass. His voice was deliberate, challenging: 'Here's to plain speaking and clear understanding.'

The fat man chuckled and they drank. The fat man sat down. He held his glass against his belly with both hands and smiled up at Spade. He said: 'Well, sir, it's surprising, but it well may be a fact that neither of them does know exactly what that bird is, and that nobody in all this whole wide sweet world knows what it is, saving and excepting only your humble servant, Casper Gutman, Esquire.'

'Swell.' Spade stood with legs apart, one hand in his trousers pocket, the other holding his glass. 'When you've told me there'll only be two of us who know.'

'Mathematically correct, sir'—the fat man's eyes twinkled— 'but'—his smile spread—'I don't know for certain that I'm going to tell you.'

'Don't be a damned fool,' Spade said patiently. 'You know what it is. I know where it is. That's why we're here.'

'Well, sir, where is it?'

Spade ignored the question.

The fat man bunched his lips, raised his eyebrows, and cocked his head a little to the left. 'You see,' he said blandly, 'I must tell you what I know, but you will not tell me what you know. That is hardly equitable, sir. No, no, I do not think we can do business along those lines.'

Spade's face became pale and hard. He spoke rapidly in a low furious voice: 'Think again and think fast. I told that punk of yours that you'd have to talk to me before you got through. I'll tell you now that you'll do your talking to-day or you are through. What are you wasting my time for? You and your lousy secret! Christ! I know exactly what that stuff is that they keep in the subtreasury vaults, but what good does that do me? I can get along without you. God damn you! Maybe you could have got along without me if you'd kept clear of me. You can't now. Not in San Francisco. You'll come in or you'll get out—and you'll do it to-day.'

He turned and with angry heedlessness tossed his glass at the table. The glass struck the wood, burst apart, and splashed its contents and glittering fragments over the table and floor. Spade, deaf and blind to the crash, wheeled to confront the fat man again.

The fat man paid no more attention to the glass's fate than Spade did: lips pursed, eyebrows raised, head cocked a little to the left, he had maintained his pink-faced blandness throughout Spade's angry speech, and he maintained it now.

Spade, still furious, said: 'And another thing, I don't want——'

The door to Spade's left opened. The boy who had admitted Spade came in. He shut the door, stood in front of it with his hands flat against his flanks, and looked at Spade. The boy's eyes were wide open and dark with wide pupils. Their gaze ran over Spade's body from shoulders to knees and up again to settle on the handkerchief whose maroon border peeped from the breast pocket of Spade's brown coat.

'Another thing,' Spade repeated, glaring at the boy: 'Keep that gunsel away from me while you're making up your mind. I'll kill him. I don't like him. He makes me nervous. I'll kill him the first time he gets in my way. I won't give him an even break. I won't give him a chance. I'll kill him.'

The boy's lips twitched in a shadowy smile. He neither raised his eyes nor spoke.

The fat man said tolerantly: 'Well, sir, I must say you have a most violent temper.'

'Temper?' Spade laughed crazily. He crossed to the chair on which he had dropped his hat, picked up the hat, and set it on his head. He held out a long arm that ended in a thick forefinger pointing at the fat man's belly. His angry voice filled the room. 'Think it over and think like hell. You've got till five-thirty to do it in. Then you're either in or out, for keeps.' He let his arm drop, scowled at the bland fat man for a moment, scowled at the boy, and went to the door through which he had entered. When he opened the door he turned and said harshly 'Five-thirty—then the curtain.'

The boy, staring at Spade's chest, repeated the two words he had twice spoken in the Belvedere lobby. His voice was not loud. It was bitter.

Spade went out and slammed the door.

Chapter Twelve

Merry-Go-Round

Spade rode down from Gutman's floor in an elevator. His lips were dry and rough in a face otherwise pale and damp. When he took out his handkerchief to wipe his face he saw his hand trembling. He grinned at it and said 'Whew!' so loudly that the elevator operator turned his head over his shoulder and asked: 'Sir?'

Spade walked down Geary Street to the Palace Hotel, where he ate luncheon. His face had lost its pallor, his lips their dryness and his hand its trembling by the time he had sat down. He ate hungrily without haste, and then went to Sid Wise's office.

When Spade entered, Wise was biting a fingernail and staring at the window. He took his hand from his mouth, screwed his chair around to face Spade, and said: ''Lo. Push a chair up.'

Spade moved a chair to the side of the big paper-laden desk and sat down. 'Mrs. Archer come in?' he asked.

'Yes.' The faintest lights flickered in Wise's eyes. 'Going to marry the lady, Sammy?'

Spade sighed irritably through his nose. 'Christ, now you start that!' he grumbled.

A brief tired smile lifted the corners of the lawyer's mouth. 'If you don't,' he said, 'you're going to have a job on your hands.'

Spade looked up from the cigarette he was making and spoke

sourly: 'You mean you are? Well, that's what you're for. What did she tell you?'

'About you?'

'About anything I ought to know.'

Wise ran fingers through his hair sprinkling dandruff down on his shoulders. 'She told me she had tried to get a divorce from Miles so she could——'

'I know all that,' Spade interrupted him. 'You can skip it. Get to the part I don't know.'

'How do I know how much she——?'

'Quit stalling, Sid.' Spade held the flame of his lighter to the end of his cigarette. 'What did she tell you that she wanted kept from me?'

Wise looked reprovingly at Spade. 'Now, Sammy,' he began, 'that's not——'

Spade looked heavenward at the ceiling and groaned: 'Dear God, he's my own lawyer that's got rich off me and I have to get down on my knees and beg him to tell me things!' He lowered at Wise. 'What in hell do you think I sent her to you for?'

Wise made a weary grimace. 'Just one more client like you,' he complained, 'and I'd be in a sanatorium—or San Quentin.'

'You'd be with most of your clients. Did she tell you where she was the night he was killed?'

'Yes.'

'Where?'

'Following him.'

Spade sat up straight and blinked. He exclaimed incredulously: 'Jesus, these women!' Then he laughed, relaxed, and asked: 'Well, what did she see?'

Wise shook his head. 'Nothing much. When he came home for dinner that evening he told her he had a date with a girl at the St. Mark, ragging her, telling her that was her chance to get the divorce she wanted. She thought at first he was just trying to get under her skin. He knew——'

'I know the family history,' Spade said. 'Skip it. Tell me what she did.'

'I will if you'll give me a chance. After he had gone out she began to think that maybe he might have had that date. You know Miles. It would have been like him to——'

'You can skip Miles's character too.'

'I oughtn't to tell you a damned thing,' the lawyer said. 'So she got their car from the garage and drove down to the St. Mark, sitting in the car across the street. She saw him come out of the hotel and she saw that he was shadowing a man and a girl—she says she saw the same girl with you last night—who had come out just ahead of him. She knew then that he was working, had been kidding her. I suppose she was disappointed, and mad—she sounded that way when she told me about it. She followed Miles long enough to make sure he was shadowing the pair, and then she went up to your apartment. You weren't home.'

'What time was that?' Spade asked.

'When she got to your place? Between half-past nine and ten the first time.'

'The first time?'

'Yes. She drove around for half an hour or so and then tried again. That would make it, say, ten-thirty. You were still out, so she drove back downtown and went to a movie to kill time until after midnight, when she thought she'd be more likely to find you in.'

Spade frowned. 'She went to a movie at ten-thirty?'

'So she says—the one on Powell Street that stays open till one in the morning. She didn't want to go home, she said, because she didn't want to be there when Miles came. That always made him mad, it seems, especially if it was around midnight. She stayed in the movie till it closed.' Wise's words came out slower now and there was a sardonic glint in his eye. 'She says she had decided by then not to go back to your place again. She says she didn't know whether you'd like having her drop in that late. So she went to Tait's—the one on Ellis Street—had something to eat and then went home—alone.' Wise rocked back in his chair and waited for Spade to speak.

Spade's face was expressionless. He asked: 'You believe her?'

'Don't you?' Wise replied.

'How do I know? How do I know it isn't something you fixed up between you to tell me?'

Wise smiled. 'You don't cash many cheques for strangers, do you, Sammy?'

'Not basketfuls. Well, what then? Miles wasn't home. It

was at least two o'clock by then—must've been—and he was dead.'

'Miles wasn't home,' Wise said. 'That seems to have made her mad again—his not being home first to be made mad by her not being home. So she took the car out of the garage again and went back to your place.'

'And I wasn't home. I was down looking at Miles's corpse. Jesus, what a swell lot of merry-go-round riding. Then what?'

'She went home, and her husband still wasn't there, and while she was undressing your messenger came with the news of his death.'

Spade didn't speak until he had with great care rolled and lighted another cigarette. Then he said: 'I think that's an all right spread. It seems to click with most of the known facts. It ought to hold.'

Wise's fingers, running through his hair again, combed more dandruff down on his shoulders. He studied Spade's face with curious eyes and asked: 'But you don't believe it?'

Spade plucked his cigarette from between his lips. 'I don't believe it or disbelieve it, Sid. I don't know a damned thing about it.'

A wry smile twisted the lawyer's mouth. He moved his shoulders wearily and said: 'That's right—I'm selling you out. Why don't you get an honest lawyer—one you can trust?'

'That fellow's dead.' Spade stood up. He sneered at Wise. 'Getting touchy, huh? I haven't got enough to think about: now I've got to remember to be polite to you. What did I do? Forget to genuflect when I came in?'

Sid Wise smiled sheepishly. 'You're a son of a gun, Sammy,' he said.

Effie Perine was standing in the centre of Spade's outer office when he entered. She looked at him with worried brown eyes and asked: 'What happened?'

Spade's face grew stiff. 'What happened where?' he demanded.

'Why didn't she come?'

Spade took two long steps and caught Effie Perine by the shoulders. 'She didn't get there?' he bawled into her frightened face.

She shook her head violently from side to side. 'I waited and waited and she didn't come, and I couldn't get you on the phone, so I came down.'

Spade jerked his hands away from her shoulders, thrust them far down in his trousers pockets, said, 'Another merry-go-round,' in a loud enraged voice, and strode into his private office. He came out again. 'Phone your mother,' he commanded. 'See if she's come yet.'

He walked up and down the office while the girl used the telephone. 'No,' she said when she had finished. 'Did—did you send her out in a taxi?'

His grunt probably meant yes.

'Are you sure she—— Somebody must have followed her!'

Spade stopped pacing the floor. He put his hands on his hips and glared at the girl. He addressed her in a loud savage voice: 'Nobody followed her. Do you think I'm a God-damned school-boy? I made sure of it before I put her in the cab, I rode a dozen blocks with her to be more sure, and I checked her another half-dozen blocks after I got out.'

'Well, but——'

'But she didn't get there. You've told me that. I believe it. Do you think I think she did get there?'

Effie Perine sniffed. 'You certainly act like a God-damned schoolboy,' she said.

Spade made a harsh noise in his throat and went to the corridor-door. 'I'm going out and find her if I have to dig up sewers,' he said. 'Stay here till I'm back or you hear from me. For Christ's sake let's do something right.'

He went out, walked half the distance to the elevators, and retraced his steps. Effie Perine was sitting at her desk when he opened the door. He said: 'You ought to know better than to pay any attention to me when I talk like that.'

'If you think I pay any attention to you you're crazy,' she replied, 'only'—she crossed her arms and felt her shoulders, and her mouth twitched uncertainly—'I won't be able to wear an evening gown for two weeks, you big brute.'

He grinned humbly, said, 'I'm no damned good, darling,' made an exaggerated bow, and went out again.

Two yellow taxicabs were at the corner-stand to which Spade

went. Their chauffeurs were standing together talking. Spade asked: 'Where's the red-faced blond driver that was here at noon?'

'Got a load,' one of the chauffeurs said.

'Will he be back here?'

'I guess so.'

The other chauffeur ducked his head to the east. 'Here he comes now.'

Spade walked down to the corner and stood by the kerb until the red-faced blond chauffeur had parked his cab and got out. Then Spade went up to him and said: 'I got into your cab with a lady at noontime. We went out Stockton Street and up Sacramento to Jones, where I got out.'

'Sure,' the red-faced man said, 'I remember that.'

'I told you to take her to a Ninth Avenue number. You didn't take her there. Where did you take her?'

The chauffeur rubbed his cheek with a grimy hand and looked doubtfully at Spade. 'I don't know about this.'

'It's all right,' Spade assured him, giving him one of his cards. 'If you want to play safe, though, we can ride up to your office and get your superintendent's O.K.'

'I guess it's all right. I took her to the Ferry Building.'

'By herself?'

'Yeah. Sure.'

'Didn't take her anywhere else first?'

'No. It was like this: after we dropped you I went on out Sacramento, and when we got to Polk she rapped on the glass and said she wanted to get a newspaper, so I stopped at the corner and whistled for a kid, and she got her paper.'

'Which paper?'

'The *Call*. Then I went on out Sacramento some more, and just after we'd crossed Van Ness she knocked on the glass again and said take her to the Ferry Building.'

'Was she excited or anything?'

'Not so's I noticed.'

'And when you got to the Ferry Building?'

'She paid me off, and that was all.'

'Anybody waiting for her there?'

'I didn't see them if they was.'

'Which way did she go?'

'At the Ferry? I don't know. Maybe upstairs, or towards the stairs.'

'Take the newspaper with her?'

'Yeah, she had it tucked under her arm when she paid me.'

'With the pink sheet outside, or one of the white?'

'Hell, Cap, I don't remember that.'

Spade thanked the chauffeur, said 'Get yourself a smoke,' and gave him a silver dollar.

Spade bought a copy of the *Call* and carried it into an office building vestibule to examine it out of the wind.

His eyes ran swiftly over the front page headlines and over those on the second and third pages. They paused for a moment under SUSPECT ARRESTED AS COUNTERFEITER on the fourth page, and again on page five under BAY YOUTH SEEKS DEATH WITH BULLET. Pages six and seven held nothing to interest him. On eight, 3 BOYS ARRESTED AS S. F. BURG-LARS AFTER SHOOTING held his attention for a moment, and after that nothing until he reached the thirty-fifth page, which held news of the weather, shipping, produce, finance, divorce, births, marriages and deaths. He read the list of dead, passed over pages thirty-six and thirty-seven—financial news—found nothing to stop his eyes on the thirty-eighth and last page, sighed, folded the newspaper, put it in his coat pocket, and rolled a cigarette.

For five minutes he stood there in the office building vestibule smoking and staring sulkily at nothing. Then he walked up to Stockton Street, hailed a taxicab, and had himself driven to the Coronet.

He let himself into the building and into Brigid O'Shaugh-nessy's apartment with the key she had given him. The blue gown she had worn the previous night was hanging across the foot of the bed. Her blue stockings and slippers were on the bedroom floor. The polychrome box that had held jewellery in her dressing-table drawer now stood empty on the dressing-table top. Spade frowned at it, ran his tongue across his lips, strolled through the rooms, looking around but not touching anything, then left the Coronet and went downtown again.

*   *   *

In the doorway of Spade's office building he came face to face with the boy he had left at Gutman's. The boy put himself in Spade's path, blocking the entrance, and said: 'Come on. He wants to see you.'

The boy's hands were in his overcoat pockets. His pockets bulged more than his hands need have made them bulge.

Spade grinned and said mockingly: 'I didn't expect you till five-twenty-five. I hope I haven't kept you waiting.'

The boy raised his eyes to Spade's mouth and spoke in the strained voice of one in physical pain: 'Keep on riding me and you're going to be picking iron out of your navel.'

Spade chuckled. 'The cheaper the crook, the gaudier the patter,' he said cheerfully. 'Well, let's go.'

They walked up Sutter Street side by side. The boy kept his hands in his overcoat pockets. They walked a little more than a block in silence. Then Spade asked pleasantly: 'How long have you been off the gooseberry lay, son?'

The boy did not show that he had heard the question.

'Did you ever—?' Spade began, and stopped. A soft light began to glow in his yellowish eyes. He did not address the boy again. They went into the Alexandria, rode up to the twelfth floor, and walked down the corridor towards Gutman's suite. Nobody else was in the corridor.

Spade lagged a little, so that, when they were within fifteen feet of Gutman's door, he was perhaps a foot and a half behind the boy. He leaned sidewise suddenly and grasped the boy from behind by both arms, just beneath his elbows. He forced his arms forward so that the boy's hands, in his overcoat pockets, lifted the overcoat up before him. The boy struggled and squirmed, but he was impotent in the big man's grip. The boy kicked back, but his feet went between Spade's spread legs.

Spade lifted the boy straight up from the floor and brought him down hard on his feet again. The impact made little noise on the thick carpet. At the moment of impact Spade's hands slid down and got a fresh grip on the boy's wrists. The boy, teeth set hard together, did not stop straining against the man's big hands, but he could not tear himself loose, could not keep the man's hands from crawling down over his own hands. The boy's teeth ground together audibly, making a noise that mingled with the noise of Spade's breathing as Spade crushed the boy's hands.

They were tense and motionless for a long moment. Then the boy's arms became limp. Spade released him and stepped back. In each of Spade's hands, when they came out of the boy's overcoat pockets, there was a heavy automatic pistol.

The boy turned and faced Spade. His face was a ghastly white blank. He kept his hands in his overcoat pockets. He looked at Spade's chest and did not say anything.

Spade put the pistols in his own pockets and grinned derisively. 'Come on,' he said. 'This will put you in solid with your boss.'

They went to Gutman's door and Spade knocked.

Chapter Thirteen

The Emperor's Gift

Gutman opened the door. A glad smile lighted his fat face. He held out a hand and said: 'Ah, come in, sir! Thank you for coming. Come in.'

Spade shook the hand and entered. The boy went in behind him. The fat man shut the door. Spade took the boy's pistols from his pocket and held them out to Gutman. 'Here. You shouldn't let him run around with these. He'll get himself hurt.'

The fat man laughed merrily and took the pistols. 'Well, well,' he said, 'what's this?' He looked from Spade to the boy.

Spade said: 'A crippled newsie took them away from him, but I made him give them back.'

The white-faced boy took the pistols out of Gutman's hands and pocketed them. He did not speak.

Gutman laughed again. 'By Gad, sir,' he told Spade, 'you're a chap worth knowing, an amazing character. Come in. Sit down. Give me your hat.

The boy left the room by the door to the right of the entrance.

The fat man installed Spade in a green plush chair by the table, pressed a cigar upon him, held a light to it, mixed whisky and carbonated water, put one glass in Spade's hand, and, holding the other, sat down facing Spade.

'Now sir,' he said, 'I hope you'll let me apologise for——'

'Never mind about that,' Spade said. 'Let's talk about the black bird.'

The fat man cocked his head to the left and regarded Spade with fond eyes. 'All right, sir,' he agreed. 'Let's.' He took a sip from the glass in his hand. 'This is going to be the most astounding thing you've ever heard of, sir, and I say that knowing that a man of your calibre in your profession must have known some astounding things in his time.'

Spade nodded politely.

The fat man screwed up his eyes and asked: 'What do you know, sir, about the Order of the Hospital of St. John of Jerusalem, later called the Knights of Rhodes and other things?'

Spade waved his cigar. 'Not much—only what I remember from history in school—Crusaders or something.'

'Very good. Now you don't remember that Suleiman the Magnificent chased them out of Rhodes in 1523?'

'No.'

'Well, sir, he did, and they settled in Crete. And they stayed there for seven years, until 1530 when they persuaded the Emperor Charles V to give them'—Gutman held up three puffy fingers and counted them—'Malta, Gozo, and Tripoli.'

'Yes?'

'Yes, sir, but with these conditions: they were to pay the Emperor each year the tribute of one'—he held up a finger—'falcon in acknowledgment that Malta was still under Spain, and if they ever left the island it was to revert to Spain. Understand? He was giving it to them, but not unless they used it, and they couldn't give it or sell it to anybody else.'

'Yes.'

The fat man looked over his shoulders at the three closed doors, hunched his chair a few inches nearer Spade's, and reduced his voice to a husky whisper: 'Have you any conception of the extreme, the immeasurable, wealth of the Order at that time?'

'If I remember,' Spade said, 'they were pretty well fixed.'

Gutman smiled indulgently. 'Pretty well, sir, is putting it mildly.' His whisper became lower and more purring. 'They were rolling in wealth, sir. You've no idea. None of us has any idea. For years they had preyed on the Saracens, had taken nobody knows what spoils of gems, precious metals, silks, ivories—the cream of the cream of the East. That is history, sir. We all know that the Holy Wars to them, as to the Templars, were largely a matter of loot.

'Well, now, the Emperor Charles has given them Malta, and all the rent he asks is one insignificant bird per annum, just as a matter of form. What could be more natural than for these immeasurably wealthy Knights to look around for some way of expressing their gratitude? Well, sir, that's exactly what they did, and they hit on the happy thought of sending Charles for the first year's tribute, not an insignificant live bird, but a glorious golden falcon encrusted from head to foot with the finest jewels in their coffers. And—remember, sir—they had fine ones, the finest out of Asia.' Gutman stopped whispering. His sleek dark eyes examined Spade's face, which was placid. The fat man asked: 'Well, sir, what do you think of that?'

'I don't know.'

The fat man smiled complacently. 'These are facts, historical facts, not school-book history, not Mr. Wells's history, but history nevertheless.' He leaned forward. 'The archives of the Order from the twelfth century on are still at Malta. They are not intact, but what is there holds no less than three'—he held up three fingers—'references that can't be to anything else but this jewelled falcon. In J. Delaville Le Roulx's *Les Archives de l'Ordre de Saint-Jean* there is a reference to it—oblique to be sure, but a reference still. And the unpublished—because unfinished at the time of his death—supplement to Paoli's *Dell' origine ed instituto del sacro militar ordine* has a clear and unmistakable statement of the facts I am telling you.'

'All right,' Spade said.

'All right, sir. Grand Master Villiers de l'Isle d'Adam had this foot-high jewelled bird made by Turkish slaves in the castle of St. Angelo and sent it to Charles, who was in Spain. He sent it in a galley commanded by a French knight named Cormier or Corvere, a member of the Order.' His voice dropped to a whisper again. 'It never reached Spain.' He smiled with compressed lips and asked: 'You know of Barbarossa, Redbeard, Khair-ed-Din?

No? A famous admiral of buccaneers sailing out of Algiers then. Well, sir, he took the Knights' galley and he took the bird. The bird went to Algiers. That's a fact. That's a fact that the French historian Pierre Dan put in one of his letters from Algiers. He wrote that the bird had been there for more than a hundred years, until it was carried away by Sir Francis Verney, the English adventurer who was with the Algerian buccaneers for a while. Maybe it wasn't, but Pierre Dan believed it was, and that's good enough for me.

'There's nothing said about the bird in Lady Frances Verney's *Memoirs of the Verney Family during the Seventeenth Century*, to be sure. I looked. And it's pretty certain that Sir Francis didn't have the bird when he died in a Messina hospital in 1615. He was stony broke. But, sir, there's no denying that the bird *did* go to Sicily. It was there and it came into the possession there of Victor Amadeus II some time after he became king in 1713, and it was one of his gifts to his wife when he married in Chambéry after abdicating. That is a fact, sir. Carutti, the author of *Storia del Regno di Vittorio Amadeo II*, himself vouched for it.

'Maybe they—Amadeo and his wife—took it along with them to Turin when he tried to revoke his abdication. Be that as it may, it turned up next in the possession of a Spaniard who had been with the army that took Naples in 1734—the father of Don José Monino y Redondo, Count of Floridablanca, who was Charles III's chief minister. There's nothing to show that it didn't stay in that family until at least the end of the Carlist War in '40. Then it appeared in Paris at just about the time that Paris was full of Carlists who had to get out of Spain. One of them must have brought it with him, but, whoever he was, it's likely he knew nothing about its real value. It had been—no doubt as a precaution during the Carlist trouble in Spain—painted or enamelled over to look like nothing more than a fairly interesting black statuette. And in that disguise, sir, it was, you might say, kicked around Paris for seventy years by private owners and dealers too stupid to see what it was under the skin.'

The fat man paused to smile and shake his head regretfully. Then he went on: 'For seventy years, sir, this marvellous item was, as you might say, a football in the gutters of Paris—until 1911 when a Greek dealer named Charilaos Konstantinides found it in an obscure shop. It didn't take Charilaos long to learn what it was and to acquire it. No thickness of enamel could conceal value from his eyes and nose. Well, sir, Charilaos was the man who traced most of its history and who identified it as what it actually was. I got wind of it and finally forced most of the history out of him, though I've been able to add a few details since.

'Charilaos was in no hurry to convert his find into money at once. He knew that—enormous as its intrinsic value was—a far higher, a terrific price, could be obtained for it once its authenticity was established beyond doubt. Possibly he planned to do business with one of the modern descendants of the old Order—the English Order of St. John of Jerusalem, the Prussian Johanniterorden, or the Italian or German *langues* of the Sovereign Order of Malta—all wealthy orders.'

The fat man raised his glass, smiled at its emptiness, and rose to fill it and Spade's. 'You begin to believe me a little?' he asked as he worked the siphon.

'I haven't said I didn't.'

'No,' Gutman chuckled. 'But how you looked.' He sat down, drank generously, and patted his mouth with a white handkerchief. 'Well, sir, to hold it safe while pursuing his researches into its history, Charilaos had re-enamelled the bird, apparently just as it is now. One year to the very day after he had acquired it—that was possibly three months after I'd made him confess to me—I picked up *The Times* in London and read that his establishment had been burglarised and he murdered. I was in Paris the next day.' He shook his head sadly. 'The bird was gone. By Gad, sir, I was wild. I didn't believe anybody else knew what it was. I didn't believe he had told anybody but me. A great quantity of stuff had been stolen. That made me think that the thief had simply taken the bird along with the rest of his plunder, not knowing what it was. Because I assure you that a thief who knew its value would not burden himself with anything else—no, sir—at least not anything less than crown jewels.

He shut his eyes and smiled complacently at an inner thought. He opened his eyes and said: 'That was seventeen years ago. Well, sir, it took me seventeen years to locate that bird, but I did it. I wanted it, and I'm not a man that's easily discouraged when he wants something.' His smile grew broad. 'I wanted it and I found it. I want it and I'm going to have it.' He drained his glass, dried his lips again, and returned his handkerchief to his pocket. 'I traced it to the home of a Russian general—one Kemidov—in a Constantinople suburb. He didn't know a thing about it. It was nothing but a black enamelled figure to him, but his natural contrariness—the natural contrariness of a Russian general—kept him from selling it to me when I made him an offer. Perhaps in my eagerness I was a little unskilful, though not very. I don't know about that. But I did know I wanted it and I was afraid this stupid soldier might begin to investigate his property, might chip off some of the enamel. So I sent some—ah—agents to get it. Well, sir, they got it and I haven't got it.' He stood up and carried his empty glass to the table. 'But I'm going to get it. Your glass, sir.'

'Then the bird doesn't belong to any of you?' Spade asked, 'but to a General Kemidov?'

'Belong?' the fat man said jovially. 'Well, sir, you might say it belonged to the King of Spain, but I don't see how you can honestly grant anybody else clear title to it—except by right of possession.' He chuckled. 'An article of that value that has passed from hand to hand by such means is clearly the property of whoever can get hold of it.'

'Then it's Miss O'Shaughnessy's now?'

'No, sir, except as my agent.'

Spade said, 'Oh,' ironically.

Gutman looked thoughtfully at the stopper of the whisky bottle in his hand, asked: 'There's no doubt that she's got it now?'

'Not much.'

'Where?'

'I don't know exactly.'

The fat man set the bottle on the table with a bang. 'But you said you did,' he protested.

Spade made a careless gesture with one hand. 'I meant to say I know where to get it when the time comes.'

The pink bulbs of Gutman's face arranged themselves more happily. 'And you do?' he asked.

'Yes.'

'Where?'

Spade grinned and said: 'Leave that to me. That's my end.'

'When?'

'When I'm ready.'

The fat man pursed his lips and, smiling with only slight uneasiness, asked: 'Mr. Spade, where is Miss O'Shaughnessy now?'

'In my hands, safely tucked away.'

Gutman smiled with approval. 'Trust you for that, sir,' he said. 'Well now, sir, before we sit down to talk prices, answer me this: how soon can you—or how soon are you willing to—produce the falcon?'

'A couple of days.'

The fat man nodded. 'That is satisfactory. We—— But I forget our nourishment.' He turned to the table, poured whisky, squirted charged water into it, set a glass at Spade's elbow and held his own aloft. 'Well, sir, here's to a fair bargain and profits large enough for both of us.'

They drank. The fat man sat down. Spade asked: 'What's your idea of a fair bargain?'

Gutman held his glass up to the light, looked affectionately at it, took another long drink, and said: 'I have two proposals to make, sir, and either is fair. Take your choice. I will give you twenty-five thousand dollars when you deliver the falcon to me, and another twenty-five thousand as soon as I get to New York; or I will give you one quarter—twenty-five per cent—of what I realise on the falcon. There you are, sir: an almost immediate fifty thousand dollars or a vastly greater sum within, say, a couple of months.'

Spade drank and asked: 'How much greater?'

'Vastly,' the fat man repeated. 'Who knows how much greater? Shall I say a hundred thousand, or a quarter of a million? Will you believe me if I name the sum that seems the probable minimum?'

'Why not?'

The fat man smacked his lips and lowered his voice to a purring murmur. 'What would you say, sir, to half a million?'

Spade narrowed his eyes. 'Then you think the dingus is worth two million?'

Gutman smiled serenely. 'In your own words, why not?' he asked.

Spade emptied his glass and set it on the table. He put his cigar in his mouth, took it out, looked at it, and put it back in. His yellow-grey eyes were faintly muddy. He said: 'That's a hell of a lot of dough.'

The fat man agreed: 'That's a hell of a lot of dough.' He leaned forward and patted Spade's knee. 'That is the absolute rock bottom minimum—or Charilaos Konstantinides was a blithering idiot—and he wasn't.'

Spade removed the cigar from his mouth again, frowned at it with distaste, and put it on the smoking-stand. He shut his eyes hard, opened them again. Their muddiness had thickened. He said: 'The—the minimum, huh? And the maximum?' An unmistakable *sh* followed the x in maximum as he said it.

'The maximum?' Gutman held his empty hand out, palm up. 'I refuse to guess. You'd think me crazy. I don't know. There's no telling how high it could go, sir, and that's the one and only truth about it.'

Spade pulled his sagging lower lip tight against the upper. He shook his head impatiently. A sharp frightened gleam awoke in his eyes—and was smothered by the deepening muddiness. He stood up, helping himself up with his hands on the arms of his chair. He shook his head again and took an uncertain step forward. He laughed thickly and muttered: 'God damn you.'

Gutman jumped up and pushed his chair back. His fat globes jiggled. His eyes were dark holes in an oily pink face.

Spade swung his head from side to side until his dull eyes were pointed at—if not focused on—the door. He took another uncertain step.

The fat man called sharply: 'Wilmer!'

A door opened and the boy came in.

Spade took a third step. His face was grey now, with jaw muscles standing out like tumours under his ears. His legs did not straighten again after his fourth step and his muddy eyes were almost covered by their lids. He took his fifth step.

The boy walked over and stood close to Spade, a little in front of him but not directly between Spade and the door. The boy's right hand was inside his coat over his heart. The corners of his mouth twitched.

Spade essayed his sixth step.

The boy's leg darted out across Spade's leg, in front. Spade tripped over the interfering leg and crashed face-down on the floor. The boy, keeping his right hand under his coat, looked down at Spade. Spade tried to get up. The boy drew his right foot far back and kicked Spade's temple. The kick rolled Spade over on his side. Once more he tried to get up, could not, and went to sleep.

Chapter Fourteen

'La Paloma'

Spade, coming around the corner from the elevator at a few minutes past six in the morning, saw yellow light glowing through the frosted glass of his office door. He halted abruptly, set his lips together, looked up and down the corridor, and advanced to the door with swift quiet strides.

He put his hand on the knob and turned it with care that permitted neither rattle nor click. He turned the knob until it would turn no further: the door was locked. Holding the knob still, he changed hands, taking it now in his left hand. With his right hand he brought his keys out of his pocket, carefully, so they could not jingle against one another. He separated the office key from the others and, smothering the others together in his palm, inserted the office key in the lock. The insertion was soundless. He balanced himself on the balls of his feet, filled his lungs, clicked the door open, and went in.

Effie Perine sat sleeping with her head on her forearms, her forearms on her desk. She wore her coat and had one of Spade's overcoats wrapped cape-fashion around her.

Spade blew out his breath in a muffled laugh, shut the door behind him, and crossed to the inner door. The inner office was empty. He went over to the girl and put a hand on her shoulder.

She stirred, raised her head drowsily, and her eyelids fluttered. Suddenly she sat up straight, opening her eyes wide. She saw Spade, smiled, leaned back in her chair, and rubbed her eyes with her fingers. 'So you finally got back?' she said. 'What time is it?'

'Six o'clock. What are you doing here?'

She shivered, drew Spade's overcoat closer around her, and yawned. 'You told me to stay till you got back or phoned.'

'Oh, you're the sister of the boy who stood on the burning deck?'

'I wasn't going to——' She broke off and stood up, letting his coat slide down on the chair behind her. She looked with dark excited eyes at his temple under the brim of his hat and exclaimed: 'Oh, your head! What happened?'

His right temple was dark and swollen.

'I don't know whether I fell or was slugged. I don't think it amounts to much, but it hurts like hell.' He barely touched it with his fingers, flinched, turned his grimace into a grim smile, and explained: 'I went visiting, was fed knockout-drops, and came to twelve hours later all spread out on a man's floor.'

She reached up and removed his hat from his head. 'It's terrible,' she said. 'You'll have to get a doctor. You can't walk around with a head like that.'

'It's not as bad as it looks, except for the headache, and that might be mostly from the drops.' He went to the cabinet in the corner of the office and ran cold water on a handkerchief. 'Anything turn up after I left?'

'Did you find Miss O'Shaughnessy, Sam?'

'Not yet. Anything turn up after I left?'

'The District Attorney's office phoned. He wants to see you.'

'Himself?'

'Yes, that's the way I understood it. And a boy came in with a message—that Mr. Gutman would be delighted to talk to you before five-thirty.'

Spade turned off the water, squeezed the handkerchief, and came away from the cabinet holding the handkerchief to his temple. 'I got that,' he said. 'I met the boy downstairs, and talking to Mr. Gutman got me this.'

'Is that the G. who phoned, Sam?'

'Yes.'

'And what——?'

Spade stared through the girl and spoke as if using speech to arrange his thoughts: 'He wants something he thinks I can get. I persuaded him I could keep him from getting it if he didn't make the deal with me before five-thirty. Then—uh-huh—sure—it was after I'd told him he'd have to wait a couple of days that he fed me the junk. It's not likely he thought I'd die. He'd know I'd be up and around in ten or twelve hours. So maybe the answer's that he figured he could get it without my help in that time if I was fixed so I couldn't butt in.' He scowled. 'I hope to Christ he was wrong.' His stare became less distant. 'You didn't get any word from the O'Shaughnessy?'

The girl shook her head no and asked: 'Has this got anything to do with her?'

'Something.'

'The thing he wants belongs to her?'

'Or to the King of Spain. Sweetheart, you've got an uncle who teaches history or something over at the University?'

'A cousin. Why?'

'If we brightened his life with an alleged historical secret four centuries old could we trust him to keep it dark awhile?'

'Oh, yes, he's good people.'

'Fine. Get your pencil and book.'

She got them and sat in her chair. Spade ran more cold water on his handkerchief and, holding it to his temple, stood in front of her and dictated the story of the falcon as he had heard it from Gutman, from Charles V's grant to the Hospitallers up to—but no further than—the enamelled bird's arrival in Paris at the time of the Carlist influx. He stumbled over the names of authors and their works that Gutman had mentioned, but managed to achieve some sort of phonetic likeness. The rest of the history he repeated with the accuracy of a trained interviewer.

When he had finished the girl shut her notebook and raised a flushed smiling face to him. 'Oh, isn't this thrilling?' she said. 'It's——'

'Yes, or ridiculous. Now will you take it over and read it to your cousin and ask him what he thinks of it? Has he ever run across anything that might have some connection with it? Is it probable? Is it possible—even barely possible? Or is it the bunk? If he wants more time to look it up, O.K., but get some sort of opinion out of him now. And for God's sake make him keep it under his hat.'

'I'll go right now,' she said, 'and you go see a doctor about that head.'

'We'll have breakfast first.'

'No, I'll eat over in Berkeley. I can't wait to hear what Ted thinks of this.'

'Well,' Spade said, 'don't start boo-hooing if he laughs at you.'

After a leisurely breakfast at the Palace, during which he read both morning papers, Spade went home, shaved, bathed, rubbed ice on his bruised temple, and put on fresh clothes.

He went to Brigid O'Shaughnessy's apartment at the Coronet. Nobody was in the apartment. Nothing had been changed in it since his last visit.

He went to the Alexandria Hotel. Gutman was not in. None of the other occupants of Gutman's suite was in. Spade learned that these other occupants were the fat man's secretary, Wilmer Cook, and his daughter Rhea, a brown-eyed fair-haired smallish girl of seventeen who the hotel staff said was beautiful. Spade was told that the Gutman party had arrived at the hotel, from New York, ten days before, and had not checked out.

Spade went to the Belvedere and found the hotel detective eating in the hotel café.

'Morning, Sam. Set down and bite an egg.' The hotel detective stared at Spade's temple. 'By God, somebody maced you plenty!'

'Thanks, I've had mine,' Spade said as he sat down, and then, referring to his temple: 'It looks worse than it is. How's my Cairo's conduct?'

'He went out not more than half an hour behind you yesterday and I ain't seen him since. He didn't sleep here again last night.'

'He's getting bad habits.'

'Well, a fellow like that alone in a big city. Who put the slug to you, Sam?'

'It wasn't Cairo.' Spade looked attentively at the small silver

I'd like to know if he did. I haven't seen anything that says he didn't.

'What's his racket?'

Spade shook his head. 'That's something else I'd like to know.' He crossed the room and bent down over the waste-basket. 'Well, this is our last shot.'

He took a newspaper from the basket. His eyes brightened when he saw it was the previous day's *Call*. It was folded with the classified-advertising page outside. He opened it, examined that page, and nothing there stopped his eyes.

He turned the paper over and looked at the page that had been folded inside, the page that held financial and shipping news, the weather, births, marriages, divorces, and deaths. From the lower left-hand corner, a little more than two inches of the bottom of the second column had been torn out.

Immediately above the tear was a small caption *Arrived To-day* followed by:

> 12:20 A.M.—*Capac* from Astoria.
> 5:05 A.M.—*Helen P. Drew* from Greenwood.
> 5:06 A.M.—*Albarado* from Bandon.

The tear passed through the next line, leaving only enough of its letters to make *from Sydney* inferable.

Spade put the *Call* down on the desk and looked into the waste-basket again. He found a small piece of wrapping paper, a piece of string, two hosiery tags, a haberdasher's sale-ticket for half a dozen pairs of socks, and, in the bottom of the basket, a piece of newspaper rolled into a tiny ball.

He opened the ball carefully, smoothed it out on the desk, and fitted it into the torn part of the *Call*. The fit at the sides was exact, but between the top of the crumpled fragment and the inferable *from Sydney* half an inch was missing, sufficient space to have held announcements of six or seven boats' arrival. He turned the sheet over and saw that the other side of the missing portion could have held only a meaningless corner of a stockbroker's advertisement.

Luke, leaning over his shoulder, asked: 'What's this all about?'

'Looks like the gent's interested in a boat.'

'Well, there's no law against that, or is there?' Luke said

while Spade was folding the torn page and the crumpled fragment together and putting them into his coat pocket. 'You all through here now?'

'Yes. Thanks a lot, Luke. Will you give me a ring as soon as he comes in?'

'Sure.'

Spade went to the Business Office of the *Call*, bought a copy of the previous day's issue, opened it to the shipping-news page, and compared it with the page taken from Cairo's waste-basket. The missing portion had read:

> 5:17 A.M.—*Tahiti* from Sydney and Papeete.
> 6:05 A.M.—*Admiral Peoples* from Astoria.
> 8:05 A.M.—*La Paloma* from Hongkong.
> 8:07 A.M.—*Caddopeak* from San Pedro.
> 8:17 A.M.—*Silveaado* from San Pedro.
> 9:03 A.M.—*Daisy Gray* from Seattle.

He read the list slowly and when he had finished he underscored *Hongkong* with a fingernail, cut the list of arrivals from the paper with his pocket-knife, put the rest of the paper and Cairo's sheet into the waste-basket, and returned to his office.

He sat down at his desk, looked up a number in the telephone book, and used the telephone.

'Kearny 1401, please.... Where is the *Paloma*, in from Hongkong yesterday morning, docked?' He repeated the question. 'Thanks.'

He held the receiver hook down with his thumb for a moment, released it, and said: 'Davenport 2020, please.... Detective bureau, please.... Is Sergeant Polhaus there?... Thanks.... Hello, Tom, this is Sam Spade.... Yes, I tried to get you yesterday afternoon.... Sure, suppose you go to lunch with me.... Right.'

He kept the receiver to his ear while his thumb worked the hook again.

'Davenport 0170, please.... Hello, this is Samuel Spade. My secretary got a phone message yesterday that Mr. Bryan wanted to see me. Will you ask him what time's the most convenient for him?... Yes, Spade, S-p-a-d-e.' A long pause. 'Yes.... Two-thirty?

All right. Thanks.'

He called a fourth number and said : 'Hello, darling, let me talk to Sid? ... Hello, Sid—Sam. I've got a date with the District Attorney at half-past two this afternoon. Will you give me a ring—here or there—around four, just to see that I'm not in trouble? ... Hell with your Saturday afternoon golf: your job's to keep me out of jail.... Right, Sid. 'Bye.'

He pushed the telephone away, yawned, stretched, felt his bruised temple, looked at his watch, and rolled and lighted a cigarette. He smoked sleepily until Effie Perine came in.

Effie Perine came in smiling, bright-eyed and rosy-faced. 'Ted says it could be,' she reported, 'and he hopes it is. He says he's not a specialist in that field, but the names and dates are all right, and at least none of your authorities or their works are out-and-out fakes. He's all excited over it.'

'That's swell, as long as he doesn't get too enthusiastic to see through it if it's phoney.'

'Oh, he wouldn't—not Ted! He's too good at his stuff for that.'

'Uh-huh, the whole damned Perine family's wonderful,' Spade said, 'including you and the smudge of soot on your nose.'

'He's not a Perine, he's a Christy.' She bent her head to look at her nose in her vanity-case mirror. 'I must've got that from the fire.' She scrubbed the smudge with the corner of a handkerchief.

'The Perine-Christy enthusiasm ignite Berkeley?' he asked.

She made a face at him while patting her nose with a powdered pink disc. 'There was a boat on fire when I came back. They were towing it out from the pier and the smoke blew all over our ferry-boat.'

Spade put his hands on the arms of his chair. 'Were you near enough to see the name of the boat?' he asked.

'Yes. *La Paloma*. Why?'

Spade smiled ruefully. 'I'm damned if I know why, sister,' he said.

Chapter Fifteen

Every Crackpot

Spade and Detective-Sergeant Polhaus ate pickled pigs' feet at
one of Big John's tables at the States Hof Brau.

Polhaus, balancing pale bright jelly on a fork half-way between
plate and mouth, said: 'Hey, listen, Sam! Forget about the
other night. He was dead wrong, but you know anybody's liable
to lose his head if you ride them thataway.'

Spade looked thoughtfully at the police detective. 'Was that
what you wanted to see me about?' he asked.

Polhaus nodded, put the forkful of jelly into his mouth,
swallowed it, and qualified his nod: 'Mostly.'

'Dundy send you?'

Polhaus made a disgusted mouth. 'You know he didn't. He's as
bull-headed as you are.'

Spade smiled and shook his head. 'No, he's not, Tom,' he said.
'He just thinks he is.'

Tom scowled and chopped at his pig's foot with a knife.
'Ain't you ever going to grow up?' he grumbled. 'What've you
got to beef about? He didn't hurt you. You came out on top.
What's the sense of making a grudge of it? You're just making a
lot of grief for yourself.'

Spade placed his knife and fork carefully together on his plate,
and put his hands on the table beside his plate. His smile was faint
and devoid of warmth. 'With every bull in town working over-
time trying to pile up grief for me a little more won't hurt. I won't
even know it's there.'

Polhaus's ruddiness deepened. He said: 'That's a swell thing
to say to me.'

Spade picked up his knife and fork and began to eat. Polhaus ate.
Presently Spade asked: 'See the boat on fire in the bay?'

'I saw the smoke. Be reasonable, Sam. Dundy was wrong and

he knows it. Why don't you let it go at that?'

'Think I ought to go around and tell him I hope my chin didn't hurt his fist?'

Polhaus cut savagely into his pig's foot.

Spade said: 'Phil Archer been in with any more hot tips?'

'Aw, hell! Dundy didn't think you shot Miles, but what else could he do except run the lead down? You'd've done the same thing in his place, and you know it.'

'Yes?' Malice gleamed in Spade's eyes. 'What made him think I didn't do it? What makes you think I didn't? Or don't you?'

Polhaus's ruddy face flushed again. He said: 'Thursby shot Miles.'

'You think he did.'

'He did. That Webley was his, and the slug in Miles came out of it.'

'Sure?' Spade demanded.

'Dead sure,' the police detective replied. 'We got hold of a kid—a bellhop at Thursby's hotel—that had seen it in his room just that morning. He noticed it particular because he'd never seen one just like it before. I never saw one. You say they don't make them any more. It ain't likely there'd be another around and—anyway—if that wasn't Thursby's what happened to his? And that's the gun the slug in Miles come out of.' He started to put a piece of bread into his mouth, withdrew it, and asked: 'You say you've seen them before: where was that at?' He put the bread into his mouth.

'In England before the war.'

'Sure, there you are.'

Spade nodded and said: 'Then that leaves Thursby the only one I killed.'

Polhaus squirmed in his chair and his face was red and shiny. 'Christ's sake, ain't you never going to forget that?' he complained earnestly. 'That's out. You know it as well as I do. You'd think you wasn't a dick yourself the way you bellyache over things. I suppose you don't never pull the same stuff on anybody that we pulled on you?'

'You mean that you tried to pull on me, Tom—just tried.'

Polhaus swore under his breath and attacked the remainder of his pig's foot.

Spade said: 'All right. You know it's out and I know it's out. What does Dundy know?'

'He knows it's out.'

'What woke him up?'

'Aw, Sam, he never really thought you'd—' Spade's smile checked Polhaus. He left the sentence incomplete and said: 'We dug up a record on Thursby.'

'Yes? Who was he?'

Polhaus's shrewd small brown eyes studied Spade's face. Spade exclaimed irritably: 'I wish to God I knew half as much about this business as you smart guys think I do!'

'I wish we all did,' Polhaus grumbled. 'Well, he was a St. Louis gunman the first we hear of him. He was picked up a lot of times back there for this and that, but he belonged to the Egan mob, so nothing much was ever done about any of it. I don't know howcome he left that shelter, but they got him once in New York for knocking over a row of stuss-games—his twist turned him up—and he was in a year before Fallon got him sprung. A couple of years later he did a short hitch in Joliet for pistol-whipping another twist that had given him the needle, but after that he took up with Dixie Monahan and didn't have any trouble getting out whenever he happened to get in. That was when Dixie was almost as big a shot as Nick the Greek in Chicago gambling. This Thursby was Dixie's bodyguard and he took the run-out with him when Dixie got in wrong with the rest of the boys over some debts he couldn't or wouldn't pay off. That was a couple of years back—about the time the Newport Beach Boating Club was shut up. I don't know if Dixie had any part in that. Anyways, this is the first time him or Thursby's been seen since.'

'Dixie's been seen?' Spade asked.

Polhaus shook his head. 'No.' His small eyes became sharp, prying. 'Not unless you've seen him or know somebody's seen him.'

Spade lounged back in his chair and began to make a cigarette. 'I haven't,' he said mildly. 'This is all new stuff to me.'

'I guess it is,' Polhaus snorted.

Spade grinned at him and asked: 'Where'd you pick up all this news about Thursby?'

'Some of it's on the records. The rest—well—we got it here and there.'

'From Cairo, for instance?' Now Spade's eyes held the prying gleam.

Polhaus put down his coffee-cup and shook his head. 'Not a word of it. You poisoned that guy for us.'

Spade laughed. 'You mean a couple of high-class sleuths like you and Dundy worked on that lily-of-the-valley all night and couldn't crack him?'

'What do you mean—all night?' Polhaus protested. 'We worked on him for less than a couple of hours. We saw we wasn't getting nowhere, and let him go.'

Spade laughed again and looked at his watch. He caught John's eye and asked for the check. 'I've got a date with the D.A. this afternoon,' he told Polhaus, while they waited for his change.

'He send for you?'

'Yes.'

Polhaus pushed his chair back and stood up, a barrel-bellied tall man, solid and phlegmatic. 'You won't be doing me any favour,' he said, 'by telling him I've talked to you like this.'

A lathy youth with salient ears ushered Spade into the District Attorney's office. Spade went in smiling easily, saying easily: 'Hello, Bryan!'

District Attorney Bryan stood up and held his hand out across his desk. He was a blond man of medium stature, perhaps forty-five years old, with aggressive blue eyes behind black-ribboned nose-glasses, the over-large mouth of an orator, and a wide dimpled chin. When he said, 'How do you do, Spade?' his voice was resonant with latent power.

They shook hands and sat down.

The District Attorney put his finger on one of the pearl buttons in a battery of four on his desk, said to the lathy youth who opened the door again, 'Ask Mr. Thomas and Healy to come in,' and then, rocking back in his chair, addressed Spade pleasantly: 'You and the police haven't been hitting it off so well, have you?'

Spade made a negligent gesture with the fingers of his right hand. 'Nothing serious,' he said lightly. 'Dundy gets too enthusiastic.'

The door opened to admit two men. The one to whom Spade said, 'Hello, Thomas!' was a sunburned stocky man of thirty in clothing and hair of a kindred unruliness. He clapped Spade on the shoulder with a freckled hand, asked, 'How's tricks?' and sat down beside him. The second man was younger and colourless. He took a seat a little apart from the others and balanced a stenographer's notebook on his knee, holding a green pencil over it.

Spade glanced his way, chuckled, and asked Bryan: 'Anything I say will be used against me?'

The District Attorney smiled. 'That always holds good.' He took his glasses off, looked at them, and set them on his nose again. He looked through them at Spade and asked: 'Who killed Thursby?'

Spade said: 'I don't know.'

Bryan rubbed his black eyeglass-ribbon between thumb and fingers and said knowingly: 'Perhaps you don't, but you certainly could make an excellent guess.'

'Maybe, but I wouldn't.'

The District Attorney raised his eyebrows.

'I wouldn't,' Spade repeated. He was serene. 'My guess might be excellent, or it might be crummy, but Mrs. Spade didn't raise any children dippy enough to make guesses in front of a District Attorney, an Assistant District Attorney, and a stenographer.'

'Why shouldn't you, if you've nothing to conceal?'

'Everybody,' Spade responded mildly, 'has something to conceal.'

'And you have——?'

'My guesses, for one thing.'

The District Attorney looked down at his desk and then up at Spade. He settled his glasses more firmly on his nose. He said: 'If you'd prefer not having the stenographer here we can dismiss him. It was simply as a matter of convenience that I brought him in.'

'I don't mind him a damned bit,' Spade replied. 'I'm willing to have anything I say put down and I'm willing to sign it.'

'We don't intend asking you to sign anything,' Bryan assured him. 'I wish you wouldn't regard this as a formal inquiry at all. And please don't think I've any belief—much less confidence—in those theories the police seemed to have formed.'

'No?'

'Not a particle.'

Spade sighed and crossed his legs. 'I'm glad of that.' He felt in his pockets for tobacco and papers. 'What's your theory?'

Bryan leaned forward in his chair and his eyes were hard and shiny as the lenses over them. 'Tell me who Archer was shadowing Thursby for and I'll tell you who killed Thursby.'

Spade's laugh was brief and scornful. 'You're as wrong as Dundy,' he said.

'Don't misunderstand me, Spade,' Bryan said, knocking on the desk with his knuckles. 'I don't say your client killed Thursby or had him killed, but I do say that, knowing who your client is, or was, I'll mighty soon know who killed Thursby.'

Spade lighted his cigarette, removed it from his lips, emptied his lungs of smoke, and spoke as if puzzled: 'I don't exactly get that.'

'You don't? Then suppose I put it this way: where is Dixie Monahan?'

Spade's face retained its puzzled look. 'Putting it that way doesn't help much,' he said. 'I still don't get it.'

The District Attorney took his glasses off and shook them for emphasis. He said: 'We know Thursby was Monahan's bodyguard and went with him when Monahan found it wise to vanish from Chicago. We know Monahan welshed on something like two-hundred-thousand-dollars' worth of bets when he vanished. We don't know—not yet—who his creditors were.' He put the glasses on again and smiled grimly. 'But we all know what's likely to happen to a gambler who welshes, and to his bodyguard, when his creditors find him. It's happened before.'

Spade ran his tongue over his lips and pulled his lips back over his teeth in an ugly grin. His eyes glittered under pulled-down brows. His reddening neck bulged over the rim of his collar. His voice was low and hoarse and passionate. 'Well, what do you think? Did I kill him for his creditors? Or just find him and let them do their own killing?'

'No, no!' the District Attorney protested. 'You misunder-stand me.'

'I hope to Christ I do,' Spade said.

'He didn't mean that,' Thomas said.

'Then what did he mean?'

Bryan waved a hand. 'I only mean that you might have been involved in it without knowing what it was. That could——'

'I see,' Spade sneered. 'You don't think I'm naughty. You just think I'm dumb.'

'Nonsense,' Bryan insisted. 'Suppose someone came to you and engaged you to find Monahan, telling you they had reasons for thinking he was in the city. The someone might give you a completely false story—any one of a dozen or more would do—or might say he was a debtor who had run away, without giving you any of the details. How could you tell what was behind it? How would you know it wasn't an ordinary piece of detective work? And under those circumstances you certainly couldn't be held responsible for your part in it unless'—his voice sank to a more impressive key and his words came out spaced and distinct —'you made yourself an accomplice by concealing your know-ledge of the murderer's identity or information that would lead to his apprehension.'

Anger was leaving Spade's face. No anger remained in his voice when he asked : 'That's what you meant?'

'Precisely.'

'All right. Then there's no hard feelings. But you're wrong.'

'Prove it.'

Spade shook his head. 'I can't prove it to you now. I can tell you.'

'Then tell me.'

'Nobody ever hired me to do anything about Dixie Monahan.'

Bryan and Thomas exchanged glances. Bryan's eyes came back to Spade and he said : 'But, by your own admission, somebody did hire you to do something about his bodyguard Thursby.'

'Yes, about his ex-bodyguard Thursby.'

'Ex?'

'Yes, ex.'

'You know that Thursby was no longer associated with Monahan? You know that positively?'

Spade stretched out his hand and dropped the stub of his cigarette into an ash-tray on the desk. He spoke carelessly: 'I don't know anything positively except that my client wasn't interested in Monahan, had never been interested in Monahan. I heard that Thursby took Monahan out to the Orient and lost him.'

Again the District Attorney and his assistant exchanged glances.

Thomas, in a tone whose matter-of-factness did not quite hide excitement, said: 'That opens another angle. Monahan's friends could have knocked Thursby off for ditching Monahan.'

'Dead gamblers don't have any friends,' Spade said.

'It opens up two new lines,' Bryan said. He leaned back and stared at the ceiling for several seconds, then sat upright quickly. His orator's face was alight. 'It narrows down to three things. Number one: Thursby was killed by the gamblers Monahan had welshed on in Chicago. Not knowing Thursby had sloughed Monahan—or not believing it—they killed him because he had been Monahan's associate, or to get him out of the way so they could get to Monahan, or because he had refused to lead them to Monahan. Number two: he was killed by friends of Monahan. Or number three: he sold Monahan out to his enemies and then fell out with them and they killed him.'

'Or number four,' Spade suggested with a cheerful smile: 'he died of old age. You folks aren't serious, are you?'

The two men stared at Spade, but neither of them spoke. Spade turned his smile from one to the other of them and shook his head in mock pity. 'You've got Arnold Rothstein on the brain,' he said.

Bryan smacked the back of his left hand down into the palm of his right. 'In one of those three categories lies the solution.' The power in his voice was no longer latent. His right hand, a fist except for protruding forefinger, went up and then down to stop with a jerk when the finger was levelled at Spade's chest. 'And you can give us the information that will enable us to determine the category.'

Spade said, 'Yes?' very lazily. His face was sombre. He touched his lower lip with a finger, looked at the finger, and then scratched the back of his neck with it. Little irritable lines had appeared

in his forehead. He blew his breath out heavily through his nose
and his voice was an ill-humoured growl. 'You wouldn't want
the kind of information I could give you, Bryan. You couldn't
use it. It'd poop this gambler's revenge scenario for you.'

Bryan sat up straight and squared his shoulders. His voice
was stern without blustering. 'You are not the judge of that.
Right or wrong, I am nonetheless the District Attorney.'

Spade's lifted lip showed his eyetooth. 'I thought this was an
informal talk.'

'I am a sworn officer of the law twenty-four hours a day,'
Bryan said, 'and neither formality nor informality justifies your
withholding from me evidence of crime, except of course'—
he nodded meaningly—'on certain constitutional grounds.'

'You mean if it might incriminate me?' Spade asked. His
voice was placid, almost amused, but his face was not. 'Well,
I've got better grounds than that, or grounds that suit me better.
My clients are entitled to a decent amount of secrecy. Maybe I
can be made to talk to a Grand Jury or even a Coroner's Jury, but
I haven't been called before either yet, and it's a cinch I'm not
going to advertise my client's business until I have to. Then
again, you and the police have both accused me of being mixed
up in the other night's murders. I've had trouble with both of
you before. As far as I can see, my best chance of clearing myself
of the trouble you're trying to make for me is by bringing in the
murderers—all tied up. And my only chance of ever catching
them and tying them up and bringing them in is by keeping
away from you and the police, because neither of you show any
signs of knowing what in hell it's all about.' He rose and turned
his head over his shoulder to address the stenographer: 'Getting
this all right, son? Or am I going too fast for you?'

The stenographer looked at him with startled eyes and replied:
'No, sir, I'm getting it all right.'

'Good work,' Spade said and turned to Bryan again. 'Now
if you want to go to the Board and tell them I'm obstructing
justice and ask them to revoke my licence, hop to it. You've
tried it before and it didn't get you anything but a good laugh all
around.' He picked up his hat.

Bryan began: 'But look here——'

Spade said: 'And I don't want any more of these informal

talks. I've got nothing to tell you or the police and I'm God-damned tired of being called things by every crackpot on the city payroll. If you want to see me, pinch me or subpoena me or something and I'll come down with my lawyer.' He put his hat on his head, said, 'See you at the inquest, maybe,' and stalked out.

Chapter Sixteen

The Third Murder

Spade went into the Hotel Sutter and telephoned the Alexandria. Gutman was not in. No member of Gutman's party was in. Spade telephoned the Belvedere. Cairo was not in, had not been in that day.

Spade went to his office.

A swart greasy man in notable clothes was waiting in the outer room. Effie Perine, indicating the swart man, said: 'This gentleman wishes to see you, Mr. Spade.'

Spade smiled and bowed and opened the inner door. 'Come in.' Before following the man in Spade asked Effie Perine: 'Any news on the other matter?'

'No, sir.'

The swart man was the proprietor of a moving-picture theatre in Market Street. He suspected one of his cashiers and a doorman of colluding to defraud him. Spade hurried him through the story, promised to 'take care of it,' asked for and received fifty dollars, and got rid of him in less than half an hour.

When the corridor-door had closed behind the showman Effie Perine came into the inner office. Her sunburned face was worried and questioning. 'You haven't found her yet?' she asked.

He shook his head and went on stroking his bruised temple lightly in circles with his fingertips.

'How is it?' she asked.

'All right, but I've got plenty of headache.'

She went around behind him, put his hand down, and stroked

his temple with her slender fingers. He leaned back until the back of his head over the chair top rested against her breast. He said: 'You're an angel.'

She bent her head forward over his and looked down into his face. 'You've got to find her, Sam. It's more than a day and she——'

He stirred and impatiently interrupted her: 'I haven't got to do anything, but if you'll let me rest this damned head a minute or two I'll go out and find her.'

She murmured, 'Poor head,' and stroked it in silence a while. Then she asked: 'You know where she is? Have you any idea?'

The telephone bell rang. Spade picked up the telephone and said: 'Hello.... Yes, Sid, it came out all right, thanks.... No.... Sure. He got snotty, but so did I.... He's nursing a gambler's war pipe-dream.... Well, we didn't kiss when we parted. I declared my weight and walked out on him.... That's something for you to worry about.... Right. 'Bye.' He put the telephone down and leaned back in his chair again.

Effie Perine came from behind him and stood at his side. She demanded: 'Do you think you know where she is, Sam?'

'I know where she went,' he replied in a grudging tone.

'Where?' she was excited.

'Down to the boat you saw burning.'

Her eyes opened until their brown was surrounded by white. 'You went down there.' It was not a question.

'I did not,' Spade said.

'Sam,' she cried angrily, 'she may be——'

'She went down there,' he said in a surly voice. 'She wasn't taken. She went down there instead of to your house when she learned the boat was in. Well, what the hell? Am I supposed to run around after my clients begging them to let me help them?'

'But, Sam, when I told you the boat was on fire!'

'That was at noon and I had a date with Polhaus and another with Bryan.'

She glared at him between tightened lids. 'Sam Spade,' she said, 'you're the most contemptible man God ever made when you want to be. Because she did something without confiding in you you'd sit here and do nothing when you know she's in danger, when you know she might be——'

Spade's face flushed. He said stubbornly: 'She's pretty capable of taking care of herself and she knows where to come for help when she thinks she needs it, and when it suits her.'

'That's spite,' the girl cried, 'and that's all it is! You're sore because she did something on her own hook, without telling you. Why shouldn't she? You're not so damned honest, and you haven't been so much on the level with her, that she should trust you completely.'

Spade said: 'That's enough of that.'

His tone brought a brief uneasy glint into her hot eyes, but she tossed her head and the glint vanished. Her mouth was drawn taut and small. She said: 'If you don't go down there this very minute, Sam, I will, and I'll take the police down there.' Her voice trembled, broke, and was thin and wailing. 'Oh, Sam, go!'

He stood up cursing her. Then he said: 'Christ! It'll be easier on my head than sitting here listening to you squawk.' He looked at his watch. 'You might as well lock up and go home.'

She said: 'I won't. I'm going to wait right here till you come back.'

He said, 'Do as you damned please,' put his hat on, flinched, took it off, and went out carrying it in his hand.

An hour and a half later, at twenty minutes past five, Spade returned. He was cheerful. He came in asking: 'What makes you so hard to get along with, sweetheart?'

'Me?'

'Yes, you.' He put a finger on the tip of Effie Perine's nose and flattened it. He put his hands under her elbows, lifted her straight up, and kissed her chin. He set her down on the floor again and asked: 'Anything doing while I was gone?'

'Luke—what's his name?—at the Belvedere called up to tell you Cairo has returned. That was about half an hour ago.'

Spade snapped his mouth shut, turned with a long step, and started for the door.

'Did you find her?' the girl called.

'Tell you about it when I'm back,' he replied without pausing and hurried out.

A taxicab brought Spade to the Belvedere within ten minutes

of his departure from his office. He found Luke in the lobby. The hotel detective came grinning and shaking his head to meet Spade. 'Fifteen minutes late,' he said. 'Your bird has fluttered.'

Spade cursed his luck.

'Checked out—gone bag and baggage,' Luke said. He took a battered memorandum book from a vest pocket, licked his thumb, thumbed pages, and held the book open to Spade. 'There's the number of the taxi that hauled him. I got that much for you.'

'Thanks.' Spade copied the number on the back of an envelope. 'Any forwarding address?'

'No. He just came in carrying a big suitcase and went upstairs and packed and come down with his stuff and paid his bill and got a taxi and went without anybody being able to hear what he told the driver.'

'How about his trunk?'

Luke's lower lip sagged. 'By God,' he said, 'I forgot that! Come on.'

They went up to Cairo's room. The trunk was there. It was closed, but not locked. They raised the lid. The trunk was empty.

Luke said: 'What do you know about that!'

Spade did not say anything.

Spade went back to his office. Effie Perine looked up at him, inquisitively.

'Missed him,' Spade grumbled and passed into his private room.

She followed him in. He sat in his chair and began to roll a cigarette. She sat on the desk in front of him and put her toes on a corner of his chair-seat.

'What about Miss O'Shaughnessy?' she demanded.

'I missed her too,' he replied, 'but she had been there.'

'On the *La Paloma*?"

'The *La* is a lousy combination,' he said.

'Stop it. Be nice, Sam. Tell me.'

He set fire to his cigarette, pocketed his lighter, patted her shins, and said: 'Yes, the *La Paloma*. She got down there at a little after noon yesterday.' He pulled his brows down. 'That means she went straight there after leaving the cab at the Ferry Building. It's only a few piers away. The Captain wasn't aboard. His name's Jacobi and she asked for him by name. He was uptown on business.

That would mean he didn't expect her, or not at that time anyway. She waited there till he came back at four o'clock. They spent the time from then till meal-time in his cabin and she ate with him.'

He inhaled and exhaled smoke, turned his head aside to spit a yellow tobacco flake off his lip, and went on: 'After the meal Captain Jacobi had three more visitors. One of them was Gutman and one was Cairo and one was the kid who delivered Gutman's message to you yesterday. Those three came together while Brigid was there and the five of them did a lot of talking in the Captain's cabin. It's hard to get anything out of the crew, but they had a row and somewhere around eleven o'clock that night a gun went off there, in the Captain's cabin. The watchman beat it down there, but the Captain met him outside and told him everything was all right. There's a fresh bullet-hole in one corner of the cabin, up high enough to make it likely that the bullet didn't go through anybody to get there. As far as I could learn there was only the one shot. But as far as I could learn wasn't very far.'

He scowled and inhaled smoke again. 'Well, they left around midnight—the Captain and his four visitors all together—and all of them seemed to have been walking all right. I got that from the watchman. I haven't been able to get hold of the Custom House men who were on duty there then. That's all of it. The Captain hasn't been back since. He didn't keep a date he had this noon with some shipping agent, and they haven't found him to tell him about the fire.'

'And the fire?' she asked.

Spade shrugged. 'I don't know. It was discovered in the hold, aft—in the rear basement—late this morning. The chances are it got started some time yesterday. They got it out all right, though it did damage enough. Nobody liked to talk about it much while the Captain's away. It's the——'

The corridor-door opened. Spade shut his mouth. Effie Perine jumped down from the desk, but a man opened the connecting door before she could reach it.

'Where's Spade?' the man asked.

His voice brought Spade up erect and alert in his chair. It was a voice harsh and rasping with agony and with the strain of keeping two words from being smothered by the liquid bubbling that ran under and behind them.

Effie Perine, frightened, stepped out of the man's way.

He stood in the doorway with his soft hat crushed between his head and the top of the door-frame: he was nearly seven feet tall. A black overcoat cut long and straight and like a sheath, buttoned from throat to knees, exaggerated his leanness. His shoulders stuck out, high, thin, angular. His bony face—weather-coarsened, age-lined—was the colour of wet sand and was wet with sweat on cheeks and chin. His eyes were dark and bloodshot and mad above lower lids that hung down to show pink inner membrane. Held tight against the left side of his chest by a black-sleeved arm that ended in a yellowish claw was a brown-paper-wrapped parcel bound with thin rope—an ellipsoid somewhat larger than an American football.

The tall man stood in the doorway and there was nothing to show that he saw Spade. He said, 'You know——' and then the liquid bubbling came up in his throat and submerged whatever else he said. He put his other hand over the hand that held the ellipsoid. Holding himself stiffly straight, not putting his hand out to break his fall, he fell forward as a tree falls.

Spade, wooden-faced and nimble, sprang from his chair and caught the falling man. When Spade caught him the man's mouth opened and a little blood spurted out, and the brown-wrapped parcel dropped from the man's hand and rolled across the floor until a foot of the desk stopped it. Then the man's knees bent and he bent at the waist and his thin body became limber inside the sheathlike overcoat, sagging in Spade's arms so that Spade could not hold it up from the floor.

Spade lowered the man carefully until he lay on the floor on his left side. The man's eyes—dark and bloodshot, but not now mad—were wide open and still. His mouth was open as when blood had spurted from it, but no more blood came from it, and all his long body was as still as the floor it lay on.

Spade said: 'Lock the door.'

While Effie Perine, her teeth chattering, fumbled with the corridor-door's lock Spade knelt beside the thin man, turned him over on his back, and ran a hand down inside his overcoat. When he withdrew the hand presently it came out smeared with blood.

The sight of his bloody hand brought not the least nor briefest of changes to Spade's face. Holding that hand up where it could touch nothing, he took his lighter out of his pocket with his other hand. He snapped on the flame and held the flame close to first one and then the other of the thin man's eyes. The eyes—lids, balls, irises, and pupils—remained frozen, immobile.

Spade extinguished the flame and returned the lighter to his pocket. He moved on his knees around to the dead man's side and, using his one clean hand, unbuttoned the tubular overcoat. The inside of the overcoat was wet with blood and the double-breasted blue jacket beneath it was sodden. The jacket's lapels, where they crossed over the man's chest, and both sides of his coat immediately below that point, were pierced by soggy ragged holes.

Spade rose and went to the washbowl in the outer office.

Effie Perine, wan and trembling and holding herself upright by means of a hand on the corridor-door's knob and her back against its glass, whispered: 'Is—is he——?'

'Yes. Shot through the chest, maybe half a dozen times.' Spade began to wash his hands.

'Oughtn't we——?' she began, but he cut her short: 'It's too late for a doctor now and I've got to think before we do anything.' He finished washing his hands and began to rinse the bowl. 'He couldn't have come far with those in him. If he—— Why in hell couldn't he have stood up long enough to say something?' He frowned at the girl, rinsed his hands again, and picked up a towel. 'Pull yourself together. For Christ's sake don't get sick on me now!' He threw the towel down and ran his fingers through his hair. 'We'll have a look at that bundle.'

He went into the inner office again, stepped over the dead man's legs, and picked up the brown-paper-wrapped parcel. When he felt its weight his eyes glowed. He put it on his desk turning it over so that the knotted part of the rope was uppermost. The knot was hard and tight. He took out his pocket-knife and cut the rope.

The girl had left the door and, edging around the dead man with her face turned away, had come to Spade's side. As she stood there—hands on a corner of the desk—watching him pull the rope loose and push aside brown paper, excitement began to supplant nausea in her face. 'Do you think it is?' she whispered.

'We'll soon know,' Spade said, his big fingers busy with the inner husk of coarse grey paper, three sheets thick, that the brown paper's removal had revealed. His face was hard and dull. His eyes were shining. When he had put the grey paper out of the way he had an egg-shaped mass of pale excelsior, wadded tight. His fingers tore the wad apart and then he had the foot-high figure of a bird, black as coal and shiny where its polish was not dulled by wood-dust and fragments of excelsior.

Spade laughed. He put a hand down on the bird. His wide-spread fingers had ownership in their curving. He put his other arm around Effie Perine and crushed her body against his. 'We've got the damned thing, angel,' he said.

'Ouch!' she said, 'you're hurting me.'

He took his arm away from her, picked the black bird up in both hands, and shook it to dislodge clinging excelsior. Then he stepped back holding it up in front of him and blew dust off it, regarding it triumphantly.

Effie Perine made a horrified face and screamed, pointing at his feet.

He looked down at his feet. His last backward step had brought his left heel into contact with the dead man's hand, pinching a quarter-inch of flesh at a side of the palm between heel and floor. Spade jerked his foot away from the hand.

The telephone bell rang.

He nodded at the girl. She turned to the desk and put the receiver to her ear. She said: 'Hello.... Yes.... Who?... Oh, yes!' Her eyes became large. 'Yes.... Yes.... Hold the line....' Her mouth suddenly stretched wide and fearful. She cried: 'Hello! Hello! Hello!' She rattled the prong up and down and cried, 'Hello!' twice. Then she sobbed and spun around to face Spade, who was close beside her by now. 'It was Miss O'Shaughnessy,' she said wildly. 'She wants you. She's at the Alexandria—in danger. Her voice was—oh, it was awful Sam!—and something happened to her before she could finish. Go help her, Sam!'

Spade put the falcon down on the desk and scowled gloomily. 'I've got to take care of this fellow first,' he said, pointing his thumb at the thin corpse on the floor.

She beat his chest with her fists, crying: 'No, no—you've got to go to her. Don't you see, Sam? He had the thing that was hers and he came to you with it. Don't you see? He was helping her and they killed him and now she's—— Oh, you've got to go!'

'All right.' Spade pushed her away and bent over his desk, putting the black bird back into its nest of excelsior, bending the paper around it, working rapidly, making a larger and clumsy package. 'As soon as I've gone phone the police. Tell them how it happened, but don't drag any names in. You don't know. I got the phone-call and I told you I had to go out, but I didn't say where.' He cursed the rope for being tangled, yanked it into straightness, and began to bind the package. 'Forget this thing. Tell it as it happened, but forget he had a bundle.' He chewed his lower lip. 'Unless they pin you down. If they seem to know about it you'll have to admit it. But that's not likely. If they do then I took the bundle away with me, unopened.' He finished tying the knot and straightened up with the parcel under his left arm. 'Get it straight, now. Everything happened the way it did happen, but without this dingus unless they already know about it. Don't deny it—just don't mention it. And I got the phone-call—not you. And you don't know anything about anybody else having any connection with this fellow. You don't know anything about him and you can't talk about my business until you see me. Got it?'

'Yes, Sam. Who—do you know who he is?'

He grinned wolfishly. 'Uh-uh,' he said, 'but I'd guess he was Captain Jacobi, master of *La Paloma*. He picked up his hat and put it on. He looked thoughtfully at the dead man and then around the room.

'Hurry, Sam,' the girl begged.

'Sure,' he said absent-mindedly. 'I'll hurry. Might not hurt to get those few scraps of excelsior off the floor before the police come. And maybe you ought to try to get hold of Sid. No.' He rubbed his chin. 'We'll leave him out of it for awhile. It'll look better. I'd keep the door locked till they come.' He took his hand from under his chin and rubbed her cheek. 'You're a damned good man, sister,' he said and went out.

Chapter Seventeen

Saturday Night

Carrying the parcel lightly under his arm, walking briskly with only the ceaseless shifting of his eyes to denote wariness, Spade went, partly by way of an alley and a narrow court, from his office building to Kearny and Post Streets, where he hailed a passing taxicab.

The taxicab carried him to the Pickwick Stage terminal in Fifth Street. He checked the bird at the Parcel Room there, put the check into a stamped envelope, wrote *M. F. Holland* and a San Francisco Post Office box-number on the envelope, sealed it, and dropped it into a mail-box. From the stage terminal another taxicab carried him to the Alexandria Hotel.

Spade went up to suite 12C and knocked on the door. The door was opened, when he had knocked a second time, by a small fair-haired girl in a shimmering yellow dressing gown—a small girl whose face was white and dim and who clung desperately to the inner doorknob with both hands and gasped: 'Mr. Spade?'

Spade said, 'Yes,' and caught her as she swayed.

Her body arched back over his arm and her head dropped straight back so that her short fair hair hung down her scalp and her slender throat was a firm curve from chin to chest.

Spade slid his supporting arm higher up her back and bent to get his other arm under her knees, but she stirred then, resisting, and between parted lips that barely moved blurred words came: 'No! Ma' me wa'!'

Spade made her walk. He kicked the door shut and he walked her up and down the green-carpeted room from wall to wall. One of his arms around her small body, that hand under her armpit, his other hand gripping her other arm, held her erect when she stumbled, checked her swaying, kept urging her forward, but made her tottering legs bear all her weight they could bear. They walked across and across the floor, the girl falteringly, with inco-ordinate steps, Spade surely on the balls of his feet with balance unaffected by her staggering. Her face was chalk-white and eyeless, his sullen, with eyes hardened to watch everywhere at once.

He talked to her monotonously: 'That's the stuff. Left, right, left, right. That's the stuff. One, two, three, four, one, two, three, now we turn.' He shook her as they turned from the wall. 'Now back again. One, two, three, four. Hold your head up. That's the stuff. Good girl. Left, right, left, right. Now we turn again.' He shook her again. 'That's the girl. Walk, walk, walk, walk. One, two, three, four. Now we go around.' He shook her more roughly, and increased their pace. 'That's the trick. Left, right, left, right. We're in a hurry. One, two, three. . . .'

She shuddered and swallowed audibly. Spade began to chafe her arm and side and he put his mouth nearer her ear. 'That's fine. You're doing fine. One, two, three, four. Faster, faster, faster, faster. That's it. Step, step, step, step. Pick them up and lay them down. That's the stuff. Now we turn. Left, right, left, right. What'd they do—dope you? The same stuff they gave me?'

Her eyelids twitched up then for an instant over dulled golden-brown eyes and she managed to say all of 'Yes' except the final consonant.

They walked the floor, the girl almost trotting now to keep up with Spade. Spade slapping and kneading her flesh through yellow silk with both hands, talking and talking while his eyes remained hard and aloof and watchful. 'Left, right, left, right, left, right, turn. That's the girl. One, two, three, four, one, two, three, four. Keep the chin up. That's the stuff. One, two. . .'

Her lids lifted again a bare fraction of an inch and under them her eyes moved weakly from side to side.

'That's fine,' he said in a crisp voice, dropping his monotone. 'Keep them open. Open them wide—wide!' He shook her.

She moaned in protest, but her lids went farther up, though her eyes were without inner light. He raised his hand and slapped her cheek half a dozen times in quick succession. She moaned again and tried to break away from him. His arm held her and swept her along beside him from wall to wall.

'Keep walking,' he ordered in a harsh voice, and then: 'Who are you?'

Her 'Rhea Gutman' was thick but intelligible.

'The daughter?'

'Yes.' Now she was no farther from the final consonant than *sh*.

'Where's Brigid?'

She twisted convulsively around in his arms and caught at one of his hands with both of hers. He pulled his hand away quickly and looked at it. Across its back was a thin red scratch an inch and a half or more in length.

'What the hell?' he growled and examined her hands. Her left hand was empty. In her right hand, when he forced it open, lay a three-inch jade-headed steel bouquet-pin. 'What the hell?'

When she saw the pin she whimpered and opened her dressing-gown. She pushed aside the cream-coloured pyjama coat under it and showed him her body below her left breast—white flesh criss-crossed with thin red lines, dotted with tiny red dots where the pin had scratched and punctured it. 'To stay awake.... walk .... till you came.... She said you'd come... were so long.' She swayed.

Spade tightened his arm around her and said: 'Walk.'

She fought against his arm, squirming around to face him again. 'No...tell you...sleep...save her...'

'Brigid?' he demanded.

'Yes ... took her ... Bur-Burlingame ... twenty-six Ancho . . . hurry...too late...' Her head fell over on her shoulder.

Spade pushed her head up roughly. 'Who took her there? Your father?'

'Yes...Wilmer...Cairo.' She writhed and her eyelids twitched but did not open. '...kill her.' Her head fell over again and again he pushed it up.

'Who shot Jacobi?'

She did not seem to hear the question. She tried pitifully to hold her head up, to open her eyes. She mumbled: 'Go ... she ...'

He shook her brutally. 'Stay awake till the doctor comes.'

Fear opened her eyes and pushed for a moment the cloudiness from her face. 'No, no,' she cried thickly, 'father...kill me... swear you won't...he'd know...I did...for her...promise... won't...sleep...all right...morning...'

He shook her again. 'You're sure you can sleep the stuff off all right?'

'Ye'.' Her head fell down again.

'Where's your bed?'

She tried to raise a hand, but the effort had become too much for her before the hand pointed at anything except the carpet. With the sigh of a tired child she let her whole body relax and crumple.

Spade caught her up in his arms—scooped her up as she sank—and, holding her easily against his chest, went to the nearest of the three doors. He turned the knob far enough to release the catch, pushed the door open with his foot and went into a passage-way that ran past an open bathroom door to a bedroom. He looked into the bathroom, saw it was empty, and carried the girl into the bedroom. Nobody was there. The clothing that was in sight and things on the chiffonier said it was a man's room.

Spade carried the girl back to the green-carpeted room and tried the opposite door. Through it he passed into another passage-way, past another empty bathroom, and into a bedroom that was feminine in its accessories. He turned back the bedclothes and laid the girl on the bed, removed her slippers, raised her a little to slide the yellow dressing-gown off, fixed a pillow under her head, and put the covers up over her.

Then he opened the room's two windows and stood with his back to them staring at the sleeping girl. Her breathing was heavy but not troubled. He frowned and looked around, working his lips together. Twilight was dimming the room. He stood there in the weakening light for perhaps five minutes. Finally he shook his thick sloping shoulders impatiently and went out, leaving the suite's outer door unlocked.

Spade went to the Pacific Telephone and Telegraph Company's station in Powell Street and called Davenport 2020. 'Emergency Hospital, please.... Hello, there's a girl in suite 12c at the Alexandria Hotel who has been drugged.... Yes, you'd better send somebody to take a look at her.... This is Mr. Hooper of the Alexandria.'

He put the receiver on its prong and laughed. He called another number and said: 'Hello, Frank. This is Sam Spade....

Can you let me have a car with a driver who'll keep his mouth shut?... To go down the peninsula right away.... Just a couple of hours.... Right. Have him pick me up at John's, Ellis Street, as soon as he can make it.'

He called another number—his office's—held the receiver to his ear for a little while without saying anything, and replaced it on its hook.

He went to John's Grill, asked the waiter to hurry his order of chops, baked potato, and sliced tomatoes, ate hurriedly, and was smoking a cigarette with his coffee when a thick-set youngish man with a plaid cap set askew above pale eyes and a tough cheery face came into the Grill and to his table.

'All set, Mr. Spade. She's full of gas and rearing to go.'

'Swell.' Spade emptied his cup and went out with the thick-set man. 'Know where Ancho Avenue, or Road, or Boulevard, is in Burlingame?'

'Nope, but if she's there we can find her.'

'Let's do that,' Spade said as he sat beside the chauffeur in the dark Cadillac sedan. 'Twenty-six is the number we want, and the sooner the better, but we don't want to pull up at the front door.'

'Correct.'

They rode half a dozen blocks in silence. The chauffeur said: 'Your partner got knocked off, didn't he, Mr. Spade?'

'Uh-huh.'

The chauffeur clucked. 'She's a tough racket. You can have it for mine.'

'Well, hack-drivers don't live forever.'

'Maybe that's right,' the thick-set man conceded, 'but just the same, it'll always be a surprise to me if I don't.'

Spade stared ahead at nothing and thereafter, until the chauffeur tired of making conversation, replied with uninterested yeses and noes.

At a drugstore in Burlingame the chauffeur learned how to reach Ancho Avenue. Ten minutes later he stopped the sedan near a dark corner, turned off the lights, and waved his hand at the block ahead. 'There she is,' he said. 'She ought to be on the other side, maybe the third or fourth house.'

Spade said, 'Right,' and got out of the car. 'Keep the engine going. We may have to leave in a hurry.'

He crossed the street and went up the other side. Far ahead a lone street-light burned. Warmer lights dotted the night on either side where houses were spaced half a dozen to a block. A high thin moon was cold and feeble as the distant street-light. A radio droned through the open windows of a house on the other side of the street.

In front of the second house from the corner Spade halted. On one of the gateposts, that were massive, out of all proportion to the fence flanking them, a 2 and a 6 of pale metal caught what light there was. A square white card was nailed over them. Putting his face close to the card, Spade could see that it was a *For Sale or Rent* sign. There was no gate between the posts. Spade went up the cement walk to the house. He stood still on the walk at the foot of the porch steps for a long moment. No sound came from the house. The house was dark except for another pale square card nailed on the door.

Spade went up to the door and listened. He could hear nothing. He tried to look through the glass of the door. There was no curtain to keep his gaze out, but inner darkness. He tiptoed to a window and then to another. They, like the door, were un-curtained except by inner darkness. He tried both windows. They were locked. He tried the door. It was locked.

He left the porch and, stepping carefully over dark unfamiliar ground, walked through weeds around the house. The side windows were too high to be reached from the ground. The back door and the one back window he could reach were locked.

Spade went back to the gatepost and, cupping the flame between his hands, held his lighter up to the *For Sale or Rent* sign. It bore the printed name and address of a San Mateo real-estate dealer and a line pencilled in blue: *Key at 31.*

Spade returned to the sedan and asked the chauffeur: 'Got a flashlight?'

'Sure.' He gave it to Spade. 'Can I give you a hand at anything?'

'Maybe.' Spade got into the sedan. 'We'll ride up to number thirty-one. You can use your lights.'

Number 31 was a square grey house across the street from,

but a little further up than, 26. Lights glowed in its downstairs windows. Spade went up on the porch and rang the bell. A dark-haired girl of fourteen or fifteen opened the door. Spade, bowing and smiling, said: 'I'd like to get the key to number twenty-six.'

'I'll call Papa,' she said and went back into the house calling: 'Papa!'

A plump red-faced man, bald-headed and heavily moustached, appeared, carrying a newspaper.

Spade said: 'I'd like to get the key to twenty-six.'

The plump man looked doubtful. He said: 'The juice is not on. You couldn't see anything.'

Spade patted his pocket. 'I've a flashlight.'

The plump man looked more doubtful. He cleared his throat uneasily and crumpled the newspaper in his hand.

Spade showed him one of his business cards, put it back in his pocket, and said in a low voice: 'We got a tip that there might be something hidden there.'

The plump man's face and voice were eager. 'Wait a minute,' he said. 'I'll go over with you.'

A moment later he came back carrying a brass key attached to a black-and-red tag. Spade beckoned to the chauffeur as they passed the car and the chauffeur joined them.

'Anybody been looking at the house lately?' Spade asked.

'Not that I know of,' the plump man replied. 'Nobody's been to me for the key in a couple of months.'

The plump man marched ahead with the key until they had gone up on the porch. Then he thrust the key into Spade's hand, mumbled, 'Here you are,' and stepped aside.

Spade unlocked the door and pushed it open. There was silence and darkness. Holding the flashlight—dark—in his left hand, Spade entered. The chauffeur came close behind him and then, at a little distance, the plump man followed them. They searched the house from bottom to top, cautiously at first, then, finding nothing, boldly. The house was empty—unmistakably—and there was nothing to indicate that it had been visited in weeks.

Saying, 'Thanks, that's all,' Spade left the sedan in front of the Alexandria. He went into the hotel, to the desk where a tall young man with a dark grave face said: 'Good evening, Mr. Spade.'

'Good evening.' Spade drew the young man to one end of the desk. 'These Gutmans—up in 12C—are they in?'

The young man replied, 'No,' darting a quick glance at Spade. Then he looked away, hesitated, looked at Spade again, and murmured: 'A funny thing happened in connection with them this evening, Mr. Spade. Somebody called the Emergency Hospital and told them there was a sick girl up there.'

'And there wasn't?'

'Oh, no, there was nobody up there. They went out earlier in the evening.'

Spade said: 'Well, these practical jokers have to have their fun. Thanks.'

He went to a telephone booth, called a number, and said: 'Hello.... Mrs. Perine?... Is Effie there?... Yes, please.... Thanks.

'Hello, angel! What's the good word? ... Fine, fine! Hold it. I'll be out in twenty minutes.... Right.'

Half an hour later Spade rang the door-bell of a two-storey brick building in Ninth Avenue. Effie Perine opened the door. Her boyish face was tired and smiling. 'Hello, boss,' she said. 'Enter.' She said in a low voice: 'If Ma says anything to you, Sam, be nice to her. She's all up in the air.'

Spade grinned reassuringly and patted her shoulder.

She put her hands on his arm. 'Miss O'Shaughnessy?'

'No,' he growled. 'I ran into a plant. Are you sure it was her voice?'

'Yes.'

He made an unpleasant face. 'Well, it was hooey.'

She took him into a bright living-room, sighed, and slumped down on one end of a Chesterfield, smiling cheerfully up at him through her weariness.

He sat beside her and asked: 'Everything went O.K.? Nothing said about the bundle?'

'Nothing. I told them what you told me to tell them, and they seemed to take it for granted that the phone-call had something to do with it, and that you were out running it down.'

'Dundy there?'

'No. Hoff and O'Gar and some others I didn't know. I talked to the Captain too.'

'They took you down to the Hall?'

'Oh, yes, and they asked me loads of questions, but it was all—you know—routine.'

Spade rubbed his palms together. 'Swell,' he said and then frowned, 'though I guess they'll think up plenty to put to me when we meet. That damned Dundy will, anyway, and Bryan.' He moved his shoulders. 'Anybody you know, outside of the police, come around?'

'Yes.' She sat up straight. 'That boy—the one who brought the message from Gutman—was there. He didn't come in, but the police left the corridor-door open while they were there and I saw him standing there.'

'You didn't say anything?'

'Oh, no. You had said not to. So I didn't pay any attention to him and the next time I looked he was gone.'

Spade grinned at her. 'Damned lucky for you, sister, that the coppers got there first.'

'Why?'

'He's a bad egg, that lad—poison. Was the dead man Jacobi?'

'Yes.'

He pressed her hands and stood up. 'I'm going to run along. You'd better hit the hay. You're all in.'

She rose. 'Sam, what is——?'

He stopped her words with his hand on her mouth. 'Save it till Monday,' he said. 'I want to sneak out before your mother catches me and gives me hell for dragging her lamb through gutters.'

Midnight was a few minutes away when Spade reached his home. He put his key into the street-door's lock. Heels clicked rapidly on the sidewalk behind him. He let go the key and wheeled. Brigid O'Shaughnessy ran up the steps to him. She put her arms around him and hung on him, panting: 'Oh, I thought you'd never come!' Her face was haggard, distraught, shaken by the tremors that shook her from head to foot.

With the hand not supporting her he felt for the key again,

opened the door, and half lifted her inside. 'You've been waiting?' he asked.

'Yes.' Panting spaced her words. 'In a—doorway—up the—street.'

'Can you make it all right?' he asked. 'Or shall I carry you?'

She shook her head against his shoulder. 'I'll be—all right—when I—get where—I can—sit down.'

They rode up to Spade's floor in the elevator and went around to his apartment. She left his arm and stood beside him—panting, both hands to her breast—while he unlocked his door. He switched on the passage-way light. They went in. He shut the door and, with his arms around her again, took her back towards the living-room. When they were within a step of the living-room door the light in the living-room went on.

The girl cried out and clung to Spade.

Just inside the living-room door fat Gutman stood smiling benevolently at them. The boy Wilmer came out of the kitchen behind them. Black pistols were gigantic in his small hands. Cairo came from the bathroom. He too had a pistol.

Gutman said: 'Well, sir, we're all here, as you can see for yourself. Now let's come in and sit down and be comfortable and talk.'

Chapter Eighteen

The Fall-Guy

Spade, with his arms around Brigid O'Shaughnessy, smiled meagrely over her head and said: 'Sure, we'll talk.'

Gutman's bulbs jounced as he took three waddling backward steps away from the door.

Spade and the girl went in together. The boy and Cairo followed them in. Cairo stopped in the doorway. The boy put away one of the pistols and came up close behind Spade.

Spade turned his head far around to look down over his shoulder at the boy and said : 'Get away. You're not going to frisk me.'

The boy said : 'Stand still. Shut up.'

Spade's nostrils went in and out with his breathing. His voice was level. 'Get away. Put your paw on me and I'm going to make you use the gun. Ask your boss if he wants me shot up before we talk.'

'Never mind, Wilmer,' the fat man said. He frowned indulgently at Spade. 'You are certainly a most headstrong individual. Well, let's be seated.'

Spade said, 'I told you I didn't like that punk,' and took Brigid O'Shaughnessy to the sofa by the windows. They sat close together, her head against his left shoulder, his left arm around her shoulders. She had stopped trembling, had stopped panting. The appearance of Gutman and his companions seemed to have robbed her of that freedom of personal movement and emotion that is animal, leaving her alive, conscious, but quiescent as a plant.

Gutman lowered himself into the padded rocking-chair. Cairo chose another armchair by the table. The boy Wilmer did not sit down. He stood in the doorway where Cairo had stood, letting his one visible pistol hang down at his side, looking under curling lashes at Spade's body. Cairo put his pistol on the table beside him.

Spade took off his hat and tossed it to the other end of the sofa. He grinned at Gutman. The looseness of his lower lip and the droop of his upper eyelids combined with the v's in his face to making his grin lewd as a satyr's. 'That daughter of yours has a nice belly,' he said, 'too nice to be scratched up with pins.'

Gutman's smile was affable if a bit oily.

The boy in the doorway took a short step forward, raising his pistol as far as the hip. Everybody in the room looked at him. In the dissimilar eyes with which Brigid O'Shaughnessy and Joel Cairo looked at him there was, oddly, something identically reproving. The boy blushed, drew back his advanced foot, straightened his legs, lowered the pistol and stood as he had stood before, looking under lashes that hid his eyes at Spade's chest. The blush was pale enough and lasted for only an instant, but it was startling on his face that habitually was so cold and composed.

Gutman turned his sleek-eyed fat smile on Spade again. His

voice was a suave purring. 'Yes, sir, that was a shame, but you must admit it served its purpose.'

Spade's eyebrows twitched together. 'Anything would've,' he said. 'Naturally I wanted to see you as soon as I had the falcon. Cash customers—why not? I went to Burlingame expecting to run into this sort of meeting. I didn't know you were blundering around, half an hour late, trying to get me out of the way so you could find Jacobi again before he found me.'

Gutman chuckled. His chuckle seemed to hold nothing but satisfaction. 'Well, sir,' he said, 'in any case, here we are having our little meeting, if that's what you wanted.'

'That's what I wanted. How soon are you ready to make the first payment and take the falcon off my hands?'

Brigid O'Shaughnessy sat up straight and looked at Spade with surprised blue eyes. He patted her shoulder inattentively. His eyes were steady on Gutman's. Gutman's twinkled merrily between sheltering fat-puffs. He said: 'Well, sir, as to that,' and put a hand inside the breast of his coat.

Cairo, hands on thighs, leaned forward in his chair, breathing between parted soft lips. His dark eyes had the surface-shine of lacquer. They shifted their focus warily from Spade's face to Gutman's, from Gutman's to Spade's.

Gutman repeated, 'Well, sir, as to that,' and took a white envelope from his pocket. Ten eyes—the boy's now only half obscured by his lashes—looked at the envelope. Turning the envelope over in his swollen hands, Gutman studied for a moment its blank white front and then its back, unsealed, with the flap tucked in. He raised his head, smiled amiably, and scaled the envelope at Spade's lap.

The envelope, though not bulky, was heavy enough to fly true. It struck the lower part of Spade's chest and dropped down on his thighs. He picked it up deliberately and opened it deliberately, using both hands, having taken his left arm from around the girl. The contents of the envelope were thousand-dollar bills, smooth and stiff and new. Spade took them out and counted them. There were ten of them. Spade looked up smiling. He said mildly: 'We were talking about more money than this.'

'Yes, sir, we were,' Gutman agreed, 'but we were talking then. This is actual money, genuine coin of the realm, sir. With a dollar of this you can buy more than with ten dollars of talk.' Silent laughter shook his bulbs. When their commotion stopped he said more seriously, yet not altogether seriously : 'There are more of us to be taken care of now.' He moved his twinkling eyes and his fat head to indicate Cairo. 'And—well, sir, in short—the situation has changed.'

While Gutman talked Spade had tapped the edges of the ten bills into alignment and had returned them to their envelope, tucking the flap in over them. Now, with forearms on knees, he sat hunched forward, dangling the envelope from a corner held lightly by finger and thumb down between his legs. His reply to the fat man was careless : 'Sure. You're together now, but I've got the falcon.'

Joel Cairo spoke. Ugly hands grasping the arms of his chair, he leaned forward and said primly in his high-pitched thin voice : 'I shouldn't think it would be necessary to remind you, Mr. Spade, that though you may have the falcon yet we certainly have you.'

Spade grinned. 'I'm trying to not let that worry me,' he said. He sat up straight, put the envelope aside—on the sofa—and addressed Gutman : 'We'll come back to the money later. There's another thing that's got to be taken care of first. We've got to have a fall-guy.'

The fat man frowned without comprehension, but before he could speak Spade was explaining : 'The police have got to have a victim—somebody they can stick for those three murders. We——'

Cairo, speaking in a brittle excited voice, interrupted Spade. 'Two—only two—murders, Mr. Spade. Thursby undoubtedly killed your partner.'

'All right, two,' Spade growled. 'What difference does that make? The point is we've got to feed the police some——'

Now Gutman broke in, smiling confidently, talking with good-natured assurance : 'Well, sir, from what we've seen and heard of you I don't think we'll have to bother ourselves about that. We can leave the handling of the police to you, all right. You won't need any of our inexpert help.'

'If that's what you think,' Spade said, 'you haven't seen or heard enough.'

'Now come, Mr. Spade. You can't expect us to believe at

this late date that you are the least bit afraid of the police, or that you are not quite able to handle——'

Spade snorted with throat and nose. He bent forward, resting forearms on knees again, and interrupted Gutman irritably: 'I'm not a damned bit afraid of them and I know how to handle them. That's what I'm trying to tell you. The way to handle them is to toss them a victim, somebody they can hang the works on.'

'Well, sir, I grant you that's one way of doing it, but——'

'But, hell!' Spade said. 'It's the only way.' His eyes were hot and earnest under a reddened forehead. The bruise on his temple was liver-coloured. 'I know what I'm talking about. I've been through it all before and expect to go through it again. At one time or another I've had to tell everybody from the Supreme Court down to go to hell, and I've got away with it. I got away with it because I never let myself forget that a day of reckoning was coming. I never forget that when the day of reckoning comes I want to be all set to march into headquarters pushing a victim in front of me, saying: "Here, you chumps, is your criminal." As long as I can do that I can put my thumb to my nose and wriggle my fingers at all the laws in the book. The first time I can't do it my name's Mud. There hasn't been a first time yet. This isn't going to be it. That's flat.'

Gutman's eyes flickered and their sleekness became dubious, but he held his other features in their bulbous pink smiling complacent cast and there was nothing of uneasiness in his voice. He said: 'That's a system that's got a lot to recommend it, sir—by Gad, it has! And if it was anyway practical this time I'd be the first to say: "Stick to it by all means, sir." But this just happens to be a case where it's not possible. That's the way it is with the best of systems. There comes a time when you've got to make exceptions, and a wise man just goes ahead and makes them. Well, sir, that's just the way it is in this case and I don't mind telling you that I think you're being very well paid for making an exception. Now maybe it will be a little more trouble to you than if you had your victim to hand over to the police, but'—he laughed and spread his hands—'you're not a man that's afraid of a little bit of trouble. You know how to do things and you know you'll land on your feet in the end, no matter what happens.' He pursed his lips and partly closed one eye. 'You'll manage that, sir.'

Spade's eyes had lost their warmth. His face was dull and lumpy. 'I know what I'm talking about,' he said in a low, consciously patient tone. 'This is my city and my game. I could manage to land on my feet—sure—this time, but the next time I tried to put over a fast one they'd stop me so fast I'd swallow my teeth. Hell with that. You birds'll be in New York or Constantinople or some place else. I'm in business here.'

'But surely,' Gutman began, 'you can——'

'I can't,' Spade said earnestly. 'I won't. I mean it.' He sat up straight. A pleasant smile illuminated his face, erasing its dull lumpishness. He spoke rapidly in an agreeable, persuasive, tone: 'Listen to me, Gutman. I'm telling you what's best for all of us. If we don't give the police a fall-guy it's ten to one they'll sooner or later stumble on information about the falcon. Then you'll have to duck for cover with it—no matter where you are—and that's not going to help you make a fortune off it. Give them a fall-guy and they'll stop right there.'

'Well, sir, that's just the point,' Gutman replied, and still only in his eyes was uneasiness faintly apparent. 'Will they stop right there? Or won't the fall-guy be a fresh clue that as likely as not will lead them to information about the falcon? And, on the other hand, wouldn't you say they were stopped right now, and that the best thing for us to do is leave well enough alone?'

A forked vein began to swell in Spade's forehead. 'Jesus! you don't know what it's all about either,' he said in a restrained tone. 'They're not asleep, Gutman. They're lying low, waiting. Try to get that. I'm in it up to my neck and they know it. That's all right as long as I do something when the time comes. But it won't be all right if I don't.' His voice became persuasive again. 'Listen, Gutman, we've absolutely got to give them a victim. There's no way out of it. Let's give them the punk.' He nodded pleasantly at the boy in the doorway. 'He actually did shoot both of them—Thursby and Jacobi—didn't he? Anyway, he's made to order for the part. Let's pin the necessary evidence on him and turn him over to them.'

The boy in the doorway tightened the corners of his mouth in what may have been a minute smile. Spade's proposal seemed to have no other effect on him. Joel Cairo's dark face was open-mouthed, open-eyed, yellowish, and amazed. He breathed through his mouth, his round effeminate chest rising and falling, while he gaped at Spade. Brigid O'Shaughnessy had moved away from Spade and had twisted herself around on the sofa to stare at him. There was a suggestion of hysterical laughter behind the startled confusion in her face.

Gutman remained still and expressionless for a long moment. Then he decided to laugh. He laughed heartily and lengthily, not stopping until his sleek eyes had borrowed merriment from his laughter. When he had stopped laughing he said: 'By Gad, sir, you're a character, that you are!' He took a white handkerchief from his pocket and wiped his eyes. 'Yes, sir, there's never any telling what you'll do or say next, except that it's bound to be something astonishing.'

'There's nothing funny about it.' Spade did not seem offended by the fat man's laughter, nor in any way impressed. He spoke in the manner of one reasoning with a recalcitrant, but not altogether unreasonable, friend. 'It's our best bet. With him in their hands, the police will——'

'But, my dear man,' Gutman objected, 'can't you see? If I even for a moment thought of doing it—— But that's ridiculous too. I feel towards Wilmer just exactly as if he were my own son. I really do. But if I even for a moment thought of doing what you propose, what in the world do you think would keep Wilmer from telling the police every last detail about the falcon and all of us?'

Spade grinned with stiff lips. 'If we had to,' he said softly, 'we could have him killed resisting arrest. But we won't have to go that far. Let him talk his head off. I promise you nobody'll do anything about it. That's easy enough to fix.'

The pink flesh on Gutman's forehead crawled in a frown. He lowered his head, mashing his chins together over his collar, and asked: 'How?' Then, with an abruptness that set all his fat bulbs to quivering and tumbling against one another, he raised his head, squirmed around to look at the boy, and laughed uproariously. 'What do you think of this, Wilmer? It's funny, eh?'

The boy's eyes were cold hazel gleams under his lashes. He said in a low distinct voice: 'Yes, it's funny—the son of a bitch.'

Spade was talking to Brigid O'Shaughnessy: 'How do you feel now, angel? Any better?'

'Yes, much better, only'—she reduced her voice until the last words would have been unintelligible two feet away—'I'm frightened.'

'Don't be,' he said carelessly and put a hand on her grey-stockinged knee. 'Nothing very bad's going to happen. Want a drink?'

'Not now, thanks.' Her voice sank again. 'Be careful, Sam.'

Spade grinned and looked at Gutman, who was looking at him. The fat man smiled genially, saying nothing for a moment, and then asked: 'How?'

Spade was stupid. 'How what?'

The fat man considered more laughter necessary then, and an explanation: 'Well, sir, if you're really serious about this—this suggestion of yours, the least we can do in common politeness is to hear you out. Now how are you going about fixing it so that Wilmer'—he paused here to laugh again—'won't be able to do us any harm?'

Spade shook his head. 'No,' he said, 'I wouldn't want to take advantage of anybody's politeness, no matter how common, like that. Forget it.'

The fat man puckered his facial bulbs. 'Now come, come,' he protested, 'you make me decidedly uncomfortable. I shouldn't have laughed, and I apologise most humbly and sincerely. I wouldn't want to seem to ridicule anything you'd suggest, Mr. Spade, regardless of how much I disagreed with you, for you must know that I have the greatest respect and admiration for your astuteness. Now mind you, I don't see how this suggestion of yours can be in any way practical—even leaving out the fact that I couldn't feel any different towards Wilmer if he was my own flesh and blood—but I'll consider it a personal favour as well as a sign that you've accepted my apologies, sir, if you'll go ahead and outline the rest of it.'

'Fair enough,' Spade said. 'Bryan is like most district attorneys. He's more interested in how his record will look on paper than in anything else. He'd rather drop a doubtful case than try it and have it go against him. I don't know that he ever deliberately framed anybody he believed innocent, but I can't imagine him letting himself believe them innocent if he could scrape up, or twist into shape, proof of their guilt. To be sure of convicting one man he'll let half a dozen equally guilty accomplices go free—if trying to convict them all might confuse his case.

'That's the choice we'll give him and he'll gobble it up. He wouldn't want to know about the falcon. He'll be tickled pink to persuade himself that anything the punk tells him about it is a lot of chewing-gum, in an attempt to muddle things up. Leave that end to me. I can show him that if he starts fooling around trying to gather up everybody he's going to have a tangled case that no jury will be able to make heads or tails of, while if he sticks to the punk he can get a conviction standing on his head.'

Gutman wagged his head sidewise in a slow smiling gesture of benign disapproval. 'No, sir,' he said, 'I'm afraid that won't do, won't do at all. I don't see how this District Attorney of yours can link Thursby and Jacobi and Wilmer together without having to——'

'You don't know district attorneys,' Spade told him. 'The Thursby angle is easy. He was a gunman and so's your punk. Bryan's already got a theory about that. There'll be no catch there. Well, Christ! they can only hang the punk once. Why try him for Jacobi's murder after he's been convicted of Thursby's? They simply close the record by writing it up against him and let it go at that. If, as is likely enough, he used the same gun on both, the bullets will match up. Everybody will be satisfied.'

'Yes, but——' Gutman began, and stopped to look at the boy.

The boy advanced from the doorway, walking stiff-legged, with his legs apart, until he was between Gutman and Cairo, almost in the centre of the floor. He halted there, leaning forward slightly from the waist, his shoulders raised towards the front. The pistol in his hand still hung at his side, but his knuckles were white over its grip. His other hand was a small hard fist down at his other side. The indelible youngness of his face gave an indescribably vicious—and inhuman—turn to the white-hot hatred and the cold white malevolence in his face. He said to Spade in a voice cramped by passion: 'You bastard, get up on your feet and go for your heater!'

Spade smiled at the boy. His smile was not broad, but the amusement in it seemed genuine and unalloyed.

The boy said: 'You bastard, get up and shoot it out if you've got the guts. I've taken all the riding from you I'm going to take.'

The amusement in Spade's smile deepened. He looked at Gutman and said: 'Young Wild West.' His voice matched his smile. 'Maybe you ought to tell him that shooting me before you get your hands on the falcon would be bad for business.'

Gutman's attempt at a smile was not successful, but he kept the resultant grimace on his mottled face. He licked his lips with a dry tongue. His voice was too hoarse and gritty for the paternally admonishing tone it tried to achieve. 'Now, now, Wilmer,' he said, 'we can't have any of that. You shouldn't let yourself attach so much importance to these things. You——'

The boy, not taking his eyes from Spade, spoke in a choked voice out the side of his mouth: 'Make him lay off me then. I'm going to fog him if he keeps it up and there won't be anything that'll stop me from doing it.'

'Now, Wilmer,' Gutman said and turned to Spade. His face and voice were under control now. 'Your plan is, sir, as I said in the first place, not at all practical. Let's not say anything more about it.'

Spade looked from one of them to the other. He had stopped smiling. His face held no expression at all. 'I say what I please,' he told them.

'You certainly do,' Gutman said quickly, 'and that's one of the things I've always admired in you. But this matter is, as I say, not at all practical, so there's not the least bit of use of discussing it any further, as you can see for yourself.'

'I can't see it for myself,' Spade said, 'and you haven't made me see it, and I don't think you can.' He frowned at Gutman. 'Lets get this straight. Am I wasting time talking to you? I thought this was your show. Should I do my talking to the punk? I know how to do that.'

'No, sir,' Gutman replied, 'you're quite right in dealing with me.'

Spade said: 'All right. Now I've got another suggestion. It's not as good as the first, but it's better than nothing. Want to hear it?'

'Most assuredly.'

'Give them Cairo.'

Cairo hastily picked up his pistol from the table beside him. He held it tight in his lap with both hands. Its muzzle pointed at the floor a little to one side of the sofa. His face had become yellowish again. His black eyes darted their gaze from face to face. The opaqueness of his eyes made them seem flat, two-dimensional.

Gutman, looking as if he could not believe he had heard what he had heard, asked: 'Do what?'

'Give the police Cairo.'

Gutman seemed about to laugh, but he did not laugh. Finally he exclaimed: 'Well, by Gad, sir!' in an uncertain tone.

'It's not as good as giving them the punk,' Spade said. 'Cairo's not a gunman and he carries a smaller gun than Thursby and Jacobi were shot with. We'll have to go to more trouble framing him, but that's better than not giving the police anybody.'

Cairo cried in a voice shrill with indignation: 'Suppose we give them you, Mr. Spade, or Miss O'Shaughnessy? How about that if you're so set on giving them somebody?'

Spade smiled at the Levantine and answered him evenly: 'You people want the falcon. I've got it. A fall-guy is part of the price I'm asking. As for Miss O'Shaughnessy'—his dispassionate glance moved to her white perplexed face and then back to Cairo and his shoulders rose and fell a fraction of an inch— 'if you think she can be rigged for the part I'm perfectly willing to discuss it with you.'

The girl put her hands to her throat, uttered a short strangled cry, and moved farther away from him.

Cairo, his face and body twitching with excitement, exclaimed: 'You seem to forget that you are not in a position to insist on anything.'

Spade laughed, a harsh derisive snort.

Gutman said, in a voice that tried to make firmness ingratiating: 'Come now, gentlemen, let's keep our discussion on a friendly basis; but there certainly is'—he was addressing Spade—'something in what Mr. Cairo says. You must take into consideration the——'

'Like hell I must.' Spade flung his words out with a brutal sort of carelessness that gave them more weight than they could have got from dramatic emphasis or from loudness. 'If you kill me, how are you going to get the bird? If I know you can't afford to kill me till you have it, how are you going to scare me into giving it to you?'

Gutman cocked his head to the left and considered these questions. His eyes twinkled between puckered lips. Presently he gave his genial answer: 'Well, sir, there are other means of persuasion besides killing and threatening to kill.'

'Sure,' Spade agreed, 'but they're not much good unless the threat of death is behind them to hold the victim down. See what I mean? If you try anything I don't like I won't stand for it. It'll make it a matter of your having to call it off or kill me, knowing you can't afford to kill me.'

'I see what you mean.' Gutman chuckled. 'That is an attitude, sir, that calls for the most delicate judgment on both sides, because, as you know, sir, men are likely to forget in the heat of action where their best interest lies and let their emotions carry them away.'

Spade too was all smiling blandness. 'That's the trick, from my side,' he said, 'to make my play strong enough that it ties you up, but yet not make you mad enough to bump me off against your better judgment.'

Gutman said fondly: 'By Gad, sir, you are a character!'

Joel Cairo jumped up from his chair and went around behind the boy and behind Gutman's chair. He bent over the back of Gutman's chair and, screening his mouth and the fat man's ear with his empty hand, whispered. Gutman listened attentively, shutting his eyes.

Spade grinned at Brigid O'Shaughnessy. Her lips smiled feebly in response, but there was no change in her eyes; they did not lose their numb stare. Spade turned to the boy: 'Two to one they're selling you out, son.'

The boy did not say anything. A trembling in his knees began to shake the knees of his trousers.

Spade addressed Gutman: 'I hope you're not letting yourself be influenced by the guns these pocket-edition desperadoes are waving.'

Gutman opened his eyes. Cairo stopped whispering and stood erect behind the fat man's chair.

Spade said: 'I've practised taking them away from both of them, so there'll be no trouble there. The punk is——'

In a voice choked horribly by emotion the boy cried, 'All right!' and jerked his pistol up in front of his chest.

Gutman flung a fat hand out at the boy's wrist, caught the wrist, and bore it and the gun down while Gutman's fat body was rising in haste from the rocking-chair. Joel Cairo scurried around to the boy's other side and grasped his other arm. They wrestled with the boy, forcing his arms down, holding them down, while he struggled futilely against them. Words came out of the struggling group: fragments of the boy's incoherent speech— 'right ... go ... bastard ... smoke'—Gutman's 'Now, now, Wilmer!' repeated many times; Cairo's 'No, please, don't' and 'Don't do that, Wilmer.'

Wooden-faced, dreamy-eyed, Spade got up from the sofa and went over to the group. The boy, unable to cope with the weight against him, had stopped struggling. Cairo, still holding the boy's arm, stood partly in front of him, talking to him soothingly. Spade pushed Cairo aside gently and drove his left fist against the boy's chin. The boy's head snapped back as far as it could while his arms were held, and then came forward. Gutman began a desperate. 'Here, what——?' Spade drove his right fist against the boy's chin.

Cairo dropped the boy's arm, letting him collapse against Gutman's great round belly. Cairo sprang at Spade, clawing at his face with the curved stiff fingers of both hands. Spade blew his breath out and pushed the Levantine away. Cairo sprang at him again. Tears were in Cairo's eyes and his red lips worked angrily, forming words, but no sound came from between them.

Spade laughed, grunted, 'Jesus, you're a pip!' and cuffed the side of Cairo's face with an open hand, knocking him over against the table. Cairo regained his balance and sprang at Spade the third time. Spade stopped him with both palms held out on long rigid arms against his face. Cairo, failing to reach Spade's face with his shorter arms, thumped Spade's arms.

'Stop it,' Spade growled. 'I'll hurt you.'

Cairo cried, 'Oh, you big coward!' and backed away from him.

Spade stooped to pick up Cairo's pistol from the floor, and then the boy's. He straightened up holding them in his left hand, dangling them upside-down by their trigger-guards from his forefinger.

Gutman had put the boy in the rocking-chair and stood looking at him with troubled eyes in an uncertainly puckered face. Cairo went down on his knees beside the chair and began to chafe one of the boy's limp hands.

Spade felt the boy's chin with his fingers. 'Nothing cracked,' he said. 'We'll spread him on the sofa.' He put his right arm under the boy's arm and around his back, put his left forearm under the boy's knees, lifted him without apparent effort, and carried him to the sofa.

Brigid O'Shaughnessy got up quickly and Spade laid the boy there. With his right hand Spade patted the boy's clothes, found his second pistol, added it to the others in his left hand, and turned his back on the sofa. Cairo was already sitting beside the boy's head.

Spade clinked the pistols together in his hand and smiled cheerfully at Gutman. 'Well,' he said, 'there's our fall-guy.'

Gutman's face was grey and his eyes were clouded. He did not look at Spade. He looked at the floor and did not say anything.

Spade said: 'Don't be a damned fool again. You let Cairo whisper to you and you held the kid while I pasted him. You can't laugh that off and you're likely to get yourself shot trying to.'

Gutman moved his feet on the rug and said nothing.

Spade said: 'And the other side of it is that you'll either say yes right now or I'll turn the falcon and the whole God-damned lot of you in.'

Gutman raised his head and muttered through his teeth: 'I don't like that, sir.'

'You won't like it,' Spade said. 'Well?'

The fat man sighed and made a wry face and replied sadly: 'You can have him.

Spade said: 'That's swell.'

Chapter Nineteen

The Russian's Hand

The boy lay on his back on the sofa, a small figure that was—except for its breathing—altogether corpselike to the eye. Joel Cairo sat beside the boy, bending over him, rubbing his cheeks and wrists, smoothing his hair back from his forehead, whispering to him, and peering anxiously down at his white still face.

Brigid O'Shaughnessy stood in an angle made by table and wall. One of her hands was flat on the table, the other to her breast. She pinched her lower lip between her teeth and glanced furtively at Spade whenever he was not looking at her. When he looked at her she looked at Cairo and the boy.

Gutman's face had lost its troubled cast and was becoming rosy again. He had put his hands in his trousers pockets. He stood facing Spade, watching him without curiosity.

Spade, idly jingling his handful of pistols, nodded at Cairo's rounded back and asked Gutman: 'It'll be all right with him?'

'I don't know,' the fat man replied placidly. 'That part will have to be strictly up to you, sir.'

Spade's smile made his v-shaped chin more salient. He said: 'Cairo.'

The Levantine screwed his dark anxious face around over his shoulder.

Spade said: 'Let him rest awhile. We're going to give him to the police. We ought to get the details fixed before he comes to.'

Cairo asked bitterly: 'Don't you think you've done enough to him without that?'

Spade said: 'No.'

Cairo left the sofa and went close to the fat man. 'Please don't do this thing, Mr. Gutman,' he begged. 'You must realise that——'

Spade interrupted him: 'That's settled. The question is, what are you going to do about it? Coming in? Or getting out?'

Though Gutman's smile was a bit sad, even wistful in its way, he nodded his head. 'I don't like it either,' he told the Levantine, 'but we can't help ourselves now. We really can't.'

Spade asked: 'What are you doing, Cairo? In or out?'

Cairo wet his lips and turned slowly to face Spade. 'Suppose,' he said, and swallowed. 'Have I——? Can I choose?'

'You can,' Spade assured him seriously, 'but you ought to know that if the answer is *out* we'll give you to the police with your boy-friend.'

'Oh, come, Mr. Spade,' Gutman protested, 'that is not——'

'Like hell we'll let him walk out on us,' Spade said. 'He'll either come in or he'll go in. We can't have a lot of loose ends hanging around.' He scowled at Gutman and burst out irritably: 'Good God! is this the first thing you guys ever stole? You're a fine lot of lollipops! What are you going to do next—get down and pray?' He directed his scowl at Cairo. 'Well? Which?'

'You give me no choice.' Cairo's narrow shoulders moved in a hopeless shrug. 'I come in.'

'Good,' Spade said and looked at Gutman and at Brigid O'Shaughnessy. 'Sit down.'

The girl sat down gingerly on the end of the sofa by the unconscious boy's feet. Gutman returned to the padded rocking-chair, and Cairo to the armchair. Spade put his handful of pistols on the table and sat on the table corner beside them. He looked at the watch on his wrist and said: 'Two o'clock. I can't get the falcon till daylight, or maybe eight o'clock. We've got plenty of time to arrange everything.'

Gutman cleared his throat. 'Where is it?' he asked and then added in haste: 'I don't really care, sir. What I had in mind was that it would be best for all concerned if we did not get out of each other's sight until our business has been transacted.' He looked at the sofa and at Spade again, sharply. 'You have the envelope?'

Spade shook his head, looking at the sofa and then at the girl. He smiled with his eyes and said: 'Miss O'Shaughnessy has it.'

'Yes, I have it,' she murmured, putting a hand inside her coat. 'I picked it up....'

'That's all right,' Spade told her. 'Hang on to it.' He addressed Gutman : 'We won't have to lose sight of each other. I can have the falcon brought here.'

'That will be excellent,' Gutman purred. 'Then, sir, in exchange for the ten thousand dollars and Wilmer you will give us the falcon and an hour or two of grace—so we won't be in the city when you surrender him to the authorities.'

'You don't have to duck,' Spade said. 'It'll be air-tight.'

'That may be, sir, but nevertheless we'll feel safer well out of the city when Wilmer is being questioned by your District Attorney.'

'Suit yourself,' Spade replied. 'I can hold him here all day if you want.' He began to roll a cigarette. 'Let's get the details fixed. Why did he shoot Thursby? And why and where and how did he shoot Jacobi?'

Gutman smiled indulgently, shaking his head and purring: 'Now come, sir, you can't expect that. We've given you the money and Wilmer. That is our part of the agreement.'

'I do expect it,' Spade said. He held his lighter to his cigarette. 'A fall-guy is what I asked for, and he's not a fall-guy unless he's a cinch to take the fall. Well, to cinch that I've got to know what's what.' He pulled his brows together. 'What are you belly-aching about? You're not going to be sitting so damned pretty if you leave him an out.'

Gutman leaned forward and wagged a fat finger at the pistols on the table beside Spade's legs. 'There's ample evidence of his guilt, sir. Both men were shot with those weapons. It's a very simple matter for the police-department experts to determine that the bullets that killed the men were fired from those weapons. You know that; you've mentioned it yourself. And that, it seems to me, is ample proof of his guilt.'

'Maybe,' Spade agreed, 'but the thing's more complicated than that and I've got to know what happened so I can be sure the parts that won't fit in are covered up.'

Cairo's eyes were round and hot. 'Apparently you've forgotten that you assured us it would be a very simple affair,' Cairo said. He turned his excited dark face to Gutman. 'You see! I advised you not to do this. I don't think——'

'It doesn't make a damned bit of difference what either of you think,' Spade said bluntly. 'It's too late for that now and you're in too deep. Why did he kill Thursby?'

Gutman interlaced his fingers over his belly and rocked his chair. His voice, like his smile, was frankly rueful. 'You are an uncommonly difficult person to get the best of,' he said. 'I begin to think that we made a mistake in not letting you alone from the very first. By Gad, I do, sir!'

Spade moved his hand carelessly. 'You haven't done so bad. You're staying out of jail and you're getting the falcon. What do you want?' He put a cigarette in a corner of his mouth and said around it: 'Anyhow you know where you stand now. Why did he kill Thursby?'

Gutman stopped rocking. 'Thursby was a notorious killer and Miss O'Shaughnessy's ally. We knew that removing him in just that manner would make her stop and think that perhaps it would be best to patch up her differences with us after all, besides leaving her without so violent a protector. You see, sir. I am being candid with you.'

'Yes. Keep it up. You didn't think he might have the falcon?'

Gutman shook his head so that his round cheeks wobbled. 'We didn't think that for a minute,' he replied. He smiled benevolently. 'We had the advantage of knowing Miss O'Shaughnessy far too well for that and, while we didn't know then that she had given the falcon to Captain Jacobi in Hongkong to be brought over on the *Paloma* while they took a faster boat, still we didn't for a minute think that, if only one of them knew where it was, Thursby was the one.'

Spade nodded thoughtfully and asked: 'You didn't try to make a deal with him before you gave him the works?'

'Yes, sir, we certainly did. I talked to him myself that night. Wilmer had located him two days before and had been trying to follow him to wherever he was meeting Miss O'Shaughnessy, but Thursby was too crafty for that even if he didn't know he was being watched. So that night Wilmer went to his hotel, learned he wasn't in, and waited outside for him. I suppose Thursby returned immediately after killing your partner. Be that as it may, Wilmer brought him to see me. We could do nothing with him. He was quite determinedly loyal to Miss O'Shaughnessy.

Well sir, Wilmer followed him back to his hotel and did what he did.'

Spade thought for a moment. 'That sounds all right. Now Jacobi.'

Gutman looked at Spade with grave eyes and said: 'Captain Jacobi's death was entirely Miss O'Shaughnessy's fault.'

The girl gasped, 'Oh!' and put a hand to her mouth.

Spade's voice was heavy and even. 'Never mind that now. Tell me what happened.'

After a shrewd look at Spade, Gutman smiled. 'Just as you say, sir,' he said. 'Well, Cairo, as you know, got in touch with me—I sent for him—after he left police headquarters the night—or morning—he was up here. We recognised the mutual advantage of pooling forces.' He directed his smile at the Levantine. 'Mr. Cairo is a man of nice judgment. The *Paloma* was his thought. He saw the notice of its arrival in the papers that morning and remembered that he had heard in Hongkong that Jacobi and Miss O'Shaughnessy had been seen together. That was when he had been trying to find her there, and he thought at first that she had left on the *Paloma*, though later he learned that she hadn't. Well, sir, when he saw the notice of arrival in the paper he guessed just what had happened: she had given the bird to Jacobi to bring here for her. Jacobi did not know what it was, of course. Miss O'Shaughnessy is too discreet for that.'

He beamed at the girl, rocked his chair twice, and went on: 'Mr. Cairo and Wilmer and I went to call on Captain Jacobi and were fortunate enough to arrive while Miss O'Shaughnessy was there. In many ways it was a difficult conference, but finally, by midnight we had persuaded Miss O'Shaughnessy to come to terms, or so we thought. We then left the boat and set out for my hotel, where I was to pay Miss O'Shaughnessy and receive the bird. Well, sir, we mere men should have known better than to suppose ourselves capable of coping with her. *En route*, she and Captain Jacobi and the falcon slipped completely through our fingers.' He laughed merrily. 'By Gad, sir, it was neatly done.'

Spade looked at the girl. Her eyes, large and dark with pleading, met his. He asked Gutman: 'You touched off the boat before you left?'

'Not intentionally, no, sir,' the fat man replied, 'though I dare say we—or Wilmer at least—were responsible for the fire. He had been out trying to find the falcon while the rest of us were talking in the cabin and no doubt was careless with matches.'

'That's fine,' Spade said. 'If any slip-up makes it necessary for us to try him for Jacobi's murder we can also hang an arson-rap on him. All right. Now about the shooting.'

'Well, sir, we dashed around town all day trying to find them and we found them late this afternoon. We weren't sure at first that we'd found them. All we were sure of was that we'd found Miss O'Shaughnessy's apartment. But when we listened at the door we heard them moving around inside, so we were pretty confident we had them and rang the bell. When she asked us who we were and we told her—through the door—we heard a window going up.

'We knew what that meant, of course; so Wilmer hurried downstairs as fast as he could and around to the rear of the building to cover the fire escape. And when he turned into the alley he ran right plumb smack into Captain Jacobi running away with the falcon under his arm. That was a difficult situation to handle, but Wilmer did every bit as well as he could. He shot Jacobi—more than once—but Jacobi was too tough to either fall or drop the falcon, and he was too close for Wilmer to keep out of his way. He knocked Wilmer down and ran on. And this was in broad daylight, you understand, in the afternoon. When Wilmer got up he could see a policeman coming up from the block below. So he had to give it up. He dodged into the open back door of the building next the Coronet, through into the street, and then up to join us—and very fortunate he was, sir, to make it without being seen.

'Well, sir, there we were—stumped again. Miss O'Shaughnessy had opened the door for Mr. Cairo and me after she had shut the window behind Jacobi, and she——' He broke off to smile at a memory. 'We persuaded—that is the word, sir—her to tell us that she had told Jacobi to take the falcon to you. It seemed very unlikely that he'd live to go that far, even if the police didn't pick him up, but that was the only chance we had, sir. And so, once more, we persuaded Miss O'Shaughnessy to give us a little assistance. We—well—persuaded her to phone your office in an attempt to draw you away before Jacobi got there, and we sent

Wilmer after him. Unfortunately it had taken us too long to
decide and to persuade Miss O'Shaughnessy to——'

The boy on the sofa groaned and rolled over on his side. His
eyes opened and closed several times. The girl stood up and
moved into the angle of the table and wall again.

'—co-operate with us,' Guttman concluded hurriedly, 'and so
you had the falcon before we could reach you.'

The boy put one foot on the floor, raised himself on an elbow,
opened his eyes wide, put the other foot down, sat up, and looked
around. When his eyes focused on Spade bewilderment went
out of them.

Cairo left his armchair and went over to the boy. He put his
arm on the boy's shoulders and started to say something. The
boy rose quickly to his feet, shaking Cairo's arm off. He glanced
around the room once and then fixed his eyes on Spade again.
His face was set hard and he held his body so tense that it seemed
drawn in and shrunken.

Spade, sitting on the corner of the table, swinging his legs
carelessly, said: 'Now listen, kid. If you come over here and
start cutting up I'm going to kick you in the face. Sit down and
shut up and behave and you'll last longer.'

The boy looked at Gutman.

Gutman smiled benignly at him and said: 'Well, Wilmer,
I'm sorry indeed to lose you, and I want you to know that I
couldn't be any fonder of you if you were my own son; but—
well, by Gad!—if you lose a son it's possible to get another—
and there's only one Maltese falcon.'

Spade laughed.

Cairo moved over and whispered in the boy's ear. The boy,
keeping his cold hazel eyes on Gutman's face, sat down on the
sofa again. The Levantine sat beside him.

Gutman's sigh did not affect the benignity of his smile. He
said to Spade: 'When you're young you simply don't understand
things.'

Cairo had an arm around the boy's shoulders again and was
whispering to him. Spade grinned at Gutman and addressed
Brigid O'Shaughnessy: 'I think it'd be swell if you'd see what
you can find us to eat in the kitchen, with plenty of coffee. Will
you? I don't like to leave my guests.'

'Surely,' she said, and started towards the door.

Gutman stopped rocking. 'Just a moment, my dear.' He held up a thick hand. 'Hadn't you better leave the envelope in here? You don't want to get grease-spots on it.'

The girl's eyes questioned Spade. He said in an indifferent tone: 'It's still his.'

She put her hand inside her coat, took out the envelope, and gave it to Spade. Spade tossed it into Gutman's lap, saying: 'Sit on it if you're afraid of losing it.'

'You misunderstand me,' Gutman replied suavely. 'It's not that at all, but business should be transacted in a business-like manner.' He opened the flap of the envelope, took out the thousand-dollar bills, counted them, and chuckled so that his belly bounced. 'For instance there are only nine bills here now.' He spread them out on his fat knees and thighs. 'There were ten when I handed it to you, as you very well know.' His smile was broad and jovial and triumphant.

Spade looked at Brigid O'Shaughnessy and asked: 'Well?'

She shook her head sidewise with emphasis. She did not say anything, though her lips moved slightly, as if she had tried to. Her face was frightened.

Spade held his hand out to Gutman and the fat man put the money into it. Spade counted the money—nine thousand-dollar bills—and returned it to Gutman. Then Spade stood up and his face was dull and placid. He picked up the three pistols on the table. He spoke in a matter-of-fact voice. 'I want to know about this. We'—he nodded at the girl, but without looking at her—'are going in the bathroom. The door will be open and I'll be facing it. Unless you want a three-storey drop there's no way out of here except past the bathroom door. Don't try to make it.'

'Really, sir,' Gutman protested, 'it's not necessary, and certainly not very courteous of you to threaten us in this manner. You must know that we've not the least desire to leave.'

'I'll know a lot when I'm through.' Spade was patient but resolute. 'This trick upsets things. I've got to find the answer. It won't take long.' He touched the girl's elbow. 'Come on.'

In the bathroom Brigid O'Shaughnessy found words. She put

her hands up flat on Spade's chest and her face up close to his and whispered: 'I did not take that bill, Sam.'

'I don't think you did,' he said, 'but I've got to know. Take your clothes off.'

'You won't take my word for it?'

'No. Take your clothes off.'

'I won't.'

'All right. We'll go back to the other room and I'll have them taken off.'

She stepped back with a hand to her mouth. Her eyes were round and horrified. 'You would?' she asked through her fingers.

'I will,' he said. 'I've got to know what happened to that bill and I'm not going to be held up by anybody's maidenly modesty.'

'Oh, it isn't that.' She came close to him and put her hands on his chest again. 'I'm not ashamed to be naked before you, but—can't you see?—not like this. Can't you see that if you make me you'll—you'll be killing something?'

He did not raise his voice. 'I don't know anything about that. I've got to know what happened to the bill. Take them off.'

She looked at his unblinking yellow-grey eyes and her face became pink and then white again. She drew herself up tall and began to undress. He sat on the side of the bath-tub watching her and the open door. No sound came from the living-room. She removed her clothes swiftly, without fumbling, letting them fall down on the floor around her feet. When she was naked she stepped back from her clothing and stood looking at him. In her mien was pride without defiance or embarrassment.

He put his pistols on the toilet-seat and, facing the door, went down on one knee in front of her garments. He picked up each piece and examined it with fingers as well as eyes. He did not find the thousand-dollar bill. When he had finished he stood up holding her clothes out in his hands to her. 'Thanks,' he said. 'Now I know.'

She took the clothing from him. She did not say anything. He picked up his pistols. He shut the bathroom door behind him and went into the living-room.

Gutman smiled amiably at him from the rocking-chair. 'Find it?' he asked.

Cairo, sitting beside the boy on the sofa, looked at Spade with questioning opaque eyes. The boy did not look up. He was leaning forward, head between hands, elbows on knees, staring at the floor between his feet.

Spade told Gutman: 'No, I didn't find it. You palmed it.'

The fat man chuckled. 'I palmed it?'

'Yes,' Spade said jingling the pistols in his hand. 'Do you want to say so or do you want to stand for a frisk?'

'Stand for——?'

'You're going to admit it,' Spade said, 'or I'm going to search you. There's no third way.'

Gutman looked up at Spade's hard face and laughed outright. 'By Gad, sir, I believe you would. I really do. You're a character, sir, if you don't mind my saying so.'

'You palmed it,' Spade said.

'Yes, sir, that I did.' The fat man took a crumpled bill from his vest-pocket, smoothed it on a wide thigh, took the envelope holding the nine bills from his coat-pocket, and put the smoothed bill in with the others. 'I must have my little joke every now and then and I was curious to know what you'd do in a situation of that sort. I must say that you passed the test with flying colours, sir. It never occurred to me that you'd hit on such a simple and direct way of getting at the truth.'

Spade sneered at him without bitterness. 'That's the kind of thing I'd expect from somebody the punk's age.'

Gutman chuckled.

Brigid O'Shaughnessy, dressed again except for coat and hat, came out of the bathroom, took a step towards the living-room, turned around, went to the kitchen, and turned on the light.

Cairo edged closer to the boy on the sofa and began whispering in his ear again. The boy shrugged irritably.

Spade, looking at the pistols in his hand and then at Gutman, went out into the passage-way, to the closet there. He opened the door, put the pistols inside on the top of a trunk, shut the door, locked it, put the key in his trousers pocket, and went to the kitchen door.

Brigid O'Shaughnessy was filling an aluminium percolator.

'Find everything?' Spade asked.

'Yes,' she replied in a cool voice, not raising her head. Then she set the percolator aside and came to the door. She blushed and her eyes were large and moist and chiding. 'You shouldn't have done that to me, Sam,' she said softly.

'I had to find out, angel.' He bent down, kissed her mouth lightly, and returned to the living-room.

Gutman smiled at Spade and offered him the white envelope, saying: 'This will soon be yours; you might as well take it now.'

Spade did not take it. He sat in the armchair and said: 'There's plenty of time for that. We haven't done enough talking about the money-end. I ought to have more than ten thousand.'

Gutman said: 'Ten thousand dollars is a lot of money.'

Spade said: 'You're quoting me, but it's not all the money in the world.'

'No, sir, it's not. I grant you that. But it's a lot of money to be picked up in as few days and as easily as you're getting it.'

'You think it's been so damned easy?' Spade asked, and shrugged. 'Well, maybe, but that's my business.'

'It certainly is,' the fat man agreed. He screwed up his eyes, moved his head to indicate the kitchen, and lowered his voice. 'Are you sharing with her?'

Spade said: 'That's my business too.'

'It certainly is,' the fat man agreed once more 'but'—he hesitated—'I'd like to give you a word of advice.'

'Go ahead.'

'If you don't—I dare say you'll give her some money in any event, but—if you don't give her as much as she thinks she ought to have, my word of advice is—be careful.'

Spade's eyes held a mocking light. He asked: 'Bad?'

'Bad,' the fat man replied.

Spade grinned and began to roll a cigarette.

Cairo, still muttering in the boy's ear, had put his arm around the boy's shoulders again. Suddenly the boy pushed his arm away and turned on the sofa to face the Levantine. The boy's face held disgust and anger. He made a fist of one small hand and struck Cairo's mouth with it. Cairo cried out as a woman might have cried and drew back to the very end of the sofa. He took a silk handkerchief from his pocket and put it to his mouth. It came away daubed with blood. He put it to his mouth once more and looked reproachfully at the boy. The boy snarled, 'Keep away from me,' and put his face between his hands again. Cairo's handkerchief released the fragrance of *chypre* in the room.

Cairo's cry had brought Brigid O'Shaughnessy to the door. Spade, grinning, jerked a thumb at the sofa and told her: 'The course of true love. How's the food coming along?'

'It's coming,' she said and went back to the kitchen.

Spade lighted his cigarette and addressed Gutman: 'Let's talk about money.'

'Willingly, sir, with all my heart,' the fat man replied, 'but I might as well tell you frankly right now that ten thousand is every cent I can raise.'

Spade exhaled smoke. 'I ought to have twenty.'

'I wish you could. I'd give it to you gladly if I had it, but ten thousand dollars is every cent I can manage, on my word of honour. Of course, sir, you understand that is simply the first payment. Later——'

Spade laughed. 'I know you'll give me millions later,' he said, 'but let's stick to this first payment now. Fifteen thousand?'

Gutman smiled and frowned and shook his head. 'Mr. Spade, I've told you frankly and candidly and on my word of honour as a gentleman that ten thousand dollars is all the money I've got—every penny—and all I can raise.'

'But you didn't say positively.'

Gutman laughed and said: 'Positively.'

Spade said gloomily: 'That's not any too good, but if it's the best you can do—give it to me.'

Gutman handed him the envelope. Spade counted the bills and was putting them in his pocket when Brigid O'Shaughnessy came in carrying a tray.

The boy would not eat. Cairo took a cup of coffee. The girl, Gutman and Spade ate the scrambled eggs, bacon, toast, and marmalade she had prepared, and drank two cups of coffee apiece. Then they settled down to wait the rest of the night through.

Gutman smoked a cigar and read *Celebrated Criminal Cases of America*, now and then chuckling over or commenting on the parts of its contents that amused him. Cairo nursed his mouth and sulked on his end of the sofa. The boy sat with his head in his hands until after four o'clock. Then he lay down with his feet towards Cairo, turned his face to the window, and went to sleep. Brigid O'Shaughnessy, in the armchair, dozed, listened to the fat man's comments, and carried on wide-spaced desultory conversations with Spade.

Spade rolled and smoked cigarettes and moved, without fidgeting or nervousness, around the room. He sat sometimes on the arm of the girl's chair, on the table-corner, on the floor at her feet, on a straight-backed chair. He was wide-awake, cheerful and full of vigour.

At half-past five he went into the kitchen and made more coffee. Half an hour later the boy stirred, awakened, and sat up yawning. Gutman looked at his watch and questioned Spade: 'Can you get it now?'

'Give me another hour.'

Gutman nodded and went back to his book.

At seven o'clock Spade went to the telephone and called Effie Perine's number. 'Hello, Mrs. Perine? ... This is Mr. Spade. Will you let me talk to Effie, please?... Yes, it is.... Thanks.' He whistled two lines of *En Cuba*, softly. 'Hello, angel. Sorry to get you up.... Yes, very. Here's the plot: in our Holland box at the Post Office you'll find an envelope addressed in my scribble. There's a Pickwick Stage parcel-room check in it—for the bundle we got yesterday. Will you get the bundle and bring it to me— p. d. q.? ... Yes, I'm home.... That's the girl—hustle.... 'Bye.'

The street-door bell rang at ten minutes to eight. Spade went to the telephone-box and pressed the button that released the lock. Gutman put down his book and rose smiling. 'You don't mind if I go to the door with you?' he asked.

'O.K.,' Spade told him.

Gutman followed him down to the corridor-door. Spade opened it. Presently Effie Perine, carrying the brown-wrapped parcel came from the elevator. Her boyish face was gay and bright and she came forward quickly, almost trotting. After one glance she did not look at Gutman. She smiled at Spade and gave him the parcel.

He took it saying: 'Thanks a lot, lady. I'm sorry to spoil your day of rest, but this——'

'It's not the first one you've spoiled,' she replied, laughing, and then, when it was apparent that he was not going to invite her in, asked: 'Anything else?'

He shook his head. 'No, thanks.'

She said, 'Bye-bye,' and went back to the elevator.

Spade shut the door and carried the parcel into the living-room. Gutman's face was red and his cheeks quivered. Cairo and Brigid O'Shaughnessy came to the table as Spade put the parcel there.

They were excited. The boy rose, pale and tense, but he remained by the sofa, staring under curling lashes at the others.

Spade stepped back from the table saying: 'There you are.'

Gutman's fat fingers made short work of cord and paper and excelsior, and he had the black bird in his hands. 'Ah,' he said huskily, 'now, after seventeen years!' His eyes were moist.

Cairo licked his red lips and worked his hands together. The girl's lower lip was between her teeth. She and Cairo, like Gutman, and like Spade and the boy, were breathing heavily. The air in the room was chilly and stale, and thick with tobacco smoke.

Gutman set the bird down on the table again and fumbled at a pocket. 'It's it,' he said, 'but we'll make sure.' Sweat glistened on his round cheeks. His fingers twitched as he took out a gold pocket-knife and opened it.

Cairo and the girl stood close to him, one on either side. Spade stood back a little where he could watch the boy as well as the group at the table.

Gutman turned the bird upside-down and scraped an edge of its base with his knife. Black enamel came off in tiny curls, exposing blackened metal beneath. Gutmans knife-blade bit into the metal, turning back a thin curved shaving. The inside of the shaving, and the narrow plane its removal had left, had the soft grey sheen of lead.

Gutman's breath hissed between his teeth. His face became turgid with hot blood. He twisted the bird around and hacked at its head. There too the edge of his knife bared lead. He let knife and bird bang down on the table while he wheeled to confront Spade. 'It's a fake,' he said hoarsely.

Spade's face had become sombre. His nod was slow, but there was no slowness in his hand's going out to catch Brigid O'Shaughnessy's wrist. He pulled her to him and grasped her chin with his other hand, raising her face roughly. 'All right,' he growled into her face. 'You've had *your* little joke. Now tell us about it.'

She cried: 'No, Sam, no! That is the one I got from Kemidov. I swear——'

Joel Cairo thrust himself between Spade and Gutman and began to emit words in a shrill spluttering stream: 'That's it! That's it! It was the Russian! I should have known! What a fool we thought him, and what fools he made of us!' Tears rolled down the Levantine's cheeks and he danced up and down. 'You bungled it!' he screamed at Gutman. 'You and your stupid attempt to buy it from him! You fat fool! You let him know it was valuable and he found out how valuable and made a duplicate for us! No wonder we had so little trouble stealing it! No wonder he was so willing to send me off around the world looking for it! You imbecile! You bloated idiot!' He put his hands to his face and blubbered.

Gutman's jaw sagged. He blinked vacant eyes. Then he shook himself and was—by the time his bulbs had stopped jouncing—again a jovial fat man. 'Come, sir,' he said good-naturedly, 'there's no need of going on like that. Everybody errs at times and you may be sure this is every bit as severe a blow to me as to anyone else. Yes, that is the Russian's hand, there's no doubt of it. Well, sir, what do you suggest? Shall we stand here and shed tears and call each other names? Or shall we'—he paused and his smile was a cherub's—'go to Constantinople?'

Cairo took his hands from his face and his eyes bulged. He stammered: 'You are——?' Amazement coming with full comprehension made him speechless.

Gutman patted his fat hands together. His eyes twinkled. His voice was a complacent throaty purring: 'For seventeen years I have wanted that little item and have been trying to get it. If I must spend another year on the quest—well, sir—that will be an additional expenditure in time of only'—his lips moved silently as he calculated—'five and fifteen-seventeenths per cent.'

The Levantine giggled and cried: 'I go with you!'

Spade suddenly released the girl's wrist and looked around the room. The boy was not there. Spade went into the passage-way. The corridor-door stood open. Spade made a dissatisfied mouth, shut the door, and returned to the living-room. He leaned against the door-frame and looked at Gutman and Cairo. He looked at Gutman for a long time, sourly. Then he spoke, mimicking the fat man's throaty purr: 'Well, sir, I must say you're a swell lot of thieves!'

Gutman chuckled. 'We've little enough to boast about, and that's a fact, sir,' he said. 'But, well, we're none of us dead yet and there's not a bit of use thinking the world's come to an end just because we've run into a little setback.' He brought his left hand from behind him and held it out towards Spade, pink smooth hilly palm up. 'I'll have to ask you for that envelope, sir.'

Spade did not move. His face was wooden. He said: 'I held up my end. You got your dingus. It's your hard luck, not mine, that it wasn't what you wanted.'

'Now come, sir,' Gutman said persuasively, 'we've all failed and there's no reason for expecting any one of us to bear the brunt of it, and——' He brought his right hand from behind him. In the hand was a small pistol, an ornately engraved and inlaid affair of silver and gold and mother-of-pearl. 'In short, sir, I must ask you to return my ten thousand dollars.'

Spade's face did not change. He shrugged and took the envelope from his pocket. He started to hold it out to Gutman, hesitated, opened the envelope, and took out one thousand-dollar bill. He put that bill into his trousers pocket. He tucked the envelope's flap in over the other bills and held them out to Gutman. 'That'll take care of my time and expenses,' he said.

Gutman, after a little pause, imitated Spade's shrug and accepted the envelope. He said: 'Now, sir, we will say good-bye to you, unless'—the fat puffs around his eyes crinkled—'you care to undertake the Constantinople expedition with us. You don't? Well, sir, frankly I'd like to have you along. You're a man to my liking, a man of many resources and nice judgment. Because we know you're a man of nice judgment we know we can say good-bye with every assurance that you'll hold the details of our little enterprise in confidence. We know we can count on you to appreciate the fact that, as the situation now stands, any legal difficulties that come to us in connection with these last few days would likewise and equally come to you and the charming Miss O'Shaughnessy. You're too shrewd not to recognise that, sir, I'm sure.'

'I understand that,' Spade replied.

'I was sure you would. I'm also sure that, now there's no alternative, you'll somehow manage the police without a fall-guy.'

'I'll make out all right,' Spade replied.

'I was sure you would. Well, sir, the shortest farewells are the best. Adieu.' He made a portly bow. 'And to you, Miss O'Shaughnessy, adieu. I leave you the *rara avis* on the table as a little memento.'

Chapter Twenty

If They Hang You

For all of five minutes after the outer door had closed behind Casper Gutman and Joel Cairo, Spade, motionless, stood staring at the knob of the open living-room door. His eyes were gloomy under a forehead drawn down. The clefts at the root of his nose were deep and red. His lips protruded loosely, pouting. He drew them in to make a hard v and went to the telephone. He had not looked at Brigid O'Shaughnessy, who stood by the table looking with uneasy eyes at him.

He picked up the telephone, set it on its shelf again, and bent to look into the telephone directory hanging from a corner of the shelf. He turned the pages rapidly until he found the one he wanted, ran his finger down a column, straightened up, and lifted the telephone from the shelf again. He called a number and said:

'Hello, is Sergeant Polhaus there? ... Will you call him, please? This is Samuel Spade. ...' He stared into space, waiting 'Hello, Tom, I've got something for you. ... Yes, plenty. Here it is: Thursby and Jacobi were shot by a kid named Wilmer Cook.' He described the boy minutely. 'He's working for a man named Casper Gutman.' He described Gutman. 'That fellow Cairo you met here is in with them too. ... Yes, that's it. ... Gutman's staying at the Alexandria, suite 12C, or was. They've just left here and they're blowing town, so you'll have to move fast, but I don't think they're expecting a pinch.... There's a girl in it too—Gutman's daughter.' He described Rhea Gutman. 'Watch yourself when you go up against the kid. He's supposed to be pretty good with the gun.... That's right, Tom, and I've got some stuff here for you. I think I've got the guns he used.... That's right. Step on it—and luck to you!'

Spade slowly replaced receiver on prong, telephone on shelf. He wet his lips and looked down at his hands. Their palms were wet. He filled his deep chest with air. His eyes were glittering between straightened lids. He turned and took three long swift steps into the living-room.

Brigid O'Shaughnessy, startled by the suddenness of his approach, let her breath out in a little laughing gasp.

Spade, face to face with her, very close to her, tall, big-boned and thick-muscled, coldly smiling, hard of jaw and eye, said: 'They'll talk when they're nailed—about us. We're sitting on dynamite, and we've only got minutes to get set for the police. Give me all of it—fast. Gutman sent you and Cairo to Constantinople?'

She started to speak, hesitated, and bit her lip.

He put a hand to her shoulder. 'God damn you, talk!' he said. 'I'm in this with you and you're not going to gum it. Talk. He sent you to Constantinople?'

'Y-yes, he sent me. I met Joe there and—and asked him to help me. Then we——'

'Wait. You asked Cairo to help you get it from Kemidov?'

'Yes.'

'For Gutman?'

She hesitated again, squirmed under the hard angry glare of his eyes, swallowed, and said: 'No, not then. We thought we would get it for ourselves.'

'All right. Then?'

'Oh, then I began to be afraid that Joe wouldn't play fair with me, so—so I asked Floyd Thursby to help me.'

'And he did. Well?'

'Well, we got it and went to Hongkong.'

'With Cairo? Or had you ditched him before that?'

'Yes. We left him in Constantinople, in jail—something about a cheque.'

'Something you fixed up to hold him there?'

She looked shamefacedly at Spade and whispered. 'Yes.'

'Right. Now you and Thursby are in Hongkong with the bird.'

'Yes, and then—I didn't know him very well—I didn't know whether I could trust him. I thought it would be safer—anyway, I met Captain Jacobi and I knew his boat was coming here, so I asked him to bring a package for me—and that was the bird. I wasn't sure I could trust Thursby, or that Joe or—or somebody working for Gutman might not be on the boat we came on—and that seemed the safest plan.'

'All right. Then you and Thursby caught one of the fast boats over. Then what?'

'Then—then I was afraid of Gutman. I knew he had people—connections—everywhere, and he'd soon know what we had done. And I was afraid he'd have learned that we had left Hongkong for San Francisco. He was in New York and I knew if he heard that by cable he would have plenty of time to get here by the time we did, or before. He did. I didn't know that then, but I was afraid of it, and I had to wait here until Captain Jacobi's boat arrived. And I was afraid Gutman would find me—or find Floyd and buy him over. That's why I came to you and asked you to watch him for——'

'That's a lie,' Spade said. 'You had Thursby hooked and you knew it. He was a sucker for women. His record shows that—the only falls he took were over women. And once a chump, always a chump. Maybe you didn't know his record, but you'd know you had him safe.'

She blushed and looked timidly at him.

He said: 'You wanted to get him out of the way before Jacobi came with the loot. What was your scheme?'

'I—I knew he'd left the States with a gambler after some trouble. I didn't know what it was, but I thought that if it was anything serious and he saw a detective watching him he'd think it was on account of the old trouble, and would be frightened into going away. I didn't think——'

'You told him he was being shadowed,' Spade said confidently. 'Miles hadn't any brains, but he wasn't clumsy enough to be spotted the first night.

'I told him, yes. When we went out for a walk that night I pretended to discover Mr. Archer following us and pointed him out to Floyd.' She sobbed. 'But please believe, Sam, that I wouldn't have done it if I thought Floyd would kill him. I thought he'd be frightened into leaving the city. I didn't for a minute think he'd shoot him like that.'

Spade smiled wolfishly with his lips, but not at all with his eyes. He said: 'If you thought he wouldn't you were right, angel.'

The girl's upraised face held utter astonishment.

Spade said: 'Thursby didn't shoot him.'

Incredulity joined astonishment in the girl's face.

Spade said: 'Miles hadn't any brains, but, Christ! he had too many years' experience as a detective to be caught like that by the man he was shadowing. Up a blind alley with his gun tucked away on his hip and his overcoat buttoned? Not a chance. He was as dumb as any man ought to be, but he wasn't quite that dumb. The only two ways out of the alley could be watched from the edge of Bush Street over the tunnel. You'd told us Thursby was a bad actor. He couldn't have tricked Miles into the alley like that, and he couldn't have driven him in. He was dumb, but not dumb enough for that.'

He ran his tongue over the inside of his lips and smiled affectionately at the girl. He said: 'But he'd have gone there with you, angel, if he was sure nobody else was up there. You were his client, so he would have had no reason for not dropping the shadow on your say-so, and if you caught up with him and asked him to go up there he'd've gone. He was just dumb enough for that. He'd've looked you up and down and licked his lips and gone grinning from ear to ear—and then you could've stood as close to him as you liked in the dark and put a hole through him with the gun you had got from Thursby that evening.'

Brigid O'Shaughnessy shrank back from him until the edge of the table stopped her. She looked at him with terrified eyes and cried: 'Don't—don't talk to me like that, Sam! You know I didn't! You know——'

'Stop it.' He looked at the watch on his wrist. 'The police will be blowing in any minute now and we're sitting on dynamite. Talk!'

She put the back of a hand to her forehead. 'Oh, why do you accuse me of such a terrible——?'

'Will you stop it?' he demanded in a low impatient voice. 'This isn't the spot for the schoolgirl act. Listen to me. The pair of us are sitting under the gallows.' He took hold of her wrists and made her stand up straight in front of him. 'Talk!'

'I—I—— How did you know he—he licked his lips and looked——?'

Spade laughed harshly. 'I knew Miles. But never mind that. Why did you shoot him?'

She twisted her wrists out of Spade's fingers and put her hands up around the back of his neck, pulling his head down until his mouth all but touched hers. Her body was flat against his from knees to chest. He put his arms around her, holding her tight to him. Her dark-lashed lids were half down over velvet eyes. Her voice was hushed, throbbing: 'I didn't mean to, at first. I didn't, really. I meant what I told you, but when I saw Floyd couldn't be frightened I——'

Spade slapped her shoulder. He said: 'That's a lie. You asked Miles and me to handle it ourselves. You wanted to be sure the shadower was somebody you knew and who knew you, so they'd go with you. You got the gun from Thursby that day—that night. You had already rented the apartment at the Coronet. You had trunks there and none at the hotel and when I looked the apartment over I found a rent receipt dated five or six days before the time you told me you rented it.'

She swallowed with difficulty and her voice was humble. 'Yes, that's a lie, Sam. I did intend to if Floyd—— I—I can't look at you and tell you this, Sam.' She pulled his head farther down until her cheek was against his cheek and her mouth by his ear, and whispered: 'I knew Floyd wouldn't be easily frightened, but I thought that if he knew somebody was shadowing him either he'd—— Oh, I can't say it, Sam!' She clung to him, sobbing.

Spade said: 'You thought Floyd would tackle him and one or the other of them would go down. If Thursby was the one then you were rid of him. If Miles was, then you could see that Floyd was caught and you'd be rid of him. That it?'

'S-something like that.'

'And when you found that Thursby didn't mean to tackle

him you borrowed the gun and did it yourself. Right?'

'Yes—though not exactly.'

'But exact enough. And you had that plan up your sleeve rrom the first. You thought Floyd would be nailed for the killing.'

'I—I thought they'd hold him at least until after Captain Jacobi had arrived with the falcon and——'

'And you didn't know then that Gutman was here hunting for you. You didn't suspect that or you wouldn't have shaken your gunman. You knew Gutman was here as soon as you heard Thursby had been shot. Then you knew you needed another protector, so you came back to me. Right?'

'Yes, but—oh, sweetheart!—it wasn't only that. I would have come back to you sooner or later. From the first instant I saw you I knew——'

Spade said tenderly: 'You angel! Well, if you get a good break you'll be out of San Quentin in twenty years and you can come back to me then.'

She took her cheek away from his, drawing her head far back to stare up without comprehension at him.

He was pale. He said tenderly: 'I hope to Christ they don't hang you, precious, by that sweet neck.' He slid his hands up to caress her throat.

In an instant she was out of his arms, back against the table, crouching, both hands spread over her throat. Her face was wild-eyed, haggard. Her mouth opened and closed. She said in a small parched voice: 'You're not——' She could get no other words out.

Spade's face was yellow-white now. His mouth smiled and there were smile-wrinkles around his glittering eyes. His voice was soft, gentle. He said: 'I'm going to send you over. The chances are you'll get off with life. That means you'll be out again in twenty years. You're an angel. I'll wait for you.' He cleared his throat. 'If they hang you I'll always remember you.'

She dropped her hands and stood erect. Her face became smooth and untroubled except for the faintest of dubious glints in her eyes. She smiled back at him, gently. 'Don't, Sam, don't say that even in fun. Oh, you frightened me for a moment! I really thought you—— You know you do such wild and unpredictable things that——' She broke off. She thrust her face forward and stared deep into his eyes. Her cheeks and the flesh around her mouth shivered and fear came back into her eyes. 'What——? Sam!' She put her hands to her throat again and lost her erectness.

Spade laughed. His yellow-white face was damp with sweat and though he held his smile he could not hold softness in his voice. He croaked: 'Don't be silly. You're taking the fall. One of us has got to take it after the talking those birds will do. They'd hang me sure. You're likely to get a better break. Well?'

'But—but, Sam, you can't! Not after what we've been to each other. You can't——'

'Like hell I can't.'

She took a long trembling breath. 'You've been playing with me? Only pretending you cared—to trap me like this? You didn't—care at all? You didn't—don't—l-love me?'

'I think I do,' Spade said. 'What of it?' The muscles holding his smile in place stood out like weals. 'I'm not Thursby. I'm not Jacobi. I won't play the sap for you.'

'That is not just,' she cried. Tears came to her eyes. 'It's unfair. It's contemptible of you. You know it was not that. You can't say that.'

'Like hell I can't,' Spade said. 'You came into my bed to stop me asking questions. You led me out yesterday for Gutman with that phony call for help. Last night you came here with them and waited outside for me and came in with me. You were in my arms when the trap was sprung—I couldn't have gone for a gun if I'd had one on me and couldn't have made a fight of it if I had wanted to. And if they didn't take you away with them it was only because Gutman's got too much sense to trust you except for short stretches when he has to and because he thought I'd play the sap for you and—not wanting to hurt you—wouldn't be able to hurt him.'

Brigid O'Shaughnessy blinked her tears away. She took a step towards him and stood looking him in the eyes, straight and proud. 'You called me a liar,' she said. 'Now you are lying. You're lying if you say you don't know down in your heart that, in spite of anything I've done, I love you.'

Spade made a short abrupt bow. His eyes were becoming bloodshot, but there was no other change in his damp and yellowish fixedly smiling face: 'Maybe I do,' he said. 'What of it? I should trust you? You who arranged that nice little trick for— for my predecessor, Thursby? You who knocked off Miles, a man you had nothing against, in cold blood, just like swatting a fly, for the sake of double-crossing Thursby? You who double-crossed Gutman, Cairo, Thursby—one, two, three? You who've never played square with me for half an hour at a stretch since I've known you? I should trust you? No, no, darling. I wouldn't do it even if I could. Why should I?'

Her eyes were steady under his and her hushed voice was steady when she replied: 'Why should you? If you've been playing with me, if you do not love me, there is no answer to that. If you did, no answer would be needed.'

Blood streaked Spade's eyeballs now and his long-held smile had become a frightful grimace. He cleared his throat huskily and said: 'Making speeches is no damned good now.' He put a hand on her shoulder. The hand shook and jerked. 'I don't care who loves who. I'm not going to play the sap for you. I won't walk in Thursby's and Christ knows who else's footsteps. You killed Miles and you're going over for it. I could have helped you by letting the others go and standing off the police the best way I could. It's too late for that now. I can't help you now. And I wouldn't if I could.'

She put a hand on his hand on her shoulder. 'Don't help me then,' she whispered, 'but don't hurt me. Let me go away now.'

'No,' he said. 'I'm sunk if I haven't got you to hand over to the police when they come. That's the only thing that can keep me from going down with the others.'

'You won't do that for me?'

'I won't play the sap for you.'

'Don't say that, please.' She took his hand from her shoulder and held it to her face. 'Why must you do this to me, Sam? Surely Mr. Archer wasn't as much to you as——'

'Miles,' Spade said hoarsely, 'was a son of a bitch. I found that out the first week we were in business together and I meant to kick him out as soon as the year was up. You didn't do me a damned bit of harm by killing him.'

'Then what?'

Spade pulled his hand out of hers. He no longer either smiled or grimaced. His wet yellow face was set hard and deeply lined. His eyes burned madly. He said: 'Listen. This isn't a damned bit of good. You'll never understand me, but I'll try once more and then we'll give up. Listen. When a man's partner is killed he's supposed to do something about it. It doesn't make any difference what you thought of him. He was your partner and you're supposed to do something about it. Then it happens we were in the detective business. Well, when one of your organisation gets killed it's bad business to let the killer get away with it. It's bad all around—bad for that one organisation, bad for every detective everywhere. Third, I'm a detective and expecting me to run criminals down and then let them go free is like asking a dog to catch a rabbit and let it go. It can be done, all right, and sometimes it is done, but it's not the natural thing. The only way I could have let you go was by letting Gutman and Cairo and the kid go. That's——'

'You're not serious,' she said. 'You don't expect me to think that these things you're saying are sufficient reason for sending me to the——'

'Wait till I'm through and then you can talk. Fourth, no matter what I wanted to do now it would be absolutely impossible for me to let you go without having myself dragged to the gallows with the others. Next, I've no reason in God's world to think I can trust you and if I did this and got away with it you'd have something on me that you could use whenever you happened to want to. That's five of them. The sixth would be that, since I've also got something on you, I couldn't be sure you wouldn't decide to shoot a hole in *me* some day. Seventh, I don't even like the idea of thinking that there might be one chance in a hundred that you'd played me for a sucker. And eighth—but that's enough. All those to one side. Maybe some of them are unimportant. I won't argue about that. But look at the number of them. Now on the other side we've got what? All we've got is the fact that maybe you love me and maybe I love you.'

'You know,' she whispered, 'whether you do or not.'

'I don't. It's easy enough to be nuts about you.' He looked hungrily from her hair to her feet and up to her eyes again. 'But I don't know what that amounts to. Does anybody ever? But suppose I do? What of it? Maybe next month I won't. I've been through it before—when it lasted that long. Then what? Then I'll think I played the sap. And if I did it and get sent over then I'd be sure I was the sap. Well, if I send you over I'll be sorry as hell—I'll have some rotten nights—but that'll pass. Listen.' He took her by the shoulders and bent her back leaning over her. 'If that doesn't mean anything to you forget it and we'll make it this: I won't because all of me wants to—wants to say to hell with the consequences and do it—and because—God damn you— you've counted on that with me the same as you counted on that with the others.' He took his hands from her shoulders and let them fall to his sides.

She put her hands up to his cheeks and drew his face down again. 'Look at me,' she said, 'and tell me the truth. Would you have done this to me if the falcon had been real and you had been paid your money?'

'What difference does that make now? Don't be too sure I'm as crooked as I'm supposed to be. That kind of reputation might be good business—bringing in high-priced jobs and making it easier to deal with the enemy.'

She looked at him, saying nothing.

He moved his shoulders a little and said: 'Well, a lot of money would have been at least one more item on the other side of the scales.'

She put her face up to his face. Her mouth was slightly open with lips a little thrust out. She whispered: 'If you loved me you'd need nothing more on that side.'

Spade set the edges of his teeth together and said through them: 'I won't play the sap for you.'

She put her mouth to his, slowly, her arms around him, and came into his arms. She was in his arms when the door-bell rang.

Spade, left arm around Brigid O'Shaughnessy, opened the corridor-door. Lieutenant Dundy, Detective-Sergeant Tom Polhaus, and two other detectives were there.

Spade said: 'Hello, Tom. Get them?'

Polhaus said: 'Got them.'

'Swell. Come in. Here's another one for you.' Spade pressed the girl forward. 'She killed Miles. And I've got some exhibits—the boy's guns, one of Cairo's, a black statuette that all the hell was about, and a thousand-dollar bill that I was supposed to be bribed with.' He looked at Dundy, drew his brows together, leaned forward to peer into the Lieutenant's face, and burst out laughing. 'What in hell's the matter with your little playmate, Tom? He looks heartbroken.' He laughed again. 'I bet, by God! when he heard Gutman's story he thought he had me at last.'

'Cut it out, Sam,' Tom grumbled. 'We didn't think——'

'Like hell he didn't,' Spade said merrily. 'He came up here with his mouth watering, though you'd have sense enough to know I'd been stringing Gutman.'

'Cut it out,' Tom grumbled again, looking uneasily sidewise at his superior. 'Anyways we got it from Cairo. Gutman's dead. The kid had just finished shooting him up when we got there.'

Spade nodded. 'He ought to have expected that,' he said.

Effie Perine put down her newspaper and jumped out of Spade's chair when he came into the office at a little after nine o'clock Monday morning.

He said: 'Morning, angel.'

'Is that—what the papers have—right?' she asked.

'Yes, ma'am.' He dropped his hat on the desk and sat down. His face was pasty in colour, but its lines were strong and cheerful and his eyes, though still somewhat red-veined, were clear.

The girl's brown eyes were peculiarly enlarged and there was a queer twist to her mouth. She stood beside him, staring down at him.

He raised his head, grinned, and said mockingly: 'So much for your woman's intuition.'

Her voice was queer as the expression on her face. 'You did that, Sam, to her?'

He nodded. 'Your Sam's a detective.' He looked sharply at her. He put his arm around her waist, his hand on her hip. 'She did kill Miles, angel,' he said gently, 'off-hand, like that.' He snapped the fingers of his other hand.

She escaped from his arm as if it had hurt her. 'Don't, please, don't touch me,' she said brokenly. 'I know—I know you're right. You're right. But don't touch me now—not now.'

Spade's face became pale as his collar.

The corridor-door's knob rattled. Effie Perine turned quickly and went into the outer office, shutting the door behind her. When she came in again she shut it behind her.

She said in a small flat voice: 'Iva is here.'

Spade, looking down at his desk, nodded almost imperceptibly. 'Yes,' he said, and shivered. 'Well, send her in.'